th R Roberts was born in North Wales in 1969 and ht up in the sleepy seaside town of Llandudno.

18 the bright lights of London beckoned and he went study politics at the LSE. Upon graduation he worked Parliament as a speech writer and researcher, before aining to be a barrister and returning nearer home to ork as a criminal barrister in Chester.

roughout his life, music (he was bassist with pre-Brit-p band The Lovelies) and storytelling have been his sion.

ow lives in Rossett on the Welsh/English border with ife Inès and two young sons Reuben and Ianto.

ISBN 1-905988-43-5   978-1-905988-43-3

Cover by Peter Thaines

Published by Libros International

www.librosinternational.com

That Immortal Jukebox Sensation

Gareth R Roberts

Libros
INTERNATIONAL

ACKNOWLEDGEMENTS

Iwould like to thank Maureen Moss for her patience and unerring ability to sort out my prose; all those at Libros for their support; Rhian and Sian for having such confidence in their little brother; and my two roommates at Chambers who listened politely and never once mocked.

For Inès

1

'No, seriously.

'Are you listening?

'It happened just like this.

'No, it's not bollocks.

'Listen.

'I found myself walking up this secluded corridor. I could hear the music of the concert in the background, like a murmur, like a rumour of something that was going on elsewhere. To anyone else it would have sounded exciting. Anyone else would have wanted to seek it out. Not me. I was going in the opposite direction. The corridor was quite dimly lit. There were those small round ceiling lights above me, but they weren't giving out much light. The funny thing is though, I kind of knew exactly where I was going. I knew exactly where I'd find what I was looking for. I didn't need lights or signposts or anything. Yeah, okay. You can laugh, but it's true. Anyway. I opened the door. It was his room. His dressing room. I knew that. Don't ask me how. For a few seconds part of the room was illuminated. Well, I say illuminated, it was more a triangle of light was thrown onto the far wall. As I opened the door wider, the triangle got bigger. I could see most of the room now. I knew it was his room. His dressing room. Fucking hell: dressing room. We once got changed in someone's kitchen. I peered through the gloomy half light. The room was empty, but I could see signs of him. I knew he'd been here, even though I haven't seen him, haven't been part of him for years. There was a half emptied glass of red wine on a dressing table. Some food. There were discarded clothes hanging, rejected on the back of a chair. A CD player flickered green lights, though the CD had finished playing. It was a room that had seen recent action. It was a Marie Celeste of a room. No, that's wrong, these people would return. They'd return and I would be waiting. I closed the door. The light poured out like an emptying glass of water. The distant noise of the music and the crowd became even fainter and disappeared altogether. Suddenly I was alone in the room. His room. There was an armchair in the corner. I sat down in it and crossed my legs. I lit a cigarette. I waited. Alone. The only light the firefly lit end of my fag. The only sound my breathing. Calm, but audible. I waited.

'I finished my cigarette. I lit another. I awaited my fate. Our fate. Eventually he came. I knew he would. The door opened, casting the triangle of light once more against the back wall. In flooded the noise of the crowd once again. The sound of outside. The sound of air and life, normality and weirdness, death and movement.

'For a second he was unaware of my presence. Then he must have sensed me. He turned directly to where I was sitting, in that armchair in the corner. His eyes squinted as he tried to focus on me. As he tried to remember my name, my personality, the conversations we had, the dreams we shared.'

'What happened then?'

'Sorry?'

'What happened then?'

'I shot him.'

'What!'

'Yes. Once, right through the forehead. Just like you see in the films.'

'Bollocks!'

'No, his head. Just left a single blood red circular mark - just like in the films. About the size of a twenty pence piece. I shot him. And, for a second he looked at me, like, like, he knew that he deserved it.'

'What did he do then?'

'Well, not a lot really, seeing as I'd just put a bullet in his brain.'

'Fucking hell, Richie. I can't believe what I've just heard.'

'You are one fucked up bastard.'

My three mates sitting alongside me in the pub were shocked. I couldn't blame them. The pub talk was about our wildest fantasies, and two of my mates had given theirs. First was Ray, 35, laboratory assistant, divorced, two kids, disenchanted, skint and fast running to fat. Ray had wanted to shag some bird from some awful manufactured pop band he'd seen on the telly.

Then there was Alec, 36, happy, recently married and fighting the good fight. Alec wanted to turn back time and play in Liverpool's glorious European Cup Final Team of 1977 (God love the soft get, he wanted to play at left back; what sad bastard wants to turn back time to play left back?).

We hadn't got onto James, and judging by his outrage at my murder fantasy, I didn't think we ever would. James: nice, worthy, fresh-faced fucking James, 32, long-term girlfriend, still canvassing for the Labour Party, no plans to marry, no plans to ever shag anyone else - probably fantasises about helping Tony Blair deliver world peace.

I laugh at them, flashing an evil set of pointy teeth, and get up.

'Bollocks to you, you sad bastards, I didn't start the conversation. Now, who wants another pint?'

I don't think it was my revelation, more the fact that we'd been out since going home from work time - 5.30pm - and it was now 9 o'rock'n'rollin' clock and they all had to be home. They got up and put their coats on. They drank the last dregs of their pints and put their hands towards me.

'No, Richie. I've got to go, the missus will kill me,' said nice James in a self-congratulatory, slightly but not offensively smug tone that says he has a significant other who gives enough of a shit about what time he arrives home to pulp him with a Teflon pan. He *is a* great guy. I don't want to kill him.

The three of them troop off. I get up to join them. But then I stop. I don't know why. Yes I do. I stop because I don't want to go home yet.

I get up and walk to the bar, my back to my departing mates and my hand raised upwards, bent at the elbow in some kind of unwitting nonchalant Nazi salute to the lads.

I know I'm half pissed. I haven't drunk that much but the only food I've eaten has been a packet of pork scratchings, so as I stand up the lager surges to my brain, creating that feeling that although my legs might give way, I am still the most interesting person in the world.

Bar. Pint. Bogs for a slash. Hand on wall to steady myself, head balanced gently, sleepily against my forearm.

Christ, if someone was looking down at me now, if someone was above me peering at me, what kind of sight would I present? Richie Strafe, 35-year-old solicitor, with no interest whatsoever in anything to do with matters legal; long time partner of Angela, with absolutely no interest in getting married; drunk and alone, having waved goodbye to my mates, and fantasising about killing my erstwhile best friend, the current star of British rock and pop music, the wonderful, fucking gorgeous, now hailed as a cerebral artist by serious music critics, Danny 'fucking' Cappaldi.

I washed my hands and looked at myself in the mirror - Richie Strafe, thinning on top, but getting bastard-well fatter everywhere else in another one of life's wonderful little ironies. I used to have hair like Johnny Marr, cheekbones like David Bowie. Now I've got hair like Andrew Marr and cheekbones like David Mellor.

I read recently that more blokes in their mid-thirties than ever before are seeking counselling from psychologists. Who can blame us? Being thirty odd in this new shiny millennium is the worst age imaginable - too young to have given up all hope, but old enough to know that your life has more than likely been sucked dry of all its best parts. You're like an island that has long been explored, all its interesting animals and plants discovered, leaving only a detailed analysis of the crop rotation techniques of the indigenous population left to do.

You have vague memories of the awful wonder of your first sloppy kiss, the veiled excitement of your first beer, but you don't understand music anymore, or clothes or even language - it's not meant for you. It's years since you felt a sense of injustice about anything, cared about anyone, wrote a shite poem about the disappearing rainforest or the unemployed or third world poverty or anything that really really means something. You're fucked, you know you're fucked, really you do, but you're not going to admit it. Not yet, not whilst there is still the echo of defiance and hope coming out of your stereo. At least not until you're forty.

I stagger out of the cloistered confines of the Gents and back into the main bar. I should definitely go home now, I really should. I check my watch, it's still only 9pm. That's hours before bedtime, hours before back-to-work time. I decide on one for the road and take my place back at the bar holding a crisp fiver in my hand, and lean comfortably amongst the laughing office workers who should also have gone home ages ago and the sour-faced princesses who dislike having to wait to be served.

It is then that I noticed the man in the cream slacks. It wasn't just the cream slacks though; it was everything about this man. I stared at him intently as I waited for the barmaid's attention. On his feet he was wearing a pair of white slip-on shoes, complete with a frayed tassel just underneath the white lip. I followed the cream slacks on an elegant and sartorial journey to a yellow and white hooped T-shirt upon the shoulders of which was casually draped a yellow woollen jumper. It was quite hideous. But it wasn't just this man's clothes, it wasn't just that he was dressed as golf club nightmare meets aging Mediterranean Lothario that was

13

causing me to stare, it was his face and hair. His face was a deep and leathery tan and from within it shone two bright blue eyes that were able to illuminate the darkness of the pub. His hair was brilliant white, like snow, like a perfectly coiffed pile of flour on his head. He caught me staring and I quickly looked away. Instinctively I glanced around to see if anyone else was aware of this man - no one was. All around me the office workers, the princesses, the locals, were going about their way utterly oblivious to the strange man who was standing amongst them at the bar. I turned to face the bar again; somehow I felt neither as pissed nor as in need of another drink as I did a few seconds earlier. Still the crisp fiver was in my thrusting hand inviting the bar staff to choose me; still my elbow was resting, happily and unconsciously, in a small pool of spilt lager on the bar as I adopted my stance of relaxed bloke in need of a drink.

I hear the voice clearly.

'You would never do it that way.'

It has a strong accent. My first assumption is that it is a French accent, or failing that, Italian. I knew it would be the man in the slacks.

I turn. 'Sorry?'

'You would never do it that way,' he repeated.

I had no idea what he was talking about. I knew he was not some misguided foreign poof chancing his arm: his tone was more fatherly, his face soft, friendly - though a bit too daytime TV presenter to put me fully at ease. In the back of my mind my subconscious age calculator tried to gauge how old he was and shot the figure 68 to my consciousness. There was wisdom in his lips.

I tried to talk and suddenly felt incredibly pissed again. 'I'm sorry, I really have no idea.... What?'

He smiled and turned slightly to one side away from me and away from the throng at the bar, but in a way that invited me to move with him. It was slick, because I did exactly as he encouraged. Now in a slightly quieter part of the bar, he fixed his stare upon me. 'You would never kill your friend by hiding in his room and shooting him in the head.'

I felt my eyes widen. Fucking hell. What a thing to say. I was only joking. It was only a weird little fantasy of mine. Fucking hell. I'm a solicitor.

The next sounds that came out of my mouth were an incomprehensible and stuttering mixture of nonsense and ineloquent defence of the conversation with my friends.

'Fgumph, er, gnnph, I wasn't - eh?! Grrr, you've got it wrong.'

Slacksman smiled at me again.

'Don't worry, at the moment the question for you is not how you should kill this man, but why you want to kill him.'

I was stung into articulacy. 'I don't want to kill anyone. It was just a joke.'

I realise how defensive I sounded. Who the fuck was this bloke, and what right did he have to comment on *my* pub talk conversation? It just isn't done. I should have told him to fuck off, I should have made a witty yet derogatory comment about his attire - but I didn't. Something about him kept me from telling him to fuck off; something about the way he stood looking at me made me feel I had to listen to him.

'If you don't want to kill him,' he asked, 'then why do you spend so much time thinking about it?'

His accent made the question so straightforward it seemed like a statement of fact - like something that I couldn't possibly deny.

'What?' I said, affecting my best look of shocked outrage before lapsing again into gibberish. 'How? What? Who are you?'

As cross-examination, statement of defence or term of abuse, my response was an abject failure. He looked at me and a slight smile developed at the corner of his lips.

'I'm sorry, mate. I don't know what the fuck you're talking about.'

This was a lie - it is a fact that I do spend a suspiciously large amount of my time fantasising about killing Danny Cappaldi - but that's not the point, it's my time - how the fuck did this strange, slack-wearing, chunky knit, grey-haired old bastard know what thoughts went through *my* head? It was too awful to contemplate.

I wished I had some mates with me. I wished that I wasn't standing alone still clutching a crisp fiver. I wished I had the power of speech. I really needed somewhere to go to; anywhere would do.

I walked purposefully out of the pub without buying my drink and without saying another word to the strange bloke with white hair. As I walked through the door my mind briefly considered why this man said what he did, and whether my flouncing out of a crowded pub having just queued up to buy a drink looked in some way suspicious or guilty.

I filled my head with sensible thoughts. What the fuck was I feeling guilty about? I hadn't killed anyone. I hadn't even hurt anyone. For fuck's sake I hadn't even been in a fight since the fourth year at school when Daz Ginge called me a poof after I played my guitar with the school choir. And if I'm honest, I can't remember causing him a great deal of pain during our two-minute mêlée.

The skin underneath my nose was the first to register the frosty night-time January air as I stepped into the street.

I continued along the road. I thought about and dismissed the idea of a taxi. It would be a fifteen-minute walk home from town to my nice two-bedroomed flat and my nice girlfriend Angela. A walk would do me good.

I pulled my coat tightly around me; it was bloody cold. A group of lads were kicking the bus stop across the road. I glanced at them, and one of them called me a wanker. Maybe I'll get a cab after all.

2

The thing I hate most about growing older is the hangovers. Oh, for the days when the hangover would comprise of waking up feeling shite, going back to sleep for a while, then idly masturbating before dragging yourself up for a bucket of tea and a hundredweight of toast. Hangovers affect you in a different way as you age - a sneaky, more pernicious way. Yes, the cardboard tongue still slaps the pallet of your throat, yes, the stomach still complains as you shit tar, the legs and arms still ache - all of that and more, but what is worse is the feeling of guilt. The voice in the back of your head that reminds you of every stupid, idiotic word you said the night before.

On this particular morning, I had no knowledge of my taxi ride home, but I could remember in vivid technicoloured detail the way in which I described to my mates my fantasies about killing Danny Cappaldi. Why the fuck did I say that? What was I thinking? Why couldn't I have played safe, stuck to the script and regurgitated some sporting or sexual fantasy? For the love of God, I was with my mates down the pub - conversations aren't supposed to go beyond football and shagging.

Gingerly, I put my hand up to my head. I was knackered due to the fitful sleep I had endured for the last three hours, lying there, hating myself and dying for a piss or a drop of water.

Angela was up and getting ready for work. So far, she had ignored my desperate attempts to feign the role of cheerful loving boyfriend. A memory of a row came back to me. She accusing me of not growing up, me accusing her of failing to understand the tortured soul of my desperate psyche. Fucking hell. I remembered my last conversation with the boys, I remembered shouting some bollocks about the 'tortured soul of my desperate psyche', yet I remembered nothing about my taxi journey home or how much it cost - funny how the human mind works when it is being fuelled by lager.

'Angie,' I said, 'I don't suppose anyone phoned for me last night?' She ignored me. She had had her back to me since she got up - this was a clear sign: she was pissed off.

'Angie?' I repeated pathetically. God, I loathe myself, even my use of the shortened form of her name is pathetic, knowing as I do that she likes being called Angie, thinking it sounds like some kind of 1970s pop poppet, whereas 'Ange' she hates, saying that it reminds her of some ropey Eastend barmaid, with peroxide hair and shag-me eyeliner.

I repeated my question. This time, without turning round, she shook her head in exaggerated despair. 'What?' I said. 'What's the matter?' Now she turned around. There was cold venom in her eyes. 'I thought you said that you weren't pissed last night?'

'I wasn't pissed,' I lied as I realised my fundamental schoolboy error.

'Well, why don't you remember me telling you that your boss phoned?'

I had no answer to that. The conversation flooded back. My boss, Howard McPhee, the McPhee of McPhee, Fox and Phillips, solicitors to the imminently guilty and perennially skint criminals, and litigators of South London. Howard 'fucking scary' McPhee, who it is generally agreed is one step ahead of the Law Society Misconduct Committee and two steps ahead of the loony bin - a man whom I have been steadfastly avoiding during my five years as a solicitor in his dead-end firm. I remember the conversation clearly now. 'McPhee? What did he want?'

'Probably wants to get rid of you just like I do, you lazy fat bastard.' I was more concerned about the prospect of my boss phoning my flat than my girlfriend's insult.

Angela is the same age as me - 35. She is an accountant. She is nice really. Perhaps that is the problem. Nice. You don't marry someone and declare before God, his assembled angels, cherubim, seraphim and all the other fuckers who sit in the Heavenly Choir, that you will cherish, obey and honour, just because someone is nice.

We met at a party twelve years ago. It will be thirteen years ago in March. I know that because it was my mate Alec's (36, happy, recently married, fighting the good fight, wants to turn back time and play in Liverpool's glorious European Cup Final Team of 1977) birthday party. He was 23 then, I was 22. I was 22, and already bitterness had set in.

HE had just released his second album. The second album. The old cliché is that the second album is the most difficult. It's not: the most difficult album is the third. The first is the easiest. The first album encapsulates the energy of raw youth. The references are still close enough to touch. The influences - and I don't mean the musical influences, I mean the *real* things that make your heart beat: the girls you wanted to shag but couldn't, the half-arsed revolutionary politics and hippy-shit ideas that made your wide eyes glisten and your beautiful uncluttered brain buzz - scream out in the first album. Parents and drink and school and drugs and trying to be cool and being ignored are all there in every chord, every beat, in every rubbish rhyme that passes for a lyric - this is what makes the first album easy. The second, though never quite as vibrant, still has the echo of those feelings. Then, when the corporations take over, when *everyone* wants to shag you, when the fear of failure overcomes the arrogance of youth, the real influences are lost. I could still hear me in Cappaldi's second album. I could still hear us.

We listened to his second album at Alec's party. It was the musical event of the year. I got pissed and pretended to be cool about the fact that I knew him, that I had played in his first band. People asked me about him. I said he was a cunt and laughed as though I didn't mean it. No one asked me why I wasn't in his band anymore. No one asked me if I had written any of the songs that were now making him famous. No one wanted to know about me. So I talked about him. I told them how we were in the same class at school. I told them how we both got our guitars at the same time. I told them about practising in his dad's basement. They listened and some girl, a small girl with red hair, asked if it had been difficult being his mate, because all the girls would have ignored me and fancied him. I laughed, but I wanted to plunge a knife in her eye.

Later, when everyone was pissed and stoned, I met Angela. She didn't ask me about Danny Cappaldi, she asked me about being a law student. She was nice. Pretty, too. We slept together in a spare room in Alec's flat. Nothing happened, well nothing much. The next day we made plans.

That was nearly thirteen years ago.

Now I watched as she applied her make-up. Could I detect a little bit more care than in years gone by? Was she a little more reticent about showing me her body than in those carefree days of early blossoming passion? I chased away these thoughts. Now was not the time.

'What did he sound like to you?'

'What?'

'McPhee. What did he sound like?'

At last she turned towards me. 'Fucking hell, Richie, we went through all this last night. He sounded like a bloke who was phoning up asking for another bloke.'

'Yes, but...' I whined, then stopped: I knew I sounded like a twat.

I took the slow morning bus from our flat in Balham south towards Streatham and the uninspiring concrete box that is the home of McPhee, Fox and Phillips. On the bus my hangover got a second wind. Every squealing school kid seemed to scratch my brain, every moment spent in endless traffic sent a wave of painful desperation through my whole body. A gang of young lads got on the bus and started abusing passers-by. I watched them in their uniform of baseball caps and baggy trousers; I listened to their affected, stilted English and defiant swear words. Fucking hell, I fucking hate kids. I want to tell them that shouting 'Oi, you nonce!' at random middle-aged men is not cool. But, of course, I don't.

The bus carried on its crawling journey up Streatham High Street - possibly the horriblest place in the world. Outside I saw the uniform drabness of MacDonalds and Pizza Hut, Curry's and Superdrug sitting cheek by dirty jowl with the newsagents, Hal-Al butchers, greasy caffs and top-price convenience stores. Outside I could see the desperate faces of the morning Londoners dragging themselves to work, farting out gusts of dirty breath in the January coldness. The drunks and winos, illegal immigrants and trendy South London types who all, like me, put up with the stinking ugly city.

I remembered that my CD player was in my briefcase and clamoured to get it out. I plugged into an album by some new Indie band. They are resplendent with jingly jangly guitars and a singer with unfeasibly high cheekbones. It was quite good. The music gave London a backbeat, a rhythm. Perhaps it's not so bad; perhaps London does have a purpose. Perhaps the grime is the detritus of an exciting, pulsating world; the people interesting, with stories to tell and vast skills and knowledge to impart. Do I love this stinking ugly city? Yes, I tell myself and praise the day that I upped and left the boring backwater of my birth.

I thought about last night again. Why did they all leave so abruptly? I had to phone Alec and James, make things cool again. I had to stop being such an arse when pissed. Then I remembered Slacksman.

Slacksman.

I thought that he could read my mind. What was I like? My tired dog-eared face broke out into a smile as I reminded myself how I believed that this man could read my mind.

Weird old poof listening to other people's conversations.

I arrived at the office and made my way quickly to the upstairs room that I shared with Tony Bowden. I skipped past the receptionist who shouted something as I passed. Did she shout that Mr McPhee wanted to see me in his office? No, surely not.

Tony was already hard at work. Well, he was at work. Together me and him make up the Personal Injury and Contentious Litigation Section of McPhee, Fox and Phillips.

It is not a big firm: it has a criminal department which is McPhee; a family department which is Fox; a conveyancing and probate department that is Phillips and our department, which is... well, our department. I sometimes feel sorry for Tony. By rights it should be McPhee, Fox, Phillips and Bowden. They all worked at the same large City firm and Tony just happened to be with them down the pub one lunchtime when they decided to leave and form their own firm. Tony tells me he just got caught up in the whole thing. One minute he was getting three pints of lager and a gin and tonic from the bar, the next he was handing in his resignation and agreeing to single-handedly set up a Personal Injury department.

Fair play to him though, he rarely complains about the absence of his moniker from the letterhead.

I arrived a year later. I was his first trainee but our relationship has never been employer/employee: Tony is my work buddy. It is one of the things that makes the job bearable. We have our routine. I make the coffee in the morning; he makes the tea in the afternoon.

We both moan about the senior partners, the secretaries and above all the clients. We both lament the absence of any good-looking birds in the office now that Sharine, the hopeless trainee with the big norks and a penchant for leather mini-skirts, wasn't taken on. We even have our own language. Rather than speak in normal everyday Queen's English which might encourage us to have a serious conversation about our work, or even - heaven forbid - a meaningful conversation about our lives (I have no idea if Tony is happy in his marriage to Julie-Anne, or whether he misses his dad who died a couple of years ago; I don't know if he wants children, or if he fears death - that is not what a work buddy talks about). We communicate in - depending upon our moods - the style of either a politician addressing a party conference, a football manager in post-match interview, a prophet from the Old Testament or a bloke called Ted Ward, who none of you will have heard of, but who had unimpeachable opinions about everything. It's a routine. It helps the time go from 9 to 5, from Monday to Friday, from Christmas party to Christmas party, from cradle to......

I knew that Tony wouldn't give a monkey's about the fact that on this particular morning I was twenty minutes late. I like to think that he knows that despite my resounding mediocrity and absolute lack of interest in any matters concerning the firm, its clients and my career, I do get my job done.

He looked up at me from his desk and sat back in his chair.

'Ah, though he doth walk amidst the hop-fuelled stench of lager-flavoured halitosis and though his face is red like the morning sun over the Sea of Galilee, he couldst not ignore the call from on high.' Tony had chosen Old Testament Prophet, and had been busy composing in the last twenty minutes. He continued, 'For from on high came the shrill clarion call of the angel of no mercy who didst say to him, "Where is the one who slithers on his belly like a serpent, for I have news of great import to impart upon him?"'

I didn't want to play along; my alcohol-induced dehydration had shrunk my brain, rendering me incapable of any kind of witty response in Tony's game. 'Fuck, McPhee? What does he want?' was my only response.

Tony continued in the same vein. 'And from beneath the small clouds of prawn cocktail flavoured crisps...'

I had to stop him. 'Seriously, Tony, fucking hell, what does McPhee want?'

'He wants *you,* mate,' said Tony, adopting the style of Lord Kitchener to point at me.

'Why?'

'That I don't know.'

I sat at my desk slumped back in my chair and put my hands together in prayer-like contemplation. Tony stared at me from his desk, a look of amusement on his face.

'Christ, Richie, don't worry about it. It's probably a bit of Personal Injury advice, that's all.'

I sat up and looked up at him. 'You're right. It's probably nothing.' I stood up. 'Coffee?'

'I'd love to, mate, but your 9.15 is sat in the conference room.'

I looked at my watch, swore and rushed out of the room, grabbing my pen and pad as I did.

3

'You're not from around 'ere, are you?'

I had just finished my five-minute opening spiel to Ernest Hetherington (60s, clearly a pain in the arse to everyone who knows him, probably lonely), who was sitting opposite me in his beige mac, gravy scarred V-neck and matching nylon pants. By his side sat the ubiquitous purple hold-all, from which I feared Mr Hetherington would produce exhibits A-Z to support whatever gripe had led him to seek my help.

Nevertheless, I adopted my usual professional yet caring voice and told him that I expected my firm to represent him with the uppermost care and professionalism, then sat back with a friendly, 'So, Mr Hetherington, tell me what this is all about.'

A question Mr Hetherington had decided to ignore.

'Are you a Scouser?' He pronounced his question in the vitriolic cockney way I had heard before, in which the first vowel sound in Scouser is changed from a mildly painful 'ow' into a screeching 'ah'.

'No, Mr Hetherington. I'm from the Wirral. Now please tell me how you think we can help you.'

He looked quizzically at me. I could tell he was trying to work out if he was satisfied with my denial of being from Liverpool.

'You sound like a Scouser.'

'Well, I'm not. Now..'

His expression changed from one of suspicion to one of resignation.

'It's me legs,' he said, moving backwards on his chair and rubbing his thigh as if to justify his complaint.

For no pressing reason I wrote down the word 'legs' and continued my examination.

'What happened to your legs?'

'They got broke in an accident.'

'When?'

'Last year. But my son tells me that I can still claim. 'E reckons I could get a few thousand.'

I looked up from my notepad. Mr Hetherington had now adopted a certain grey sadness.

The sudden mention of his son made me feel pity towards him. I pictured uncaring offspring harbouring ideas of cashing in on whatever unfortunate accident fate had dished out to this man.

I smiled at the aging, shabbily dressed man. 'That depends, Mr Hetherington. Please, tell me what happened.'

'Well, it's like this,' he started emphatically, then stalled. 'It was a Tuesday, or perhaps it was Thursday. Yes, it was definitely a Thursday, because I was going to meet me mates Jacko and Arthur down the Horses, nice pint down the Horses, even after Whitbreads took over.'

Any sympathy I had briefly held for Ernest Hetherington was evaporating. I knew that he was about to tell me in forensic and tortuous detail everything that occurred on the day something happened to his legs. I knew that we were about to wade through the myriad of his prejudices and opinions until the pertinent facts could be extracted like stubborn teeth.

'Are you sure you're not a Scouser?' he enquired again.

'Yes, I am sure. Please carry on, Mr Hetherington.'

'Anyway, I was crossing over by Boots and suddenly I felt this almighty shove from behind. I thought I'd been shot. I didn't stick a chance. I got knocked about six feet.'

'What happened?'

'I fell to the floor. I lost me glasses and everything.'

'Yes, but why?'

'The ambulance took forty minutes to get there. I tell you, talk about the National Health. It used to be the envy of the whole world. Not any more.'

'What?'

'I broke me legs. Both of them.'

'How?'

'When I fell over.'

By now I was losing the will to live. I tried not to sound too angry.

'What caused you to fall over?'

'The cow.'

'What cow?'

At this point I assumed that Mr Hetherington was making a derogatory remark about some woman. I was completely wrong. Ernest Hetherington, it turns out, was hit by a proper milk-producing, all-mooing dairy cow that was being transported through London by a halfwit lorry driver. A letter Mr Hetherington had carefully pulled out of his grubby inside pocket, from the owner of the cow, a company called Greencounty Agriculture Ltd, explained it all.

It transpired that, in an attempt to evade the traffic of the M25 motorway around London, the enterprising farm driver had decided to take his load of one dozen cows from a farm in Warwickshire towards Dover through London. Apparently the cows were fine going through Finchley and Golders Green, had started to grow restless when the lorry went four times around Marble Arch and were in outright rebellion by the time they crossed the river at Westminster and were heading towards the Elephant and Castle. One particular cow - I kid you not, called Edna (4 years old, likes being milked, eating grass and producing enormous pools of shite) - started to ram the back shutter of the lorry, something that the driver must have either failed to hear or decided to ignore. By the time the lorry reached Streatham High Road, which unfortunately was the exact same time Mr Ernest Hetherington was planning to meet his mates at the Horses Arms Public House, the lock on the back shutter broke and the shutter sprang open, revealing twelve cows peering nervously out towards the South Circular Road. Again, unfortunately for Mr Hetherington, just as the lorry drew parallel with him, Edna decided to make a jump for freedom. Edna, being a cow, had little idea of the concept of forward rotation, therefore it must have come as something of a shock to her when upon landing in the middle of the road, she was catapulted forward through the air, past the cab of the hapless lorry driver and straight into Mr Hetherington, who, as he rightly says, was in turn knocked a further six feet before landing and breaking both his legs.

'There was cows everywhere,' he added, as I read the explanation contained in the letter.

I felt an overwhelming desire to laugh.

I bit my lip.

When that didn't work I sucked my cheeks. I read and re-read the letter knowing that if I was forced to look up at the purple-faced pensioner across the way, I would be unable to contain myself. My stomach hurt. I became aware of him fossicking inside his purple zipped holdall. I tried to stop myself from imagining what was coming next - perhaps a sworn affidavit from some sheep. Tentatively I looked up, my eyes on stilts, my teeth boring into my bottom lip. He handed me a slightly moth-eaten copy of the South London Press. On its front page was a picture of an out-of-sorts Mr Hetherington in a hospital bed with both his legs suspended in traction. In the bottom right hand corner was an inset picture of a cow. Perhaps it was the look on the cow's face, or perhaps it was the headline 'Man Hit By Cow', but at this point I could no longer control the roaring laughter that had been welling up inside me. First my head went forward and a high-pitched wheezing sound came from some depths of my body as I tried to stifle it. It was no good, my head rocked back and I roared until my throat rasped. Then I rocked forward again, my face contorted with the uncomfortable pleasure of uncontrolled laughter. No sound emanated from me. I had gone beyond guffawing.

The next time I looked up, Mr Hetherington and his letter and bag were limping towards the door. He turned back to me as he put his hand on the handle. He looked at me as I tried to contain myself. 'They couldn't save my right leg,' he said mournfully.

I stopped laughing.

Well, almost.

4

'I thought that you Liverpudlians were supposed to have a sense of humour,' snapped the Senior Criminal Partner, Howard McPhee. I looked down furtively and muttered something about me coming from the Wirral.

'Because I've got to say, mate,' he continued in cockney staccato, ignoring my comment and slipping in the dreaded word 'mate' which meant that this bollocking was going to be one of those 'more in sorrow than in anger' ones that hit the spot like an arrow searing towards the bullseye, 'it's not fucking humorous, laughing at amputees. Especially ones with potential hundred grand claims.'

I shrugged; I had no defence. My only solace was that I knew that he had wanted me to see him before the incident with Arthur Hetherington who had left my office, gone home and immediately phoned to complain to the Senior Partner. I had snuck back to my office to await my fate. I knew that I had fucked up. I knew that I would be summoned to see someone. I had hoped that it would have been Gill Foster - who I quite fancy - or John Phillips, who had long stopped caring what happens in the firm, so when the summons came to 'pop up' to Howard McPhee's office, I feared the worst.

He looked at me now and sucked in his lips. He threw a piece of paper down onto the desk. 'These are the figures for you and Tony's department.' I feigned interest. 'They're shite.' I feigned meek disagreement.

'I mean, we have to compete now with these big firms and

insurance companies. If we can't take care of the Mr Whatever His Name Was who got hit by a sheep.'

'Cow'

'What? Oh yes, cow ..we're going to be fucked.'

McPhee was a big man with big hair and a booming voice. He liked to shout and use profanities, and, I have to admit, he was good at it. He was scary. He was without a doubt the alpha male in the office. He was the bloke in every firm who is always loudly telling someone on the other end of a telephone that he's got his dick in the door and his tits in a grinder over some big deal. Strangely, women fancied him.

I looked at him and inwardly started to defend myself. I bet that he had never played his guitar in front of two thousand fans. I bet he had never watched a woman walking from a bar to the girls' toilets and been so moved by the experience that he had to write a song.

As I fortified my ego, he broke off from his bollocking.

'To be honest though, Richie, I've not really got you here to talk about the problems of the Personal Injury Department, nor do I want to talk any more about flying cows, because I know that that is something that won't be repeated, will it?'

The twat. I was thirty fucking five, not twelve. I murmured an apology and a promise not to let it happen again.

'The reason I wanted to speak to you was this. You're from Liverpool, aren't you?'

I nodded: I was past arguing.

'Well, we've got a big trial that's going to start in Liverpool. I mean big. It's real balls on the line stuff.' I was interested, but at a total loss as to why this would include me in some way.

'One of our big clients has been accused of murdering some Scouse drug barons,' he continued, to my total confusion.

'We've got our barrister and QC up there, but I want someone from this firm to go and look after this lad throughout the trial.'

The penny put itself into a position to drop.

'Given you know the area and that and maybe could live somewhere for free for a bit, I thought that you'd be the ideal person to be our man in the North, as it were.'

The penny dropped. I had been chosen to spend God knows how long back home, in Merseyside, holding some lunatic's hand through a murder trial because I was cheap; they wouldn't have to pay for me to stay anywhere. Fair play to McPhee, he doesn't miss a trick. His mind must have mulled that one over for all of seconds as he considered which poor bastard he could send up North. Don't get me wrong, it's not a northern thing, it's not a Liverpool thing. It's a home thing.

McPhee continued, 'I've spoken to Tony and he says your department isn't busy at the moment and he can spare you for a month or two.'

The last part of his sentence screamed in my head - a month or two. A month or two. Fucking hell. This man wanted to send me back home for a month or two. I tried to put up some kind of a fight.

'I don't know, Howard. January does start to get busy. You know how it is. People make New Year's resolutions to sue some other poor bastard.'

McPhee shot me the type of incredulous look that I might have expected if I had revealed to him there and then that I was in fact a woman.

'Richie, I don't think that you fully understand. This is a big case in Liverpool. This is not some bloke getting hit by a cow. This is a murder trial. The firm has got its bollocks well and truly in a vice over this one. We can't afford to fuck up. I wouldn't send just anyone up there, you know.'

Yeah right, so the fact that I come at half price has got nothing to do with it.

'I need someone who I can trust. Someone who can do a good job. If you do alright with this I'll be prepared to let go some of your less astute antics.'

As McPhee mixed flattery and threat, my already fragile defences crumbled.

'Well, are you sure that I am up to the job? I mean, after all, don't you want a specialist criminal bod up there?'

McPhee considered my argument for a second, then dismissed it. 'No.'

He didn't care if I had never seen the inside of Crown Court in my life, indeed he wouldn't have cared if I had never seen the inside of a law book in my life. McPhee simply wanted a body up in Liverpool who could look after his precious drug dealer's every desire and be on the end of a telephone in the event of things going tits up. He reckoned that even I could do that, but what was more, I could do it at half the cost of anyone else.

I had no choice. I thought about playing the Angela card, but couldn't summon up any enthusiasm to bring my decaying relationship in to save me from my fate. I was going to Liverpool for the trial. I was going to spend the longest period back at my home with my parents since I packed my dreams in my holdall and left for University at the beautiful age of eighteen. It was a prospect that filled me with dread. I felt helpless rage build inside me like a solid brick in my stomach. I didn't want to go back for such a long time. I didn't want to revisit my failed dreams. I didn't want to have to face the things I had been avoiding for so long. I didn't want to go home.

I skulked back into my office. Tony was waiting for me.

'At the end of the day, when all is said and done, it was a dodgy penalty. Now, I'm not one to have a go at the referees of today, but McPhee's been an absolute nightmare. He couldn't referee an under seven's game, he should be on his way to SpecSavers....'

Tony had launched himself into football manager mode, but I wasn't in the mood.

'Thanks a fucking bunch, Tone. Thank you for everything, mate.' I spat the last word to leave him in no doubt of my wrath. In fairness to Bowden he looked genuinely confused.

'What?'

'You've sold me up the river to McPhee, you bastard.'

'Sold you up the river? What on earth are you going on about?'

'You told me that you had no idea what he wanted.'

'I didn't.'

'Bollocks.'

'Honestly. I didn't. No, correction - I don't know what Howard McPhee wanted with you.'

I looked at him directly, scowling at him. He is a genuinely nice bloke, Tony. He is not a liar; but I was not ready yet to back down. I still needed someone to take my mood out on. I needed someone to upset.

'You're a liar. You and McPhee have obviously discussed sending me to Liverpool to cover some poxy trial. He told me that you'd told him that I wasn't needed at the moment because we weren't very busy.'

Tony considered this. He didn't like confrontation. 'Listen, for fuck's sake. McPhee has not mentioned sending you anywhere to me. He did ask me how busy we are and, well, I told him we aren't.'

I continued to scowl at him. He was telling the truth. I knew he was telling the truth, so I ignored him and sulked like an errant toddler.

5

I am not a Scouser. I am from the Wirral, a little place called Parkgate, which is on the Dee Estuary across from the industrial part of North Wales. The nearest big town is the once resplendent Birkenhead. Parkgate was once resplendent too, or so I am told. Once upon a time it had a beach with sand, but gradually the beach became a marsh, which in turn attracted various rare birds, which attracted various ornithologists. And that is the abiding image of the area where I was brought up - blokes in green waterproofs with binoculars and weekend shopping trips to Birkenhead.

I was born in the 1970s when everything was grey. We lived in a semi-detached just up the road from the old beach: my mum, dad, big brother and me. We aren't a close family; we are like four discombobulated bobbins that spin around each other shooting off violently if they ever get close enough to touch.

Dad was an engineer and Mum cooked tea every day. There were holidays in caravans where new friends, other kids just like me, would be made and forgotten about. We went to a little primary school and laughed about the dinners and loved the teachers and put our hands up for every question and looked for comfort whenever there was pain.

I had a Chopper bike, and mates. I played footie in the park and, like all the other kids, assumed that I would naturally one day become Kenny Dalglish. We lived for war films and the splash of football stickers; we ran everywhere and longed for

Christmas. At primary school teachers called me fanciful, a dreamer. Then at my comprehensive school my dreams became more important amongst the violence of growing up.

There were girls, too. Two types of girls: the ones who were always top of the class, never had fights and seemed to have perfect handwriting, and the ones who showed you their pants in the local park and made you feel a bit strange.

We all made plans for when we were grown up but we never really thought it would happen.

Then my elder brother John got his own record player. That's when life started.

John was three years older than me. I had my own records, I seem to remember: the ubiquitous mix of Walt Disney classics and nursery rhymes that seem to be given to every child at birth and upon the cover of which every child writes his name at the first spidery opportunity with a green crayon. But John, upon being given his own record player, started to buy his own records, and I listened to everything he bought. John told me that each record was brilliant, and I naturally agreed. I would sit cross-legged on the floor and watch as the wonderful seven-inch single was gently manoeuvred out of its sleeve and placed gingerly on the turntable. I would stare in awe as the arm of the hi-fi journeyed across the record on its fantastic adventure. The Undertones, Blondie, The Cure, Clash. 'These are brilliant,' said my brother. How right he was. Even I, a ten-year-old boy, with no idea about anything, could not help but be moved by the raw energy of the songs. They were much better than my ponderous nursery rhymes; they were much better than the songs at school and Mum's Radio 2 - these songs were ours. These records were loud and fast and dirty. You listened to them in your bedroom where your parents didn't go. You looked at the pictures of the band with their long hair, their dishevelled clothes and their grimaces that said they were much harder than the hardest lads in town. I didn't understand the words, but I knew that somehow they suggested things I shouldn't know about. I loved them all. I would sneak into John's room and play them when he was out. I would turn his little speakers up until I could hear my mum shouting from the bottom of the stairs. I loved her shouting. I loved the fact that she called the music a racket. It made my possession of them even more complete.

Over the next years I made the awkward transition from boy to teenager and as I did so my music remained with me, my constant friend. The records and bands inspired me, comforted me, educated me. I judged people by what albums they bought. My little mates who I had played football and army games with would be cast aside for the crime of buying a record by Jive Bunny or Kajagoogoo or Michael Jackson. Girls would be rejected as stupid for mooning over the last pop pin-ups. They didn't understand; they didn't realise that these people were imposters, posing as their heroes, contriving to make up feelings rather than articulating real ones. These pin-ups with their perfect hair and smiles hadn't suffered, and as such they couldn't truly know what it was like to be young. They would never make parents shudder with the memories of youth. They were phoney and I knew it.

At first I thought that only I knew it - well, me and Morrissey and one or two others. I thought that only I was suffering. A suffering that manifested itself in solitude and bad poetry. I rejected all the things that I had loved as a child. I considered everything through the medium of music. I listened to Joy Division and considered my own mortality; I listened to U2 (only the first album of course; once they got big I was no longer interested), and considered politics; I listened to The Undertones and considered girls. I wondered how I could make a statement like that; I wondered how I could communicate what I was feeling, how I was suffering. I wanted to be immortal like the songs.

I badgered my father and he bought me a guitar. It was black with silver edging: a Gibson Les Paul copy. I remember it cost him twenty-five quid from a bloke in Wallasey advertising in the Liverpool Echo. I ran my hands down its fretboard, I fingered its strings, I hung it around my neck and looked at myself in the mirror and suddenly I was no longer just Richie Strafe from Parkgate. I was more, I was male. I parted my legs slightly as I struck my pose - me and my axe were going to take on the world and fuck it.

I was fourteen. After a couple of months though I realised it wasn't going to be quite as straightforward as I had thought. I had not become Johnny Marr, in fact I was a bit shite. I might have my axe, I might have my attitude, but I couldn't play a bloody thing.

For months I struggled. I couldn't form the chords properly. I couldn't strum without simply making a horrible noise that bore no resemblance to the art I was trying to create. I put the guitar away. My family claimed it had been a fad. I sulked even more.

The change came when my mate Ned (real name Phil Needham, just turned 14, good at music and physics, going steady for two months with Mandy Friar) bought a bass. I liked Ned. He was a good bloke. He had loads of friends. He had a bass guitar and I went around to his house to play with him. We learnt together, me and Ned. He learnt the bass line to the Castrol GTX advert; I learnt the guitar riff to The Cure's The Forest. He learnt the bass line to Sunday Bloody Sunday, so I taught myself the guitar part. Slowly I started to get the hang of the chords and the arpeggios, strumming and damping. Slowly I started to work out chord sequences of my own. I thought they sounded good. I wrote little choruses and verses. I wrote my first songs. They sounded suspiciously like whatever I was listening to at the time, but that didn't matter. They were songs, they were my songs. I would be immortal after all.

My confidence in the playground improved along with my guitar playing. I started to revel in my newfound position in school as a bloke who was into different music and - rumour had it - played the guitar. I even managed to get my first snog under my belt with a Goth called Donna Macey (14, mad for

Robert Smith and the poetry of Shelley, used to have a mongrel dog called Frankie that she walked every night).

Some of my classmates started to catch up as well - of course these were the 1980s and most of the lads were into Simple Minds and Level 42, and most of the girls were into Bros and Johnny Hates Jazz and other such nonsense, but some were starting to take an interest in stuff that mattered. Kev Parsons, who I had previously rejected as being a spoony maths geek, wore a Dead Kennedys T-Shirt for PE, whilst Roger Davies - who played football for the school team - started reading the NME in form class.

It was 1985. I felt that I was losing out. If everyone started to like my music, I would become pointless, just another name on the register – and I wasn't going to have that, no way. Me and Ned needed to start an actual band. In a bold move I brought my guitar into school a couple of times to play under the loose pretence that I was going straight from school to rehearsals. In fact I was using the music room to practise during lunchtime as my dad had got seriously pissed off with me since I had invested in a 'Heavy Metal' effects pedal that initially made everything I tried to play sound like the bin lorry had parked outside.

It worked though. If nothing else, girls started getting interested in me. Donna Macey had chucked me for no apparent reason but that wasn't the end of the world; there were others. Jenny Sweet was a year younger and thought I was fantastic. Paula Fitzgerald wrote my name on her Geometry book. Then Sue Ellis let me feel her tits behind the curtain of the assembly hall in the Hallowe'en disco. She never spoke to me again but I knew that she would never forget that, never ever, ever. Spandau Ballet's Gold was playing over the DJ's crummy amplifiers and I put my hand up her chunky knit sweater and copped a feel. She could live until she was ninety, die in sick dribbling confusion and then live for eternity in some ethereal paradise, but I would always be the bloke who felt her up in the fourth form disco as Tony

Hadley told us to *'always believe in your soul'*. That, I reckoned, was, after a fashion, immortality.

Into the mélange of intense emotion, insecurity and dream-like unreality appeared Danny Cappaldi. Cappaldi didn't fit into any category. He wasn't Smiths or Bros, he wasn't Dépêche Mode or Spandau Ballet - he was too fucking cool and too fucking good-looking for his own good. All the boys tried to ignore him, all the girls tried to go out with him. He had only arrived in our school at the start of that year, after his father had moved up from London to run an Italian restaurant in the area. He had a Southern accent and dark, brooding good looks. He wore his school uniform properly - I mean he didn't cut his tie or replace his slacks with black jeans. He didn't have to. His only concession to teenage insurrection was a pair of bright red Kicker boots. He arrived in our class. The swots didn't want him; the sporty types didn't want him, and I, unable to pigeon-hole him, didn't want him either. He sat at the back with Ellie Smith who wore glasses and never spoke to anyone.

Ellie Smith.

I admired Ellie. I didn't fancy her. Well, not then. I admired her.

She didn't lend herself to the sexual interest of a fifteen-year-old boy. She wore her hair scraped back in the harsh custody of a ponytail; she wore a long skirt that reached just above her Doctor Martin'd calves and a baggy jumper that left everything to the imagination. And that was the problem: most fifteen-year-old boys don't have an imagination that goes a great deal further than fantasy about the girls who wore their short skirts tight and their school shirts tarty. Ellie Smith definitely didn't come into that category. I had no idea if she was fat or thin, woman or girl, and that was the way Ellie liked it. She never smiled, never laughed and never talked to anyone. Not even me, the self-styled dark poet and teenage sufferer of our class. I admired her though, and had done so since I noticed that in a moment of rare public pronouncement she had written Cocteau Twins on her green army school bag. I admired her when she told the English teacher that DH Lawrence was a misogynist for writing Lady Chatterley's Lover. I had to look up misogynist, but I didn't have to look up the expression on Mr Parsonage's face. He was stuffed and she was cool.

Cappaldi went to sit next to Ellie Smith. Of course he did. He was cool and so was she. He was too cool to be bothered about sitting next to a girl; she was too cool to worry about the fact that she was the only person in class who had a space next to her for him to sit in. They sat next to each other and naturally he didn't talk to me either. Not for three months. Then one morning in November as I stood outside the canteen with my guitar propped up in its flight bag behind me, he walked over. I remember it; I had my personal stereo on. The Jesus and Mary Chain whispering their dark rhymes in my ear. I pulled out the plugs as he approached me. He smiled a broad charismatic smile, as though we had been best buddies forever.

'What kind of guitar have you got?'

'It's crap, just a Gibson copy.'

I instantly hated myself for saying that. Why did I demean my guitar? Why did I diss the thing that I loved as much as anything - my axe, the thing that made me me? I have thought about that over the years. I have asked myself why I didn't proclaim that my guitar was actually quite good, said something positive, something witty, something strong. No, I dissed my guitar and, as I did so, I dissed myself. The writing was on the wall, painted in thick white emulsion. Cappaldi had managed in the course of one question to put me in my place, firmly behind him. The person who makes excuses, the person who apologises, the beta male. That's where I was as I stood with my back to the school canteen.

'I've got a Strat,' he responded. This shocked me. Not the fact that he had a Fender Stratocaster, the guitar of choice, the guitar I dreamt about owning. Of course he was going to own one of them, plus a Marshall amp as well, I assumed. What surprised me was the fact that he played at all. As I considered this, possibilities entered my head like lights flickering. Initially I was hostile: he might be a rival. He might already be in a band. He continued, 'We've got this basement in our house, it's brilliant. I've got all my gear set up. You should come over and jam sometime.'

To this day, I don't think that anyone has said anything as significant as that muted, innocuous invitation. Danny Cappaldi was inviting me to jam at his house, in his basement, which was brilliant and in which all his gear was set up. I was going to form a band. I was going to play my songs with someone else. I was going to be immortal. Of course at that time I would have formed a band with just about anyone, I would have jammed with anybody who asked me - the fact that it was Cappaldi would become important later. Like today. Like now, as I consider the best ways in which I can have him killed.

6

It had been six days since I got drunk with my mates and five days since Howard McPhee broke the news to me of my imminent exile back to whence I came.

Professionally my life in the previous five days could be summarised fairly easily.

Day One: spent the morning still sulking and avoiding all conversation with Tony Bowden. Him: 'The football was crap last night.' Me: 'Yup.' Him: 'How are you getting on with the cost schedule on the Isaac case?' Me: 'Yup.' That sort of thing. Thankfully Tony went out at lunchtime and bought two enormous cream slices and gave me one. It was hard to remain surly with jam and cream all over your face, and in any event it was becoming increasingly difficult to sustain my mood in the face of such a nice bloke who had done nothing wrong.

Day Two: five large boxes arrived, each filled with four lever arch files. Attached to them was a note from Howard McPhee telling me that within these boxes were the depositions and disclosed material in the Liverpool case. I was slightly shocked by their size and hoped that if I ignored them they would go away.

Day Three: with the five boxes still stood unopened in exactly the same place, McPhee visited our room to discuss the case. Unfortunately he found me trying to fire elastic bands into Tony's open mouth. McPhee told me that it would be better if I worked on them from home. In fairness, Tony attempted to resist this, saying that I couldn't be spared; at which point McPhee told him that he was taking on a new paralegal - an eighteen-year-old female student - to work with him. Tony's resistance crumbled like a November leaf in the autumn frost.

Day Four: at home, in my own flat surrounded by five bloody boxes. Spent the morning watching television and considering masturbation. Panic at three o'clock that suddenly I was about to have McPhee on the phone, so I opened boxes and placed files in some semblance of order. Then, tired, I catalogued my CD collection again.

Day Five, today: starting to lose the will to live. The flat seemed a cold, dark, small place now that I was confined to it. I had not left the house for a day. So after an early work spurt I decided to take a walk into the High Street. Before I went I put on the TV and flicked through the music channels. That was a mistake. Cappaldi's new single was due for release and some stupid, feckless American Music Channel was dedicating a day to him. They showed early footage, they showed interviews of him being a fucking egomaniacal prick. They showed him with Nelson Manfuckingdella, smiling and talking about some worthy cause, before they showed him with some ten-foot model he'd currently got on the go. The bastard, the bastard, the bastard.

I watched for forty minutes. Forty minutes. I suppose it is like someone who is afraid of snakes or spiders insisting on watching a documentary about some rare and nasty species slithering through the jungle. I suppose it is like a kid wanting to ride the biggest roller coaster. Forty minutes, then I dragged myself away.

I left my flat and decided to take a walk up to the High Street. Outside, the January morning was crisp and cloudless. There was a pale blue sky that seemed out of place above South London. This wasn't how I normally see Balham High Road; normally I see it out of resentful, just-woken eyes, blinded by the dismal prospect of a day at work, or tired, pissed-off eyes just wanting to rest at home. Normally I look out for potential muggers on the bus and avoid the faces of the people who surround me on my journeys who are doing exactly the same as me. But that day at 10.30 in the morning, my High Street was different. There were young mothers with prams, old people who stopped and talked to one another. The atmosphere was relaxed and calm - even friendly.

I called in at a second-hand bookshop I'd been meaning to look at for ages. They have an old vinyl record section. I leafed through it enjoying the images of bands I had long forgotten. I toyed with the idea of buying a book of poetry for Angela. I left the shop empty-handed.

It was also five days since I had told Angela that I would be away for a couple of months. Of course it was no big deal. Not really. If I was in the army (a pitiful thought), I might be called away for months on a regular basis. Or even if I was a lorry driver or a international businessman, or any job that required a great deal of travel, I would be away for weeks on end. I told her this. I told her this because I hoped that it would make it easier for her, so that it would smooth things over. But I didn't have to. I didn't have to smooth anything over. I didn't have to put up with her tears or tantrums or an ultimatum about it being 'her or my goddammed job'. I told her, and she nodded. I looked right into her eyes to see some kind of response, and she asked calmly when I would be leaving. Her words struck me like a cricket bat about my temple. Why did she say 'leaving'? Why didn't she say 'going'? Or 'when will you have to go'? Or anything but 'when are you leaving?' Those were her precise words. I told her not for a few weeks, and she nodded again. Then we had spaghetti Bolognese and watched Coronation Street.

That night I lay in bed awake. I sensed that Angela was awake as well. We ignored each other, just two bodies in the dark. I thought about going back home, but I thought more about Angela and me. She was lying beside me, her breathing quiet and rhythmical. I wondered what she was thinking about, but something stopped me from asking her. Our relationship was shit, but this was the first time that I knew, that I could sense that she did not want me to hold her, or kiss her or touch her. Perhaps her indifference to my departure had made her realise, made her see that there was no need to pretend any more.

For the next couple of days we revolved around each other like two planets spiralling away in different directions. We spoke as normal. We ate, watched the TV. We asked each other about our days. It was normal, but we had to work hard to make it normal - and that was the problem.

I continued my walk up the High Street. I bought a newspaper and decided to go and read it in a café. The nearest was Star Kebabs - a particularly nasty and unhygienic establishment, resplendent with the rush of chip fat streaming through your nostrils, sticky floors and an array of strange-coloured concoctions kept in old plastic ice cream tubs under the counter. I ordered a cup of tea and sat down in the hard yellow chair that was screwed to the floor for safety.

I took a slurp from my tea and opened my paper. I took no notice of anyone else in the café. I flicked to the back page and read about football; then I read about nasty goings-on in the Middle East. Then I turned a page and it was him - Cappaldi, at the opening of a new movie.

I didn't believe it. There was me, sitting in a hard plastic screwed-down chair drinking stewed tea in a kebab shop, whilst he was in Leicester Square being photographed at the opening of a new Hollywood blockbuster.

I could have killed him. I *could* kill him.

I could strap semtex to myself and wait for him. I could wear a long coat - an overcoat - with the explosives attached to me. I would have a button attached to my explosives that would run down the arm of my coat. I would hold my button in my palm. Around me people would be screaming for him, unaware of me, unaware of my presence and my mission. I would have to have some kind of symbol, though. Yes, in the pocket of my overcoat I would have some symbol - a book perhaps, like Mark Chapman carrying The Catcher in the Rye as he gunned down John Lennon. What book? I realised that the last book I had read was Harry bleeding Potter. That wouldn't do. I could hardly commit an assassination and leave as my enigmatic symbol a book about a boy wizard and his poxy mates. No, not a book - a record. Yes, my symbol would be a record, perhaps Jeff Buckley's Grace or The Doors' LA Woman - something that people would discuss, an album that would become synonymous with my act.

In my head I pictured the scene. He would appear out of some limousine or from the entrance of a fancy club. I would confront him. I would look him in the eye - he would recognise me, he *would* recognise me. I would go towards him. He would probably be confused - it has been years. He wouldn't know what to say, how to react - he couldn't treat me like another fan. He couldn't treat me like some stalking photographer. Then I would press the button. We would become immortal together.

I considered whether it would be okay to have the album on CD, or would it somehow be more powerful if I remained pure and had it on Long Playing Vinyl?

'Your symbol would be destroyed in the explosion.'

The voice came from the table to my left.

I turned around sharply towards it. Sitting on the table next to me, unmistakeable with his leathery tan, snow-white hair and appalling dress sense was him - Slacksman.

I closed my eyes. Then slowly opened them, assuming that he would be gone by the time I had focussed again. But there he was. There he was, sipping some kind of hot beverage out of a mug. There he was, wearing a white suit over a pink pastel T-shirt. There he was, commenting on my plans for Danny Cappaldi.

How had I not noticed him before? Surely he had been there?

I tried to remember if the café had been empty a few seconds earlier. I was sure that it had.

I stared at him.

'Your symbol - it's good in theory, but in practice it will never work,' he continued as I slowly shook my head and tried to make sense of who this man was and what he wanted. At least this time I was sober.

'I don't know who you are, I don't know what you are doing, but I'm not interested.' I stood up and went to leave the café.

I knew his eyes were fixed upon me. I wanted to walk away but knew that there was no point; we would just meet again if I did. He would engineer it; somehow he would make it happen. Why? What did this strange bloke want with me? Why was he doing this?

'You are interested though, aren't you, Mr Strafe?'

His voice was calm and measured, his accent making him sound learned and wise. I sat down again. I was resigned to what was going to happen - whatever that would be. Nevertheless, I put up one last pitiful effort at opposition.

'Go on then, Mr Whateveryournameis: tell me how you do it. Is it some kind of trick? Has one of my mates put you up to this? Or is it part of some God-awful early Saturday evening light entertainment programme? Come on, is Noel Edmonds or Ant and Dec about to arrive from somewhere and invite the nation to take the piss out of me?'

Slacksman ignored my outburst, pushed his tea away. 'I don't know what they have done to this tea. It tastes like dirt,' he said, before muttering something about expecting it from a Turkish establishment.

I snorted derisorily and made another attempt to leave.

'Please sit down, Mr Strafe, and I shall try to explain.'

I sat down, this time across the table from him.

'Good. Explain away, Mr...?'

'Costas, Doctor Costas.' His title - Doctor - threw me.

'Doctor,' I snorted back at him. 'Is that like Doctor Who, Doctor No, or Carry On Doctor?'

He clearly had no idea what I was talking about at this

point, but continued politely. 'No, Mr Strafe. I am a Doctor of Philosophy.'

'Philosophy? How does that enable you to read my mind and comment on my private thoughts?'

He gave me a playful smile. 'Mr Strafe, I am Greek. We Greeks are the fathers of all knowledge. Plato was the father of Politics, Socrates the father of Philosophy, Archimedes the father of Physics, Pythagoras - Maths. Need I go on?'

I chortled. 'Hold on, let me get this right. You are Greek, and therefore by definition are able to read my mind?'

He waved his hand nonchalantly, as though the proposition I had just put to him was the most natural in the world.

'Listen Doctor fucking Slacksboy, I've been to Greece, and I've yet to meet a Greek who could read my bill, let alone my mind.'

I wasn't trying to be offensive. I had very much enjoyed my two weeks in Kos, and had found the Greeks extremely pleasant and helpful, but I was understandably perturbed by the notion that all Greeks could read my mind.

'Mr Strafe,' he replied coolly, 'of course not all Greeks can read your mind. Such a thing would be preposterous, just like the view that all Englishmen are lager-drinking, offensive, uncultured yobs.'

'So what are you saying, then?' I continued, confused.

Doctor Costas leant back in his seat and took out a packet of cigarettes from the inside pocket of his suit. He offered me one, which I declined without speaking. He lit it slowly and took a short drag before letting it smoulder at arm's length in his hand, which was placed flat on the table. He looked as though he was about to impart to me some sort of painful information that required particularly careful phrasing.

'Mr Strafe, I can't read all your thoughts.'

This was good.

'Only the thoughts which are relevant to my mission.'

This was mad.

'Your mission!' I exclaimed, with a barely concealed look of hilarity on my face. 'What is your mission?'

He took another drag on his cigarette, longer this time, and returned his hand to the table.

He ignored my question. 'I know, Mr Strafe, that you consider the meaning of life.'

I let out a chortle.

'Do you know what it is?'

This was priceless. I looked around me. Yes, up above the counter in oversized, drunk-friendly lettering, the menu still told me that a shish kebab would cost £4.50 and chips £1.20. On the tiled ceramic walls was an advert for an item of food called a Chico Burger that I had seen advertised in every kebab shop I had ever been in, but had never seen anyone ever buy. The olive-skinned bloke with a moustache was still piling a disgusting brown meaty substance onto his doner kebab spit. I was, without doubt, in a kebab shop, and I was about to be told the meaning of life.

I smelt a rat - a large, strangely-dressed, suntanned rat, and it was becoming clear now that this rat was about to tell me something about religion. His mission was clearly to convert me to some kind of Greek-based sect. Fucking hell, I thought, perhaps it was a prerequisite that everyone had to wear light grey slip-on shoes and comfortable trousers.

I shrugged my shoulders, resigned myself to hear what he had to say, and watched as a beaming smile broke out on his face. It was eerie, as though he again knew what I was thinking and found it amusing. This time he chose not to tell me. Instead, he simply smiled at me and declared that he was a 'keeper'.

'What, like a goalkeeper?' I replied sarcastically.

He ignored my comment and returned to the meaning of life. There was a degree of seriousness in his voice now. 'All creatures, Mr Strafe, have as a goal the need to live and to continue their species - yes?'

I nodded in agreement.

'Is this the meaning of life?' he added rhetorically. I

considered his question. It's true that I had espoused the 'you're born, you eat, work and shag, then you die' theory of life on more than one occasion during the 'there must be more to it all than this' conversations at dinner parties and down the pub.

'What more can there be?' I proffered, attempting to sound ambiguous.

'For a worm, Mr Strafe, nothing. For a cat or a dog or a chimpanzee, nothing.' He smiled at me and took another drag from his cigarette before continuing. 'But what is the meaning of *your* life?'

I shrugged. 'I don't know.'

I didn't know.

'Why do you think so much about killing this man Cappaldi?'

I shook my head and gritted my teeth - not this again.

'I don't think about killing this man. I don't know why you keep bloody mentioning it.' There was defiance in my voice.

Slacksman leant across the table towards me. The smile was gone. 'Mr Strafe, I don't choose to know what is in your mind. It is my mission, my job.' His tone was aggressive, menacing. I was starting to worry about where our conversation was going - what was his mission?

'Alright,' I said, 'maybe I do hate the bastard, maybe I do harbour thoughts about killing him, but that's all they are, and that's all they ever will be, and besides, what the fuck has it got to do with you? What are you talking about *"your mission"*?'

'For many of us humans, Mr Strafe, being born, eating, fornicating and working, followed by death, is not enough, is it?' I was struck dumb by his chilling ability to paraphrase one of my favourite arguments.

He continued, becoming more impassioned now, thrusting his tanned hands towards me. 'For many of us humans there is the pursuit of immortality for its own sake.' He stopped for a second as the chap from behind the counter arrived with another cup of tea. As he stirred his tea, his words resonated through my head. I tried to make sense of them.

'My mission,' he continued, still stirring his cup, 'as one of the Keepers of the Great Library of Myths and Legends, is to store, record and research people's pursuit of immortality. In the library is kept every one of our stories, each of our individual paths through life. I am, naturally, in the Section of the Immortals.'

I stared blankly at him. Fucking hell - The Great Library of Myths and Legends, Section of the Immortals. What was coming next? Elves and bloody Hobbits?

Quite clearly this person was mad. Surely he was mad?

He continued. I wanted him to.

'In some cases, though, people need to be ushered in a particular direction in their pursuit of immortality. You are one of those people. Because without their stories to be loved and cherished and passed from one generation to the next, there is no human spirit, there are no dreams for us to emulate, no reason to live. That is what makes us different from the worm, the giraffe and the chimp.'

'What?' I was totally confused now. 'What do you mean? What kind of direction? What is in this library? Where is it? What have giraffes got to do with anything?'

Doctor Costas - Slacksman - looked at his watch then smiled at me.

'I have to go,' he said, standing up.

'Go?' I was about to tell him that he couldn't go and that I needed to hear more, but I stopped myself. I wasn't the type of person who begged mad people or religious nutcases or whatever this man surely was to stay and talk about mythical libraries.

He put a sheepskin coat over his shoulders.

'We will meet again. I will explain more then.' He went out into the cold South London air. I stood up to follow him but, as I did so, the bloke from behind the counter demanded his money. I grappled with some change. I rushed outside, but he was gone.

For a few moments I stood and contemplated what had happened. I painted the picture of the Great Library of Myths and Legends in my mind. It was a large marble edifice with legions of mighty pillars leading up to its enormous, intimidating entrance. Inside, I imagined miles of corridors piled high with leather-bound volumes. For a few seconds I enjoyed this image, let it grow and live in consciousness, then cynicism took over and destroyed it, razed it to the ground. There was no Great Library of Myths and Legends, this man was no keeper of the Immortality Section, he was simply a nutcase who had overheard my conversation in the pub and had struck lucky when he had seen me a second time. That was it. Myths and Legends - fucking hell. I shook my head and smiled to myself, almost enjoying the fact that I was still naïve enough to have given this strangely-dressed nutter some minutes of my time. If I saw him again I would call the police, because obviously he was weird.

With that final thought the Great Library was destroyed and in its place in my mind came a new image: that of Howard McPhee and his fucking boxes. I felt a strange and sudden desire to start doing some work.

7

The case of *R v Hawkins* didn't immediately mean anything to me. Howard had failed to tell me anything whatsoever about it, other than the fact that it was a murder, would take up to two months to try, and would be heard in Liverpool.

I wasn't therefore prepared for the revelation when I opened the first box, took out the first ring binder and read the opening lines of the case summary:

Terence Hawkins is charged with three counts of murder – of Martin O'Kane, Graham De Voos and Jimmy Avro, whose headless corpses were found in a lock-up garage in Wavertree, Liverpool...

My eyes involuntarily widened, my heart quickened and my bottom lip dropped - this was no ordinary murder, this was the Wavertree Execution. Fucking hell, I was going to be looking after the welfare of the Wavertree Executioner - Terry Hawkins.

I read on. I read on and considered what monumental event had pushed Terry Hawkins down his particular avenue of life. What had made him choose the particular path that set into play a series of events that now led him to languish in a Liverpool jail awaiting his trial for triple murder and would bring him into contact with me?

Terry was only 27. He had been born in a nasty part of Wimbledon, a nice part of South London. Was that it? Was it his growing up in such close proximity to such affluence that made him covet it and not care what he did to get it? Or was he simply born iffy?

They said that he had executed three 'Liverpudlian businessmen': Graham De Voos, Martin O'Kane and Jimmy Avro, whose corpses had been found in a lock-up garage in a civilised part of Liverpool. They said that the lock-up had been specially modified to take on the appearance of an execution chamber and that the three men had been taken there and kept in chains for up to a week, before being forced one by one to place their heads on a large block and be executed, using an antique ceremonial axe. They said that this was a ritual murder.

The press had had a field day. **THREE MEN KILLED IN DUNGEON OF HELL**, cried one headline. **MYSTERY OF THE WAVERTREE EXECUTIONER**, cried another. They speculated. They rumbled out possibilities of bizarre sexual rituals, black magic and the crime underworld. The police, though, knew straightaway. The police knew that De Voos, O'Kane and Avro were businessmen whose nominal business was second-hand furniture but who made their money from drugs.

They were the men who controlled much of the supply in the North-West; they were the men who controlled the import of heroin and crack cocaine. They were the men who paid other men to sell drugs to other men who sold them on at street corners and crack houses on run-down estates. They were the men who cut the drugs with rat poison, chalk dust and flour, then sold it at a price they more or less fixed. They controlled the supply and they determined the demand by encouraging a few cheap freebies to be given to the vulnerable, knowing well that giving away an addictive drug is a type of loss-leader, so effective that it could have been devised by the cleverest of Harvard Business graduates.

Eventually the papers worked out that the three 'Liverpudlian businessmen' weren't quite as deserving of their sympathy as they first thought. But what did they have to do with Terry Hawkins?

Terry left school with no qualifications. But Terry was gobby and quick-witted, hard and brave. At first, his only ambition was self-preservation, which meant being the leader of the gang that hung around his estate and terrorised his school and the local shops. This Terry achieved effortlessly. He used violence when it was required - mindless, bloody violence that would leave victims scared and damaged. He would carry out the most daring thefts and appear the most defiant in court because that was what it took to maintain his position. He shagged the most, drank the most and took the most drugs; then he disappeared into a morass of junkiedom. Terry went from being the seventeen-year-old leader of the gang to just another teenage addict, stealing old people's bric-a-brac in return for smack and crack cocaine.

But there was something about Terry. Inside him still were the embers of defiance. Even when he was sitting in public lavatories sticking a used needle into his groin, or trying to sell a twenty-year-old video recorder that he had risked eighteen months in the Scrubs to steal to buy a ten-pound bag of crack, there was still the spark of resistance. After a particular nasty knife fight when he had been too smashed on drugs to properly defend himself, Terry had a moment of clarity. He realised that the way of the junkie meant death, prison or rehabilitation on *their* terms - and their terms meant becoming an honest citizen, returning to the estates he had grown up on, not as the leader of the gang, but as one of those the new leaders terrorised. That wasn't going to happen to Terry Hawkins. Terry came off the street drugs and started to sell. He became the man who cut the bags of heroin with chalk and talcum powder. He became the man who said to a fourteen-year-old girl, 'You can have this together with your dope for now, and pay me later.' He found his patch and grew strong from the depravation of others. He cut the ears off rivals who strayed on his turf, he bought a big car and learnt the two lessons you need to stay ahead of the law: never get caught with anything on you, and make sure that no one will ever grass you up.

He made money and opened a 'legitimate business' running nightclubs and bars. He bought one of the big houses he had seen and coveted as a child; he married a girl who other men fancied and had a baby daughter. Terry Hawkins never got caught.

The investigation into the deaths of De Voos, O'Kane and Avro was extensive. Police found no trace of any forensic evidence in the 'execution chamber'. Police interviewed every dealer and junkie in Liverpool, but no one knew anything. They painstakingly pored over the dead men's accounts and found their only lead. Prior to their rather gruesome demise a Mr T Hawkins had been using the accounts of the three dead men's businesses to conduct various transactions. Within days Hawkins was arrested and interviewed. They said that Terry Hawkins had been involved in a money-laundering scheme with De Voos and Co and had taken matters into his own hands when things had gone wrong.

Hawkins said it wasn't him. He told the police that he had an alibi for every day of the week in which it was alleged that the three men had been kept in the chamber. His pretty wife said that he had been with her some of the time; his business associates, friends and family offered similar accounts of his whereabouts, far away from a lock-up garage in Wavertree. The case against Hawkins would have collapsed but for one man, Colin Rutland, the one business associate of Hawkins who had decided that it was in his interests to give the police a different account of Hawkins' movements during the week when De Voos and his hapless mates were being prepared for the block.

I read the papers with a renewed interest in my job. This was exciting stuff. This wasn't old men being hit by flying farmyard animals, this was the case that had gripped the nation - the Wavertree Executions. I forgot about Slacksman. I forgot about Danny Cappaldi, I put my troubles with Angela to the back of my mind and started to consider that my months at home working on this case might not be so bad. This was, after all, a famous case. A killer, an immortal crime, a crime that would live on, that people would hear about long after all those involved had come to their own ends.

I read on - descriptions of the lock-up garage, with its heavy damp dark walls, discoloured by blood and a dim light bulb; the efforts of Scenes of Crime officers to find fingerprints amongst the gore and sinew of three decapitated bodies. I read page after page until my brain reeled with the words of police officers and their statements written in their tortuous, regimented English. I looked at photographs of headless corpses partially covered with brown rugs, at bloodstains and large blocks of wood, where I assumed the three dead men had placed their heads for the last time.

My head spun and a wave of nausea passed through me.

I lay back on the couch.

I tried to read some more. It was no use.

I slept.

In my sleep I dreamt of being chased through snowy woods by Nazis. In my dream I had to make it to a garage that I could see in the distance, where I would be safe. My feet crunched in the snow and I could sense the evil of the Nazis as they pursued me, relentless, getting closer and closer. The closer they got, the more my feet struggled in the snow. In the distance, the door of the garage swung open and out popped Sir Cliff Richard - Sir Cliff sodding Richard - why?

Sir Cliff - to his credit - seemed extremely concerned about my plight and started to beckon me towards the garage. Behind me the Nazis were now close, their bullets whistling past my ears, their bombs exploding all around me, as I focussed on Sir Cliff. Then as I started to feel a need to have a wee, something unexpected happened. Sir Cliff was transformed into Angela. She was shouting something, I could hear her voice. I could see her lips moving, her arms waving at me to hurry. What was she saying? What *was* she saying? 'Rich? Rich, what are you doing? Rich, RICH!'

Angela wasn't standing by the garage, she was standing by the door. I wasn't being chased by Nazis, of course I wasn't.

I sat up, bleary-eyed, and tried to focus on her. Her lips were thin; her face had that muted, tired look of someone who has had a hard day at work.

'Bloody hell, Richard, you've been in all day and you still haven't done that fucking washing-up in the kitchen - thanks a fucking lot.'

I ignored her statement.

'You'll never guess who it is we're representing in Liverpool - the Wavertree fucking executioner.'

She stopped for a second, considered this, before adding rather enigmatically, 'Don't forget, tomorrow night we're at Byron and Lucy's for dinner.'

I sat back on the couch. I wanted to tell her about the Wavertree Executioner. I had even been considering telling her about Slacksman, but I thought better of it. She was tired and obviously more concerned about the washing-up than about my involvement with either a triple murderer or the Great Library of Myths and Legends.

In any event she had taken her bollocking into the kitchen. I listened to her banging about. She was making a point. With each teacup that rattled against the draining board she was sending me a message. With each knife she threw violently into the cutlery drawer she was expressing her opinion of me, of us. She didn't have to - our conversation had said it all. Three statements made by two people. She told me about the undone washing-up, I told her about my murder, she told me about the dinner party round at her boss's. That wasn't interaction, that wasn't a conversation - that was an exchange of commands and observations. We might as well be two of those prototype Japanese robots that are able to do everything other than react humanely to a human situation. I wouldn't tell her about Slacksman, but I would go into the kitchen, grab a tea towel, and tell her about the Wavertree Executioner. After all, she was the girl who had been interested in me.

Well, once upon a time.

Byron Majors is Angela's boss. I hate him. I hate his poxy big Docklands apartment with its enormous windows and state-of-the-art everything. I hate his wife, the perfect Lucy, for putting up with him, and I hate the dinner parties that periodically we are invited to attend. I mean, why? No one seems to enjoy them. Perhaps Byron wakes up one morning and thinks, 'I know, I haven't patronised anyone for a while. I'll invite Angela and her strange boyfriend around for diner.'

Notwithstanding, my record at Byron and Lucy's is so bad I am amazed that they have even contemplated inviting me to their house to break bread.

On the first occasion, my misdemeanour was falling into a deep rage followed by a soundless sulk after Lucy put Simply Red on their expensive Bang & Olufsen music system when we arrived. I said nothing throughout the night. On occasion two, having been warned about my surliness and tipped off that people thought I was being shy - shy! - I was protesting over heinous crimes against popular music - I got incredibly pissed and fell heavily on the stairs, causing an embarrassing nosebleed and a fairly large stain on their white shag-pile.

I am not confident about tonight, I thought. I am just not good at dinner parties. They are the adult version of exams. You sit around a table and are tested on your knowledge of current events, culture, other people's desperate problems and the office politics. You are then required to comment warmly and sincerely about the food and the wine, the new house or décorations that the hosts invited you to coo over and, invariably, fucking invariably, over someone's new baby/precocious child/pregnancy, and all when you've drunk enough red wine to kill a small horse.

We arrived at Byron and Lucy's at five past eight. I was wearing a tie. Angela, fair play, looked pretty foxy in a small black dress. I had been warned to within an inch of my life to behave. I was not allowed to mention music, politics and my views on accountancy ('isn't that just spending your day doing sums?'). I was allowed to talk briefly and modestly about the Wavertree Executioner. I was only allowed one glass of wine per two glasses of water.

Lucy met us, grinning at the door. There then followed one of those awful kissy kissy moments that are completely alien to all men of a certain class from north of Watford - Lucy offered me her left cheek and went to kiss me on my right. Unfortunately I offered her my left cheek and went to kiss her left - there followed a brief and extremely embarrassing French kiss as we both met in the middle and I inadvertently stuck my tongue in and she mistakenly gave my top lip a little naughty nip.

We parted, me far more embarrassed than her, and made small talk about their heroic efforts to remove my blood from their stair carpet. We all chortled. 'Oh, how funny it was when Richie almost broke his nose.' Then we were led into the lounge where I was simultaneously handed a glass of champagne and introduced to a group of six others, some of whom I knew. There was Ray (40s, works with Angela, dull, dull, dull) and his wife Clare (I don't know her, but my initial impression was that she is obviously lacking in imagination having married Ray), Harry (30s, posh, already dominating the room in a way in which only the expensively educated can), who appeared to be with Emma (or was it Anna, who was already affecting an air of disinterest in a way in which only a truly posh bird can), and finally Guy (late 20s, the office spunk). Angela talks about him incessantly. She obviously fancies him. I checked him out and was glad to see that he is receding, despite his attempts to grow his hair long in Hugh Grant style. Guy was clearly being set up with Jasmine (quite fit, 20s, too much make-up, and slightly too chunky to end up with Guy, but nevertheless you probably would, well *I* would. Guy probably doesn't have to - the twat's probably got standards that would make a premiership footballer jealous). Jasmine laughed every time Guy breathed and flicked her hair back so much that I started to wonder if she might have nits. Posh birds have their place, definitely, but one thing they can't do is pull. Rough birds pull at an alarmingly successful rate.

Anyway.

I smile at no one in particular and remember Angela's words.

God, I hate these occasions. I concentrated on not drinking my champagne in two thirsty gulps. I watched Angela effortlessly add herself to the room. She was already flirting with Guy, she was already smiling happily. I hadn't seen her smile for so long.

I drank my champagne in three gulps.

We were placed in our seats at the table. I was in between Jasmine and Lucy, who appeared unfazed by our snog. She turned to me and asked me how work was. I opened my mouth to answer, but she ignored me, chastised herself and said she had forgotten to put music on. I feared the worst. I braced myself for an evening of Elton John or Phil Collins. She sauntered over to her Bang & Olufsen hi-fi and fiddled with the controls. I felt a wave of desperation pass over me. I was merely seconds from self-righteous, indulgent ballads with big drums. To my surprise, the Majors had got themselves some kind of ambient Trance/House CD. It was a little predictable, but infinitely better than Simply Red or Genesis. I clutched my champagne flute in celebration and knocked back a thirsty gulp of grapey bubbles before remembering my instructions.

The first hour was good. I remembered to drink water with each drink of booze. I remembered to smile and to comment appropriately and at the right time.

'Yes, I agree, Guy. Whatever people say about Tony Blair, the economy has never been so settled....'

'Harry, you're so right. I wouldn't want to be a first-time buyer now either..'

'Oh, you'd be amazed, Lucy. Liverpool has such a diverse range of culture...'

Blah, blah, clichéd, middle-class blah.

The second hour saw the onset of a couple of good bottles of red wine. My guard slipped slightly and I upped the pace of my wine consumption whilst allowing my water intake to drop. Still I maintained my stoical good behaviour, but I could feel myself tiring of not talking about me, or anything that interested me.

Byron was now firmly ensconced in the role of raconteur, chairman and philosopher-in-chief. He loudly told us that he and Lucy were considering selling the Docklands apartment and moving to the country. He reckoned he'd get 'a mill' for the apartment.

Unfortunately, I failed to grasp that when he said 'mill' he was not considering the acquisition of an old-fashioned flour making outbuilding.

'Byron,' I said, 'don't you think a mill will look a bit silly around here, this being a very modern development and that?'

As soon as the words left my mouth I realised what I had said. The table erupted into laughter. Even Angela was pissing herself at my faux pas. In fact she was laughing most.

Bollocks to them. I drank more wine. I stopped drinking water altogether.

Lucy, fair play to her, seemed to sense my embarrassment. She asked me about work. It was a nice polite question. It should have been my cue to talk modestly and with charm about the Wavertree Executioner. But I didn't want to be polite. I didn't want to talk modestly or charmingly about anything with these people.

'It's alright,' I grunted, like a spotty teenager being asked about his favourite lesson at school.

She held her fixed grin for a few polite seconds, realised that she wasn't going to get much more by way of a response, and got up to change the CD.

I recognised the opening guitar chords immediately. The big, open chords that linger, before being modulated ever so slightly by the gentle push of a tremolo. I recognised them immediately because they were the guitar chords of Danny Cappaldi. They were the guitar chords he played to me. They were the guitar chords we played together. Before. They were the chords that formed *his* first hit single. Only some clever DJ had mixed them with a syncopated drum box beat and the wailing of a soul singer to turn our teenage two-minute burst of energy into a dour ten-minute trance piece designed to blend pleasantly into the background of dinner parties. Not too loud or meaningful, nothing that might disturb the likes of Byron and his self-congratulatory soliloquies.

Immediately I clasped my hand to my head. 'What the fuck is this?'

The table stopped. Even Byron stopped. Angela frowned at me from behind Guy who stared as though I was quite mad.

'What the fuck is this?'

I felt like Charlton Heston discovering the remains of the Statue of Liberty in the Planet of the Apes as all the monkeys and apes look on, clueless as to what he's talking about. I was tempted to shout 'Goddamn them all to hell!' But instead a deep groan emanated from deep in my soul. 'I can't believe he has allowed this.'

I still had my hand clasped to my face. I was no longer making dinner party conversation. There was panic around the table. They didn't know whether to find my outburst fascinating or embarrassing. Apart from Angela, who was immediately embarrassed. 'Richard,' she hissed from across the table.

'I can't believe that he allowed this. Not with this song. He is such a...'

I avoid the 'c' word - the water must have done the trick there - but it didn't stop my rant. 'That's it, bollocks to it, I am definitely going to have him killed. This is the last straw.'

Byron was interested now. 'Who do you want to have killed?'

I didn't answer him. I just continued to make groaning noises as Guy, Harry and Jasmine swapped glances and started to giggle. My rage went from amber to scarlet. I felt the need to make some kind of statement. I contemplated hitting Guy, the smirking bastard, but not being one to fight, I ruled it out. Instead I made my way to the CD player and removed the offending disc. I had my back to the table now, but I knew that Angela was on her feet. I heard her shouting, 'Richard, don't!' It was too late. I was going to vent my anger on the CD.

I was going to make a scene by breaking the object of the betrayal of my youth into tiny bits.

I grabbed the disc in my fists and made to snap it.

Surprisingly, the CD was not easy to snap.

I tried to bend it. The fucker.

It refused.

In fact, the stubborn bastard proved impossible to break. I wrestled with it, but the evil - if deceptively sturdy - little prick steadfastly refused to play along with my outburst. I slammed it against my thigh. Nothing. It remained intact, its title: 'Jamie Oliver's Dinner Party Tracks Volume III' glinting at me from its indestructible surface.

The atmosphere in Lucy and Byron's dining room had gone from confusion to concern to mirth as they watched me struggling with the CD, bashing it against my head. I could hear the sounds of giggles, but above them I could hear the voice of Angela.

'Richard, just go home. Richard, go home now.'

A moment of clarity. I stopped. I turned to her. Her face was crimson with anger. I looked around the room. All eyes were upon me. I left the room. I left the pristine warmth of Byron and Lucy's Docklands apartment and walked into the night.

It was quiet outside. The night was clear, with a chilliness that you could smell and hear. I looked upwards in desperation. I could see stars, but the drink and overwhelming realisation that I had been a total prick forced me to ignore them. I started to walk home. I knew that Angela wouldn't be coming after me. She was tired of me.

8

I rushed home on the day Danny Cappaldi told me to come around and jam in his basement where all his gear was set up. I rushed home, ran up the single flight of stairs and closed my bedroom door behind me. I plugged in my guitar, and there, surrounded by posters and schoolbooks, I wrote a song. I'd had the idea for a few weeks. It was about the fat lad in the third year who'd been bullied and tried to take an overdose of his mother's contraceptive pill. The poor bastard. Everyone said that he was going to grow even bigger tits and that his voice would never break. I am proud to say that I refrained from the chants and jokes at the time. I felt genuinely sorry for the bloke; my view was that if you're going to kill yourself, do it properly.

I remember the words and the tune clearly. Only four chords. My favourites at the time: a C7th and an A minor for the verse followed by a G and B flat for the chorus. The words were my teenage take on teenage suicide.

Billy Don't
The girls in class all laugh at you,
Your ma says take a second to
Count to ten and it'll be alright,
Best to run when you just can't fight,
Billy don't

You can't stop thinking that there's better than this
You can't stop thinking that you won't be missed
You're sick and tired of hiding from the inside gang
You're thinking about leaving with a crash and a bang
Billy don't
You can't afford to fake it,
You can't afford to make it,
You can't afford to lose it,
You can't afford to choose it,
Billy don't, Billy don't, Billy don't

I was pleased with it. The lad in the third form was called
Dominic but that didn't go, so I called him Billy - which,
looking back, borrowed heavily from The Jam's Billy Hunt,
but at the time I didn't care. True, it was hardly Bob Dylan and
I'm not quite sure who the *inside gang* were, but it all rhymed
and scanned okay. I would play it to Ned and then - the big test
- to Danny Cappaldi that weekend. The weekend I had
decided we would jam.

I spoke to Danny the next day in school. An inner force, a
determination, made me overcome my shyness and cool and
invite myself and Ned around that weekend to jam. Danny's
response was amazing. 'Brilliant,' he exclaimed, smiling his
beaming smile. 'We can form a band.'

I'll never forget that first time in his basement. Me and Ned
called around at his big house at exactly eleven o'clock, the
designated hour, and were handed a can of lager each from his
fridge. Fantastic - booze. This was rock and roll. My mum
would have killed me but his dad didn't bat an eyelid. We sat
in his kitchen and I sipped the beer, not wanting to say that I
didn't really like it much. I wanted to go into his basement.
Today wasn't the day for further experiments with alcohol;
today was the day to go into Danny Cappaldi's basement
where his gear was all set up, to form a band, to play my

songs, to start on the road to immortality. But Cappaldi wanted to sit and talk for a while. He took me and Ned to his bedroom and played us his Husker Du LPs. I looked up at his posters. They were cool - Joe Strummer smashing his guitar, a poster of Led Zeppelin's The Song Remains the Same album, and some of The Smiths.

'I love The Smiths,' he said. 'Do you like The Smiths?'

Did I like The Smiths? Did I like The Smiths? Do fish swim in rivers? Do my lungs fill with air? Morrissey and The Smiths were the most important thing in my teenage life.

After a while I heard the doorbell ring. Danny jumped up. 'That'll be my cousin.'

I was starting to get anxious: what did his cousin have to do with it? Why weren't we already jamming downstairs? It was a feeling of anxiety that I was going to get used to over the next few years: Danny Cappaldi did things at his pace. Danny Cappaldi controlled everything. I shot a concerned look towards Ned, but he was engrossed with Danny's record collection.

Danny returned to the room accompanied by a tall male with long black hair.

'This is my cousin David, but everyone calls him Pim,' he told us. 'He's going to be our drummer.' Pim smiled at us. He was already holding his drumsticks. He was older than us - about seventeen - and, so we found out later, worked in one of Danny's father's pizza restaurants. I was happy, but still anxious. I concluded that I was probably still on the road to immortality, but Danny was definitely driving the car.

The rest of the morning will remain in my memory forever.

We went down into his basement. It was the most amazing place I'd ever been in my life: large and dark with a damp, musty smell of cigarettes and slowness. It was everything that I had dreamed of. It was the place where immortality is carved out.

In the corner was an already set-up drum kit - I had never been so close to a proper drum kit before. Either side of the kit were the stacked speakers from Danny's PA system that were joined by a system of leads and wires to what I assumed was a mixing desk. Fuck me, a mixing desk. I looked behind me to where Danny stood smiling.

'It belongs to the group who play in some of my dad's restaurants, but we can use it any time.'

There was a Marshall amp for my guitar, a Laney Bass amp for Ned. In a cleared area in front of the kit stood two skinny microphone stands. It looked like something I had seen on the TV. It looked like the set on The Tube where Jools Holland would announce the acts for the forthcoming show. My heart raced: the microphones were the most daunting thing of all. I contemplated the prospect of actually uttering something into a mike, something that was mine, amplified through this system so that other people could hear.

Fuck.

'You can plug into that Marshall,' Danny told me. Of course I agreed. Danny's Fender was already on a stand in front of some other amp. He watched me as I slowly unzipped my guitar case and tentatively unveiled my crappy guitar. Ned was tuning up his bass, sitting nonchalantly on one of the battered leather sofas that were dotted around the side of the room. Danny lit a fag and offered me one. I refused and felt like a twat. Ned took one.

I had to make some kind of statement. Behind me, Pim was sitting on the drum stool and hitting the snare hard while readjusting his hi-hat and bass drum pedals. Danny switched on the PA and a loud hum from the speakers added to the noise. I had to make some kind of statement. I had to assert myself.

'What shall we play then?' asked Danny above the noise of Pim rolling his sticks around the kit and Ned who was now playing the bass line to *Billy Don't*.

'Well, we could play that,' I said nervously, motioning towards Ned. 'It's just something we've written in the last few days. It's probably a bit shite, but....'

I turned my amp on and tuned my guitar. I had been tuning it all morning so there wasn't much to do. Ned continued to play the bass line and I joined him. He looked at me and grinned as Danny motioned towards the mike. 'Has it got lyrics?'

I nodded. I was shitting myself now. I had never sung through a microphone. By now Pim had joined in a drumbeat. It sounded brilliant; a real drummer putting a drumbeat to my song.

Bollocks, I had to do it. I stood by the microphone and tentatively started to sing my song about the fat lad in the third form called Dominic who had taken his mum's pill. It sounded awful, my voice sounded like a ranting cacophony of noise. The others didn't seem to care though. Pim just carried on smashing his cymbals, Ned just continued to pose with his bass and his fag, and Danny started to add little touches and trills to my rhythm chords. I stopped singing and we just played the four chords of the song. Louder and faster. By now all four of us were moving to the sound. To anyone else it would have sounded like a mess, but we were like four infants smashed out on jelly and coke, rampaging through a birthday party, making as much noise and expending as much energy as we could. After a while we stopped. I mumbled something about still working on a middle eight and a rise. I expected Danny to make some comment on my song. I expected him to be enthused. He said nothing, just continued to smile. 'I know, let's play something we all know.'

I so wanted him to say something, I so wanted him to tell me he liked the song, anything. But I suppose that he had a point; I suppose it was best for us to play a song we all knew before we started writing our own. After all, Lennon and McCartney knew everything Chuck Berry had to offer before they started on their own stuff.

We agreed on 'Don't You Forget About Me'. Pim counted us in and off we went. This time Danny took the mike. He had it positioned so that he craned his neck upwards. He closed his eyes and put his lips close to it. He looked right. He looked fantastic. He looked like a rock star, whereas I had just looked like a mad bollocks shouting. It was brilliant.

At that moment, I wasn't jealous. I was happy. It was the way it would be. Or so I thought. Danny would be the singer, the front man, and I would be the guitar hero. I would be Johnny Marr to his Morrissey, Will Sergent to his Ian McCulloch, Ernie Fucking Wise to his Eric Morecombe. That was alright. I was happy with that, if that was how immortality was going to map itself out for me.

We played for quickly disappearing hours. We played songs we knew, over and over again. We even played a couple of my songs which Danny repeated dutifully and improved immediately. We made noise, we broke strings, we drank lager and laughed at each other through the rising gloom of cigarette smoke. Then we collapsed in the leather chairs, grinning at each other.

'I tell you,' said Pim, 'I reckon we'll be gigging in three months.'

Three months. I was blissfully happy.

'What shall we call ourselves then?' added Ned.

For the next hour we went through that most wonderful rite of passage of anyone who has ever been in a band - naming it.

We started off shyly.

'How about "The Lenins"?' I suggested tentatively. Pim feigned sickness.

'What about "Cappaldi"?' added Danny, laughing. We all threw cushions at him. Becoming eponymous would happen for him later.

'I know,' said Ned, '"Dennis Thatcher's Bastard Sons".'

'Yes!' I screamed.

'No!' shouted Pim and Danny.

We grew more confident and over the next hour became briefly the 'The Lemons', 'The Waifs', 'Excelis' and 'Gum Tree'.

We rejected 'The Park Boys' immediately - too gay. And

'The Jones' - too much like The Smiths and Prague Circus - too modern romantic, yuk. We toyed with 'The Ruffians', 'Madman 4', and 'The Keegans', before finally agreeing on 'The Sensationals'.

The Sensationals.

It was Ned's idea.

I can still see him sitting on the leather chair, tiddly after his three cans of beer, his ungainly adolescent body still barely under control, shouting, 'I know, I know! "The Sensationals".'

There was a silence as we all considered it. Then a smile broke on Danny's lips.

'Yeah, The Sensationals, featuring Danny Cappaldi,' he said as he wrote it on an imaginary billboard. We all laughed, Pim nodded enthusiastically, and that was that. I was now Richie Strafe, guitarist in The Sensationals. I had taken another step towards immortality. I was going to grow my hair and write my songs and hang around graveyards. I was going to have loads of women and be on television and buy a new guitar.

I wrote 'The Sensationals' on my schoolbooks. I wrote it in all different styles imagining how it would look on our first album.

I *would* be immortal.

9

I was the most hated person on the 11.49 train from London to Liverpool. It was Friday morning and the train was packed with Scousers on their way home for the weekend, and tourists intent on lapping up every morsel of kitsch Beatlemania that the nostalgia industry can shove down their throats.

I arrived early for the train with the six boxes of files that Howard McPhee was too tight to have couriered. I struggled through the station before piling them onto the train and placing them on the three seats around me. This was a serious crime. I was taking up three seats with boxes of files because there was no other bastard place on the train to put them. So I was hated. My crime was the type of crime where people feel the need to comment and tut audibly, to scowl intensely at me. The hypocritical bastards. We all know that if I was sitting here slapping my girlfriend or abusing my children then they'd all have their heads so far into their newspapers they could practically kiss their own arses. But put a box on a seat, fucking hell, they all want to persecute me for that.

'Hey, mate,' said a broad Liverpudlian accent, 'are these seats taken?'

They were taken. Taken with my boxes. 'Um, yeah,' I stuttered. 'I'm sorry, there's nowhere else for me to put these bloody boxes. There's some seats in the next carriage I think.'

He looked at me. Judging by his neck - or the thick mountain of skin and muscle where his neck should have been - and his clothes, he had spent the week on a building site and was clearly looking forward to a relaxing journey back home in preparation for a night on the bevy with his mates. The last thing he wanted was some twat with a load of boxes preventing him from taking his seat.

'I'm sorry, mate,' he persisted, 'but I don't want to sit in the next carriage. I want to sit here.'

'Yeah, I know,' I said, beefing up the accent of my home town, the accent of my childhood, in an attempt to gain some sympathy. 'Honestly, I'm really sorry about this, mate. There's just nowhere else for me to put these boxes.' He looked at me and contemplated making a big fuss as I contemplated telling him how he shouldn't blame me, that it was Howard McPhee's fault and that if Howard McPhee was any kind of professional he would have had these boxes sent over by courier.

He shook his head and called me a knobhead as he walked away to the other carriage. Everyone else in the carriage adopted a thin-lipped expression of contempt and took a glance at me. He was on the side of righteousness. I knew this. I didn't need their dirty looks. I was not proud of taking up the three seats. I didn't want to do it. I didn't even want to be on this train.

It was five days since my 'performance' at Byron and Lucy's. They hadn't been good days.

The morning afterwards I awoke on the settee still in my clothes. My head was pounding with guilt and the painful rasping dryness brought on by too much red wine. Angela wasn't there. She hadn't come home. The flat was like a condemned man's cell. I lay still, thirsty through dehydration, dishevelled and awaiting my fate. I stared at the photographs on the wall. Me and Angela in Paris, smiling in front of the Arc de Triomphe. Me and Angela on a beach in Corfu, young and tanned. I tried to remember if we were happy. We looked happy. I tried to remember happy.

She came home eventually. I knew she would. I heard the clatter of her shoes on the wooden stairs, the silent pause as she rummaged in her handbag for her keys, then the shove of her key in the Yale lock.

I sat up on the couch and regretted not getting up and getting changed. The lounge must have smell of guilt, alcohol and that cheesy musty fragrance that boys make during the hours of sleep.

Angela came straight to the lounge and stood by the door. I got to my feet and faced her.

She held up her hand to stop me from speaking.

'I'm not staying,' she said, avoiding my glance.

I nodded, biting on my lips that I had sucked into my mouth.

'I'm just collecting some things.'

I continued to nod.

'Where are you going?' I ask.

'I'm going to my sister's until you go up to Liverpool on Friday.'

I looked at her. 'Then what?'

She looked away. I knew she was upset now and I was glad. This meant a reprieve from the bollocking she would have given me if she was angry. I knew this, because I am a sad coward.

She started to cry. 'You're just a complete mess, Richard, a complete fucking mess.'

I started to walk towards her. This was a mistake. This turned her angry.

'No, Richard,' she shouted at me, tears rolling down her cheeks. 'You don't realise what a complete tosser you've become. Last night was the most humiliating of my life.'

I considered a counter attack. I thought about telling her that if she hadn't been all over Guy, I might not have acted like such an arse, but I decided against it. She continued her bollocking. I let her rage.

'Ten minutes,' she said confusingly. 'We watched you try

and break that CD for ten minutes,' she continued. 'Ten minutes. God, Richard, at one point you were trying to bite it. Do you know what you looked like?'

I shuffled, moving my shame from my left foot to my right. I knew very well what I looked like - she didn't have to spell it out.

'Then you clasped it between your knees.' She put her hand up to her forehead and left it there as she shook her head in desperation.

I had to say something. I had to try to defend myself.

'I'm sorry, Ange,' I started. 'It was just, well, it was just hearing what Cappaldi has allowed to happen to that song.'

She shot me a look that suggested that she had given up all hope in me, in us.

'What?' she screamed, her eyes bright with disdain and anger. 'Oh, for Christ's sake, Richard, are you still going on about that? Fucking hell, can't you just grow up? Can't you just get over it? You're not a popstar, you never will be, you're nothing, just an ordinary bloke. You're nobody special, you're just a fucking solicitor and you won't be one of them for very long if you carry on like this.'

I tried to interject. I had formed in my head the speech about being too sensitive for this cruel world - unfortunately it came out differently. 'If you hadn't been all over that Guy, perhaps I would have acted differently.'

She looked exasperated.

'You just don't get it, do you?' she continued, quieter now, softer. 'I don't want Guy. He's a bigger arsehole than you are. I don't want anyone else.' She looked at me before adding, 'I just want you to stop being such a prick.'

With that, I sat back down on the settee as she stormed off into the bedroom and packed some clothes. It hurt. Her words had wounded me, for sure.

I thought about them again now as I surveyed my boxes, as the rest of the carriage looked at me with disdain.

'Nothing. Nobody special.'

I'd show her.

I went to put on my Discman as an elderly couple of Japanese tourists, both wearing baseball caps with John, Paul, George and fucking Ringo on them, approached my seats. The man pointed to the seats. 'Taken?' he said, a big friendly grin breaking out on his face.

I opened my mouth to explain. I looked at the happy grinning couple in their Fab Four hats. I looked at the thin-lipped Sanhedrin around me. I couldn't be arsed to explain. I got up and picked up the first of my boxes and dumped it in the aisle by the toilet. I repeated the journey five more times as the smiling Japanese people looked on happily and the rest of the carriageway enjoyed a victory. Then I sat down on the last box propped up against the khazi.

I'm not *'nobody'* I thought as another train thundered past, close to ours. I could feel its power resonate through my body. I started to regret giving up my seats for the tourists. The box I was sitting on was not in any way comfortable and there was a rather unpleasant smell coming from the toilet.

How could Angela be so callous? How could she call me a nobody? I'd show her. I'd still achieve my immortality. I thought about Cappaldi. I imagined him at Byron and Lucy's fucking dinner party: 'Oh, Danny - can I call you Danny? - your last album was so fantastic, so much better, if I can be so bold, than your early stuff. We play it at all our dinner parties, don't we, darling?'

'Yes, we do, darling. Tell me, Danny, do you have a mill?'

Fuck, fuck, fuck.

I'd have to kill him, there was no other way. The train. Now that would be a good idea: simple, quick. I'd follow him one day down to his railway station, then just one little push, and bingo, no more Danny Cappaldi. I'd have to be clever though, I'd have to do something about the security cameras. That shouldn't be too hard though, just a little snip. Yeah, that's all it would take, a little snip followed by a little push. I found myself smiling as I thought about it.

The flush of the lavatory brought me back to my senses. It was an absurd idea - I bet he doesn't even travel by train.

The door of the toilet opened and a familiar face peered out at me. This time, however, his expression was different. The benevolent concern of our past meetings was gone. This time he looked down at me sitting on my boxes with disdain. His shining eyes were sad; sad for me. I felt as though I had let him down.

'Dr Costas,' I said, enthusiastically, trying to get up and knocking my box over. 'What are you doing here?'

He shook his head, as a file and wad of paper spilled over the carriage corridor, causing me to grapple on my knees to retrieve them.

'I am on my way to Liverpool, of course,' he answered and started to walk away. I was amazed: my mad stalker was looking disdainfully at me, rejecting me, making me feel like I was letting him down. This couldn't be right. I grappled with my papers and pushed them back into my box.

'What do you mean, Liverpool? Why are you going to Liverpool?'

'Mr Strafe,' he answered in his Mediterranean lilt, 'Liverpool is home to the Beatles and Echo and the Bunnymen, home to the Kop and Atomic Kitten and all sorts of wonderful people who are in need of the services I provide.'

I don't know what surprised me more, his knowledge of the Bunnymen, or his new dismissive attitude towards me.

'Dr Costas,' I cried after him, 'we need to talk. There are so many questions I need to ask you.'

He turned and looked at me as I scrabbled on my hands and knees outside the foul-smelling toilet of the 11.49 train to Lime Street Station, Liverpool, picking up bits of my file. A smile crossed his lips.

'Maybe,' he said and walked away.

Home was like a dull ache. It had been so long since I had

been home for this length of time. I suppose I am typical of my generation: told that you must do as well as you can at school, you run as fast as you can to college so that you can get away from home; then you spend your days slowly coming home less and less. At first, it's every holiday; then you miss a couple of holidays as your new mates outnumber your old ones. Then you come home every time you've got a new girlfriend or something; then it becomes just Christmas because you work, and if you've got a free weekend you're fucked if you want to spend all your time on a train. It had been two years since I'd been home; it had been fifteen years since I was home for a period of over two weeks - now I faced the prospect of two months at home.

I dragged the boxes off the train and managed to get into a taxi.

The taxi driver looked over from behind the glass partition.

'What's with all the boxes, mate? Are you trying to dispose of your mother-in-law? You'll never get away with it, you know.'

He erupted into a bellowing throaty laugh at his own joke as I smiled weakly and stared out of the window. I searched for relics from my past. I stared at people I assumed were my age to see if I recognised them. I looked at pubs and bars in an attempt to provoke some kind of memory. There were none. I saw no one I knew and felt no empathy with the places I recognised from my past.

I hadn't told my parents when I was expecting to arrive home. They would have tried to pick me up from the station. There would have been questions. They would have welcomed me, and my guilt at ignoring them for the last two years would have been even more difficult to bear.

As we pulled into my home town, a profound sadness came upon me. People milled around going to and from their work and their homes. People laughed and cried and moaned - what did I expect? Did I expect everything to have stopped as soon as I had left? Did I expect the shops to remain the same? The bars and cafés to remain unchanged from the ones I had frequented in my teens? Did I hope that the corporate cloned shops and fast food restaurants would not have made it to *my* home town? I probably did. That was probably my problem: I expected to be able to walk back in time and find everything the same.

At my parents' house, I made the fundamental mistake of not tipping the taxi driver. So as I traipsed to and from my parents' house with each blessed box, he sat idly in his cab, making remarks about how my mother-in-law must have been a right fat bird.

Eventually, sweating and surly, I paid the bastard his eleven pounds, waited for my twenty pence change and returned to the house of my parents. The house of my childhood.

The inside of my mum and dad's offered no surprises to me. If everything had changed in the town, nothing had changed inside my parents' house. The same pictures hung on the walls: the twee one of the little girl saying her prayers as her dog and cat eye her breakfast, the watercolour of some mysterious castle, the horses galloping ferociously through some kind of field. There they were, all regularly dusted and ignored just as they had been twenty years earlier.

I put the last of my blessed boxes in the hall and looked around. The sideboard still had little ornamental ladies and gentlemen in Georgian dress walking coquettishly past the glass vase that sometimes had flowers put in, but not often. The family pictures of us all smiling happily at the camera wearing awful 1970s fashions still sat flanked by a picture of me on my graduation and my brother John on his wedding day. And just behind them the ceramic urn still waited for someone to put it to some kind of use. I wondered if it still contained the corpse of the Subutteo player who had been broken twenty-odd years earlier after becoming airborne attempting a thirty-yard screamer. Poor bastard, he had been brought downstairs for my dad to mend and spent two decades languishing in the urn of no purpose.

'Richard, is that you?' It was my mum's voice from the kitchen.

'Yes,' I replied, trying to summon some kind of enthusiasm. 'Hi, Mum.'

She came smiling into the hall. She looked at me and then my boxes and her smile waned.

'I'm sorry, Mum,' I said referring to the boxes, 'I thought that I could put them all up in John's old room. Where's Dad?'

'He's on the roof,' she answered as though I'd asked a particularly stupid question.

'No, I'm not,' came a slightly breathy panting voice I recognised immediately as my father's.

He walked enthusiastically towards me, drying his hands on a dishtowel and smiling.

'Hi, Dad,' I said, trying to match his smile with one of my own.

'You should have told us you were arriving, son. I'd have come to pick you up at the station.'

He called me son. He always did, and that word, together with the smile, crashed into the guilt I was now feeling in my stomach.

'Oh, Dad,' I said, 'it was last minute, and I didn't want to disturb you.'

'Nonsense,' he said, and his eyes lingered on me as though he was checking that everything was okay. God knows what conclusions he drew. I looked at him, too. There was a little more grey around the temples, that was for sure, and did I detect a little weight loss? I wasn't sure.

Mum broke the silence. 'Is that all to do with the murderer?' she added, looking again at my boxes.

'Ah, Mum,' I replied. 'He's only a murderer if the jury find him guilty of murder.'

'Yes, but he looks guilty,' she continued with a forensic analysis some judges would be proud of. 'I don't know how you can bring yourself to even talk to him.'

I was quite happy to talk to them about work; it was easier

to explain my strange presence in a murder trial than it was to explain the other fast unhinging parts of my life.

The questions came thick and fast. 'Where will you be working from?'

'From an office in Liverpool that my boss has arranged for me with another law firm.'

'When will you be seeing the murderer?'

'He's not a murderer, and next week, in prison.'

'Is the case in Liverpool?'

'Yes.'

Then, 'I suppose you'll be in contact with your old friends?'

This one was more difficult. I had no idea who was left at home. I hadn't given it much thought. Perhaps it would be a chance to meet up with people. The idea appealed to me. There were only two people I really wanted to see.

My thoughts were interrupted by the doorbell and the arrival of my brother John and his mouse family.

John has been at home for the last four years. There was no stiff small talk between Mum and Dad and him. He didn't feel my guilt. Mum kissed Sam - his wife - grabbed a toddler in her arms, and cooed whilst another slighter older boy of about five marched into a position in front of me, stood still and stared intently. I stared back.

'You've got a really big nose,' he said.

'Fuck off,' I replied as my brother John came over.

Thankfully he hadn't heard my response to his son George's observation. We shook hands, like strangers. I saw him about ten months before when he came down to London for a couple of days on business. He did something clever with petro-chemicals.

'How are you, mate?' he asked with innocent and honest enthusiasm.

'Oh, fantastic,' I lied, 'couldn't be better. It's great to be home.'

'Yes, well, we haven't seen you for a while,' he said, adding a spikey reminder of my absence to his initial enthusiasm. I tried to mumble something about being busy and making up for it now, but it had passed over. He's a sound bloke, there was no need for him to enter into some protracted bollocking. The conversation moved in a predictable direction. 'How's Ange?'

'Fine, fine,' I replied, adding, 'she sends her love to you and Sam and eh, the boys.'

He was content with this and invited me outside to look at his new people carrier. I hated it. If you want to drive a bus, then buy a proper big red thing with a double deck and a conductor and half a dozen members of the lunatic fringe. Of course I responded appropriately and told him how great it was, and it must be really practical for him and Sam and George and Whatevertheotheronesnameis. I look at him as he lovingly removed a piece of twig from the front grill.

My big brother. We were never that close, but he was, at the end of the day, the person who introduced me to Blondie and the Undertones. The person who told me that Roxanne by The Police was about a prostitute, and then told me exactly what a prostitute was (I nodded, but I had no idea what he was talking about). He was the person I once watched, mesmerised, out of our front window as he snogged Bridget Francis whilst simultaneously trying to get his hand inside her dungarees. I was finding it hard to reconcile that pioneer, that frontiersman, with this family man who was proudly telling me about the fuel consumption of his horrible oversized Japanese car.

After a few minutes of me struggling for the right response about his car and him struggling for the right response about my life, we went back inside. He helped me with my boxes. We drank more tea. We marvelled at his mousey children; he asked me about my case and I explained again the principle of innocent until guilty in increasingly pompous tones. I was starting to enjoy myself. I even predicted that Angela would be coming up in a week or so and we could have a family meal somewhere. I bounced little Whateverhisnameis on my knee.

Eventually during a lull in the conversation it was suggested that me and my dad and John went to the pub for a pint. I readily agreed and put forward The Old Swanny as the nearest pub to home and a source of a number of fond memories from times gone by. I could tell my dad was pleased with the idea of a visit to the pub by the speed with which he had his coat on.

The Old Swanny was a proper drinking pub, or rather had been a proper drinking pub the last time I had been there. It had a jukebox that only ever seemed to play Hotel California by The Eagles. It had crushed velvet seats and awful sticky patterned carpets. It had a group of old unfriendly bastards drinking pints of mild, and it had a rather lax attitude to the age when one can legally buy a drink, hence its popularity during my late teens.

When we arrived I was surprised to see a poster advertising 'DJ Marty Martin and his Karaoke Show Tunes Special - each Friday from 8pm'. At least that wouldn't offend my dad. The same couldn't be said for DJ Marty Martin's Saturday night offering of 'Pumping Hot Techno Disco'.

We entered just in time to hear DJ Marty Martin thank 'Crazy Dave from Heswall' who was singing the last few bars of 'Luck be a Lady Tonight', which he completed to whoops of delight from a crowd of well-dressed young men with short hair who were gathered round the bar drinking bottled lager.

It was immediately apparent to me, and I assumed pretty clear to my brother, that The Swanny was not the pub it had once been. Someone had clearly come along with a big skip and dumped in it the jukebox, the deep crimson crushed velvet seats, lurid sticky carpets and collection of old blokes complaining about the price of a pint of mild. The Swanny had tragically become a trendy Gay Theme Bar. The floors were stripped pine, the chairs, retro leather sofas and old blokes complaining about mild had been replaced by young gay fellas enjoying the sounds of DJ Marty Martin.

I watched my dad saunter off to the bar having insisted on getting the first round in. He gave the décor a swift inspection, seemed neither perturbed nor impressed and took his place next to a good-looking young bloke who kept waving his hands around saying 'Oh my God!' in a loud camp Liverpool accent.

He came back and placed three pints on the small glass table as me and John exchanged nervous glances, hoping that he wouldn't say something politically embarrassing. He didn't look comfortable, but I don't think that it was anything to with the boozer. The new décor actually seemed to please him, the fact that it was a gay bar had passed him by and from his humming along to 'Big Brett's' rendition of Memories, I guess he liked the music.

No, his discomfort had nothing to do with the pub or the clientèle, it was something else. He seemed ill at ease, nervous. He told us how fantastic it was that he was in a pub drinking a pint with his two sons; then in the next sentence he told us how worried he was about the fact that he didn't have a ladder to go into the loft, and about his concern that there was some kind of wasps' nest in the garden shed. We both tried to placate him, but to him these were genuine concerns. I got the next round in even though I was the only one who had finished, as Gary from Birkenhead started on 'The Girl from Ipanema'.

When I returned John had developed a serious expression and my dad was watching the karaoke. He thanked me with a thin smile as I placed his half on the table. The lines creased on his forehead and I could see for the first time the milky rim around the pale blue of his eyes.

'Listen, Rich,' he said. I knew that there was going to be news and I knew that I was going to receive it to the background of Gary from Birkenhead as he slaughtered a song cherished by millions.

'I've got to go into hospital.'

The words 'I've got to into hospital' are always shite, they become particularly shite when they are being conveyed to you by your father, but they are really, really, really shite, when they are accompanied by a young homosexual singing what, if I had been listening to him more attentively, I would have realised was not a faithful rendition of The Girl From Ipanema, but a slightly bitchy and crashingly unfunny parody.

'Short and fat and bald and pasty..........'

'Why? What's wrong?'

'They've found a lump, nothing serious.'

'..the boy from Ellesmere Port goes walking..'

'What kind of lump? Where?'

'..and when she passes each one she passes goes uugh..'

'Don't look so worried, they don't even know what it is yet. It's probably nothing.'

I looked at John. He bore the expression of someone who had known for a while and had faced up to the worst.

'..oh, how he watches so sadly....'

I looked at John, then my dad.

'How long have you known? Why didn't you tell me sooner? I would have come home.'

'..oh, how he smells like a pasty...'

Dad swallowed hard. 'There was no need. It's only an exploratory operation. Me and your mam didn't want to worry you.'

'..oh, how all his clothes are so nasty..'

John took over. 'Dad only found the lump about six months ago. He wouldn't go to see a doctor for ages, would you, Dad?'

'..da, da-da da da da dah..'

The information rushed into my consciousness like freezing cold water. I couldn't make any sense of it. I tried to consider the possibility of my father's mortality. It stretched before me like a huge dark scary chasm. I tried to imagine it, to formulate some kind of proper response, but it was no use. I couldn't see beyond the Girl from Ipanema, Gary from Birkenhead and his increasingly frisky mates. I couldn't help myself. I stood up and faced the collection of men at the bar who were by now engaged in some kind of dance routine.

'This isn't a fucking show tune. What show was this in? I thought this was show tunes karaoke? And those aren't the right words either – whoever heard of someone singing the wrong words at a karaoke night. It doesn't make sense. And why does he smell like a pasty? For fuck's sake.' They turned towards me bearing looks of confusion and I sat down again, apologising to my equally confused father and brother.

We had another few pints and tried to talk about everything other than my dad's lump. Football, beer and John's new car got us through the evening.

My dad and my brother went home. My brother to his mousey family and new Japanese car, my dad to his age, to his worries and his lump. I didn't want to go home. I decided to take a taxi into Liverpool. I told my dad and brother that I had arranged to meet up with some people. It was a lie. I travelled disconsolately in the back of a taxi. I drank alone, moving from bar to bar until they all looked the same. Until their same clean antiseptic look was uniform. I wondered why they all looked as though they had just been opened up that evening. Can the young really not bear to go anywhere with a past? Must they ignore all the scars and stains of history? Replace age and relevance with shiny aluminium, faceless chrome and past-less, spirit-less plastic? I drank alone and leerily watched young girls wearing too much make-up and not enough clothes. Why do they all giggle? What's so fucking funny all the time? I watched drunken blokes in pastel coloured shirts compete with one another. Who could drink the most, who could laugh the loudest, who could wear the pastelest shirt? I listened to the same forgettable tunes in bar after bar until I could bear it no longer. I was lucky with a taxi. I got home.

10

Sunday was just the three of us. It seemed to take an eternity to pass. I did try to talk to my dad about the lump, but he told me to forget about it, and that it was nothing. So I tried to talk to Mum about it, she told me the same, but without the same conviction. They badgered me about phoning Angela, and I made up some story about her being away for the day and that I'd phone her from work. Mum cooked Sunday lunch and we ate in grating silence, each attempt at conversation having the same effect as a nail being dragged down a blackboard.

I was glad when Monday arrived and I was able to go to work.

I drove to the offices of Linkbournes & Co. I found them in a seedy backstreet of Liverpool across the way from a lap-dancing bar. It was apt. I know what kind of solicitors they are: they are the type of solicitors who gorge themselves on the unfortunate and the nasty. I know that the victims of accidents, victims of domestic violence, drug-addled burglars, the cruel, the dishonest and the stupid will all take a sneaky look at the fluorescent sign advertising Sloppy Joe's Pole Dancing Emporium across the road (£5 entrance gets a free dance and a complimentary pint of lager) before passing through their doors seeking legal advice.

I presented myself at the reception and, after some confusion, was introduced to a Mr Truss who appeared to be the only person in the building who had ever heard of me or Howard McPhee. Mr Truss was a stooping man of about forty-five with a lazy eye and halitosis. He smiled a maggoty smile that his lazy eye couldn't keep up with and asked me if I wanted to see my office. I nodded enthusiastically; I needed a bolt-hole.

Behind Mr Truss was a ginger-haired monster who I was told was called Tommy, and who had been instructed to help me with my six boxes which, as usual, were sitting behind me waiting for something useful to happen to them. Tommy, God love him and save him, is as ugly as he is tall. He could be any age between sixteen and fifty and has been blessed with unfeasibly short and skinny legs that appear to have been shoehorned into a cheap pair of undersized nylon pants, out of which erupts a gigantic torso and gut that spills over the soiled band of his trousers. He made a face at me from beneath a head of wispy thinning ginger tufts that could be either a smile or a scowl. I was instantly scared of him, but at least he picked up a couple of the boxes. I picked up another one and followed Tommy as Mr Truss, boxless, led us to my office. Strangely, both Mr Truss and Tommy walked with a limp.

We made our way, a macabre procession, through a corridor with glass-fronted offices on either side. Through the glass I could see people at work: on telephones, typing at keyboards, writing and talking. I found myself limping along with Truss and Tommy - I don't know why. My box was starting to weigh heavily and in front of me I could see a patch of sweat grow on the back of Tommy's shirt.

We walked through a typing pool, where one of the typists - a woman in her thirties with an orange face and peroxide hair - asked Tommy how his custard was. It was quite clearly a risqué euphemistic reference, the source of which I hope I will never discover. He bellowed a laugh back at her before looking to see if Truss had reacted in some way. He hadn't.

We left the typing pool and went through another corridor, this time the doors were closed and opaque. They had nameplates on them: Scanlon LLB, Jones BA (Hons), Hagan

LLB, and others I didn't read because my arms were now killing me from the weight of my fucking box. I vowed that when I had finished with this case, I would burn every sodding piece of paper until each charred remnant begged for mercy.

At last we reached the end of the corridor with the names. Truss turned to me and gave me another one of his creepy smiles.

'We used to have a family department on the top floor of the old building, Mr Strafe, but it wasn't making any money, so we closed it.' He smiled sickly, before adding, 'No money in divorce any more.' He laughed at his last comment and I tossed him a sort of smile-cum-grimace.

What did he mean by top floor?

He meant four flights of fucking stairs, that's what he meant. I know because I and my limping weirdo companions climbed every bastard one of them, dropped off the first three boxes in a deserted, dark, damp corridor, then returned to reception, picked up the other boxes and did the same journey again.

When we had assembled all the boxes at the top of the corridor, Truss limped up past various doors with nameplates on them before eventually selecting one called Butternorth BSc (Hons). He opened Butternorth BSc (Hons), fumbled for the light switch and entered. I followed. It was like entering some kind of morgue. I wondered what fate had dealt Butternorth. I felt uneasy about being in his room, in his space. Where the fuck was he?

The room clearly hadn't seen signs of life for a number of years. On the wall was a two-year out-of-date calendar. In the middle of the room was a huge and ancient photocopy machine. It took up most of the space, leaving just enough room for a desk and chair. I wondered why it was there. There was a phone on the chair which Truss picked up to test for a ring tone, brushing off a layer of dust as he did.

'I am afraid that we don't use this corridor at all these days,' he oozed. 'I'll just let reception know what extension you are on and let you get on with things.'

I smiled, unable to find the power of speech as Truss muttered something into the receiver, replaced it, and left, together with Tommy who grinned at me the knowing grin I imagine jailors give to their captors shortly before they are executed. The hackles rose on the back of my neck. I watched as they both limped back down the corridor then closed the door.

With the door closed, the room was even smaller, even darker, even dustier. There was a strange smell emanating from a bin underneath the desk and the fluorescent light kept flickering, creating an infernal glow. Following a struggle I managed to open some shutters. Alas, the view was of the back wall and bins of the building next door.

I cleared the dust off my chair and sat by my desk, staring at the wall, at the out-of-date calendar and the light flickering from the dodgy fluorescent strip. This was bad. I got up and walked to the door, opening it onto the corridor. Outside there was silence and emptiness; just a length of closed brown doors, each with a little brass nameplate.

I was in purgatory. I was being punished. This was going to be my fate. I was going to sit alone in this grubby dusty office, on the death corridor from hell, together with six bloody boxes of folders, for all eternity. Perhaps that was what had happened to Butternorth; he had lived here in this room until he had been moved on to his next ethereal state. How long would I have to wait? Oh, why hadn't I paid more attention to Dr Costas? I had ignored his wisdom and now I would have to sit here forever.

Things couldn't get much worse.

The phone rang. And things got worse. It was Howard McPhee.

'Strafe, is that you?'

'Yes.'

'Good. Great call wasn't it, setting you up with

Linkbournes, eh? Have you got all the depositions and papers there?'

I murmured that I had.

'Good, now listen. Things have gone a bit tits up. Our client has sacked his barristers. Nothing for you to worry about, these things happen. Problem is, we need to get the depositions copied and sent to the new barristers by Friday. Okay?'

I didn't understand. What did he expect me to do about that? I glanced at the boxes resting on the ancient photocopy machine. Photocopy machine! Dawn broke in some far-off region of my brain. Fuck. That's what he wanted me to do - photocopying. McPhee was not content to make me lug the boxes around the country, he now wanted me to create new boxes - illegitimate offspring of the original ones.

McPhee continued on the other end of the phone.

'Truss has sorted you out with a photocopier?'

I murmured that he had.

'Good, excellent. He's a funny bloke Truss, gammy eye and all, but when your dick's in the door, he'll always open it for you.'

I put my hand to my forehead, accidentally coating my face with the dust from the telephone receiver as McPhee described how he wanted me to photocopy the entire contents of the six boxes by Friday.

'So you want a copy of every page of the deps done by Friday?'

'Don't be a muppet, Strafe, I want two copies by Friday, one for each barrister. Look, Strafe, this is a fucking big job here, all of our tits are in the thresher over this one, you know. This bloke's sacked two barristers. If he sacks us as well, we're all fucked. Do you understand?'

I understood. I understood that I would have to spend the next few days in this God-awful room, endlessly photocopying. That was my lot.

McPhee wasn't finished. 'There's another thing, Strafe...' I wondered what this could possibly be. Would he be asking me to become Truss's or mad Tommy's sexual plaything for the duration of the case? Though in many ways this would be preferable to photocopying, and at least it might get me out of this room.

'..... I've booked you in to visit Hawkins on Thursday.'

McPhee paused. There was clearly something extra on his mind, something significant. He was looking for the right words to impart this something to me. He continued after a few seconds, but this time without his usual frenetic Anglo-Saxon eloquence.

'Now, Strafe, the thing about Hawkins is this..' He paused again. 'He might ask you to do a few things for him, that are, well, shall we say, not in your law college textbooks. Nothing illegal, mind,' he added quickly and with force, 'just a little bit....' He stopped before telling me what 'a little bit' would entail, adding, 'You've got nothing to worry about, Richard. Just do everything he asks you and come to me, and only me, if you've got any problems. Remember, all our winkles are in the vice over this, and only you've got your fingers around the handle.'

I had been mildly concerned about meeting a criminal client for the first time. I became genuinely worried when I discovered that this client was charged with an act of psychopathic homicide. But when Howard McPhee called me by my Christian name, I shat myself.

I sat back in my chair and watched as the dust from the telephone drifted into the air. What kind of requests would Hawkins make? What would I be asked to do? Look after his axe? I contemplated this as, thankfully, the image McPhee had planted in my mind of a vice full of my colleagues' penises slowly evaporated and disappeared.

There was a knock on the door and in, uninvited, staggered mad Tommy, his ginger tufts of hair stuck to his forehead giving him a rabid look. He was carrying three large boxes. 'Truss sent you up these boxes of photocopying paper,' he told me, and plonked them heavily on the floor next to the huge copier.

'Thanks,' I said, noticing for the first time that big mad rabid Tommy was wearing a personal stereo.

I was vaguely interested now.

'What are you listening to?' I enquired innocently. I should have known. I should never have asked the question.

'Cappaldi,' he retorted immediately, 'the new album. It's boss.'

I should have fucking known.

11

1986. 1986 - ah, now that was a brilliant year. What a brilliant, heady, wonderful year.

For me, sixteen years old, my ship had just anchored off the coast of Discovery and I was intent on exploring everything.

There were parties, great extravagant orgiastic affairs of heavy petting swilled down with Strongbow cider that inevitably ended up with either a stomach-pumping visit to the hospital, an irate parent returning home unexpectedly, or a soppy girl in floods of tears.

I remember the parties in wonderful, rose-coloured detail. I remember the build-up; all week aching in anticipation for the weekend, everyone knowing that there was a party because in school everyone knows everything about everybody.

I'd plan going to a party with meticulous detail: what I was going to wear, how much of my dinner money I could put aside to fund my purchase of alcohol; even my compilation tape of sounds that I'd take with me just in case the party was being held by a sporty type or a Brosette which would mean music hell. After that, the only thing left was the consideration of who I was going to cop off with. This was vital. Going to a party was great in itself, but during the years of exploration between your voice breaking and the day you have to pay rent to someone else, a party was inevitably a means to further your studies in the opposite sex.

I remember the girls of my teens so well. If I close my eyes, I swear I can still smell the scent of their mum's perfume, or taste the mixture of bubble gum and Lambrusco on their breath. Funny, they are far more vivid than the blurry fumblings of my twenties.

Like all teens, my companions fell into three groups: those who were going steady, those who seemed to rotate between each other, and those whose rôle it was to remain on the couch, alone, clutching a can of Kestrel Lager. I was in the middle group or so I liked to think. I never seemed to have a girlfriend for more than a couple of weeks, but would always end up in a vigorous clinch with someone; albeit usually with the party coming to an end and a taxi tragically on its way.

I remember Jenny George's parties most of all. Her parents had a large hotel right by the sea in West Kirby. Each Christmas she had a party. She was a great girl was Jenny, she would invite everyone, and everyone would turn up, drink anything that they could lay their hands on (including one eventful year Windowlene, which led to Brian Higgs having his stomach pumped – ah, happy days), then pair off into one of the many rooms for two minutes of turbo-charged romping.

The best thing though about Jenny George's hotel was its huge dining room, which in the height of summer could comfortably entertain sixty guests for a sit-down full English.

For our parties all the tables were cleared away and the room would become our own disco. I had plans for that room. I was going to make that room immortal. In the late summer of 1986, just after my 'O' level results came out (eight passes of stunning mediocrity), we decided that that room at Jenny George's Christmas party would be the scene of The Sensationals' first gig. We had three months to perfect our set. We had three months to hone our songs and the rest of our lives to listen to people boasting about how they had been there. Jenny George's hotel would be our Cavern, our Hundred Club, our Marquee.

The Sensationals had become an obsession. After the wonder of our first jamming session we had played whenever we could. I *would* be the immortal guitarist and songwriter with The Sensationals and so I started to develop my own rock star persona. I tried to speak in that languid cynical manner of John Lennon; I tried to grow my hair like Johnny Marr and practised sucking my cheeks in like Bobby Gillespie. I dabbled with vegetarianism because Morrissey said so; I hated the Tories and Thatcher because Billy Bragg and Paul Weller told me at a Red Wedge concert. I constantly wore my battered biker's jacket and dreamed all day at school and at night in my bedroom of the stardom I assumed was on its way.

Now, with a gig planned, my dreams were about to become reality. Jenny had welcomed the idea with wild-eyed enthusiasm and now we had something to aim for. With each session the band got better. Ned and Pim grew so tight that at times the rhythm would be almost primeval. My guitar playing improved; I stopped simply copying everything everyone else did, and started developing my own style. I learnt that there was more to it than just playing loud, fast and furious chords, there had to be space and slowness, depth and subtlety. The three of us became quite good. But Danny, well, Danny was becoming sensational. He sang in a breathy, masculine way that made you want to listen. He commanded a room in an instant. You couldn't take your eyes off him as he strutted and preened himself behind his mike. He had bought a tambourine that he would occasionally play whilst singing. I loved this. I knew that if the band was rocking, then Danny would play his tambourine like a man possessed. It was fantastic.

We grew close, too. All four of us became mates. We swapped records and tapes and started to dress in similar fashion. We even developed a language of our own that we thought was cool, exclusive and funny, but now years later is cringingly embarrassing. Rather than urge the band to 'take it from the top', one of us would shout 'take it up the arse'. Rather than tell Pim the drummer to insert a drum fill, we would say, 'slap your plates.'

'Slap your plates,' - what was that about? I rouge now at the very thought of it. But at the time it seemed cooler than an Eskimo's nose.

It was after about six practices that Ellie Smith first came to listen. I didn't notice her come in. We had just been rattling through a rather ropey version of The Undertones' Teenage Kicks. I had gone into the guitar solo too early and we had ground to a noisy, stumbling halt. Ned had given me a look of exasperation and I was tetchy. I turned to Pim and started trying to blame him for being too loud and too fast. Eventually after a short moody exchange, I told the band to take it from the top, or, in our parlance take it up the arse. Unfortunately, as I was shouting, 'Right, let's take it up the arse,' at the top of my voice, Mrs Cappaldi had opened the door to the basement and led Ellie Smith into the gloomy, heavy-aired confines of our rehearsal room.

Pim tapped his sticks and we hit the first chord of the song. I glanced to my side and saw Ned was smiling at something behind me. I turned around and there was Ellie, sitting on the floor with her back to the wall and her chin resting on her knees. She was staring at us bright-eyed, a smile on her face. I had never seen her smile. I had never seen her out of her scowling school uniform. But here she was in our rehearsal room smiling at us as we played. Looking fantastic in her ripped blue jeans and leather jacket, her long auburn hair released from the straitjacket of its usual bun - and I had just been shouting 'let's take it up the arse.'

I felt a warm flow of blood to my cheeks and looked down at my shoes. When I looked up again she was still smiling. It was as though she couldn't believe what she was hearing. When we finished the song, she clapped and opened her mouth and smiled again. Danny bowed. Of course he did. I just looked moodily at my strings and pretended to twiddle a few knobs on my guitar.

We played another song. This time one of our own: 'Billy Don't'. Danny pouted out the words, I rocked to the rhythm of the song I had written and Ellie grinned and smiled at us.

I felt something move inside me. Something waved a white flag, surrendered, and was taken capture. I tried to catch a sneaky glance at her. She was gorgeous. Out of school uniform her steely inaccessibility had been replaced by an image of fun and possibility. Her expression was no longer surly and superior but bright and warm.

'Wow, you guys are great,' she said, genuinely enthused.

'Yeah,' said Danny, 'and if you like you can be our first groupie.'

I expected her to revert to her usual classroom frostiness at Danny's flirty remark, but amazingly, she didn't. 'Yeah, I'll say,' she cooed, and I nearly came there and then at the prospect.

I tried to be cool. 'Come on, fellas, what shall we play next?'

We played everything we knew and Ellie Smith seemed to love every song. She loved the songs I had written - 'Billy Don't', 'It's all Sensational' and 'At the Bus Stop'. She loved the way we had attempted some pop irony by covering The Pet Shop Boys 'West End Girls' at breakneck speed. She even loved our cover versions of songs by bands whose names she wrote on her English books. She loved The Sensationals, but I loved her more. I knew it, I could feel it. This was more than the lust I had felt for Joanne Hargreaves who had accidentally touched the crotch of my jeans; or the three-day passion I had felt for Susan Thomas that had manifested itself in a very bad poem called Death by Blonde and had ended when I discovered that she had Wham posters on the wall of her bedroom. No, this was different, this was very different.

I left the rehearsal feeling agitated. After we had finished, Ellie had sat on Pim's drum kit and bashed at some of his cymbals, she had flirted with Ned who had given her cigarettes, then she had stayed with Danny. She hadn't so much as talked to me. Why should she stay with Danny? Danny was going out with a girl from the university called Kathy. Everyone knew that, so there couldn't be anything untoward going on, could there? So why was I bothered?

I left the rehearsal and took the bus home. It was raining. I watched the evening lights through the drips of rain running down the windows of the bus. It was autumn now, it should have felt like summer, but it didn't - it felt like winter.

12

My three days solidly photocopying the contents of the six boxes will rank as amongst the most tedious and depressing of my life. Each day I drove my dad's Vauxhall car over to Liverpool. Each day I parked in the same parking spot. Each day I walked past the sad sight of Sloppy Joe's Pole Dancing Emporium promising the best girls in Liverpool for under a fiver. Each day I entered the reception at Linkbournes & Co and made my way down the various corridors and through the typing pool to the back staircase and up to the corridor of death.

I had hoped that the girls in the typing pool might engage me in a bit of saucy banter as they had with the big halfwit Tommy. I made a habit of slowing down as I walked past them trying to get a bit of eye contact. Alas, on each occasion I was able to walk through unhindered by any verbal molestation. I tried to tell myself that it was because they knew I was a solicitor as opposed to whatever menial position the great lummox Tommy had attained and were showing me a bit of respect. That's what I tried to tell myself.

Up on the corridor of death there was no one to show me any professional respect. There was no one and there was nothing - only me, my boxes and my photocopy machine. For three days I picked up each folder, took out the pages and placed them in a pile on top of the copier. I then put each piece of paper individually in the machine and copied it twice. I then placed each copy in a pile and the original in another pile. It was as tedious as it sounds.

As I placed each piece of paper, pushed the button and watched the gentle green light pass over the depositions and evidence in the case of the Crown versus Terry Hawkins, my mind meandered through its various corridors. I thought about my dad and about his life. About the way in which he used to live for little victories: bargains at the supermarket, free parking in the town centre, his police speed gun radar that kept him one step ahead of a ticket. I wondered if now, as he contemplated his mortality, he thought about his little victories and whether they were all really worthwhile.

I thought about Angela. She hadn't phoned me once. What was she doing? Did she mean what she said about me being a nobody? Why did she say it? Surely that wouldn't have been enough for her? Surely she would crave a 'someone'? I thought about ringing her, but decided against it. No, that's wrong; it wasn't a conscious decision, it was more of a physical manifestation of my inertia towards the concept of 'us' - in other words I couldn't be arsed to phone her.

I thought about Sloppy Joe's a few times as well. I'm a bit embarrassed about that. But being shacked up all night alone in my old single bed, and all day alone in the office from hell, photocopying tens of thousands of pieces of paper, does, in my book, provide a decent excuse for the crime of being tempted by Wendy from Kirkby and her spangly thong. Thankfully, I had spotted the crowd hanging around outside during the lunch hour - they made big Tommy with the limp and ginger waft of hair look like a paragon of normality. I owed it to myself to stay away.

Occasionally, I got the feeling that I wasn't alone. I thought I could hear voices coming from the corridor of death. I ignored them at first, assuming it was just someone retrieving files from one of the purgatorial rooms. Eventually it became too much for me. I desperately needed to talk to someone, anyone, even that huge galoot Tommy would have done. I rushed out to see who was there. There was no one. The corridor of death was empty, its heavy air just as still as when I had trudged up to my room an hour or so earlier.

I returned to my photocopying, to the room of the missing Mr Butternorth, and picked up another folder from one of my boxes.

I moved the pages again, pushed the button again and watched the machine spark into life again, its existence assured and confirmed by its ability to clone pieces of paper.

I thought about Danny as well.

About ways to kill him.

I thought about bashing his head in the photocopy machine; I thought about locking him in one of the unused offices of Linkbournes & Co and leaving him to his own sad demise. I thought about pushing him off the roof, poisoning him with photocopying ink, having him suffocated between the thighs of a stripper or crushed by a falling lift. There are, as I found out during those three tedious days, so many potential ways to kill a popstar.

On the Thursday, I had my meeting with Terry Hawkins at Liverpool Prison. I travelled over to Fazackerley in my dad's Vauxhall and parked outside. It was a fine April day. There were some gardens around the car park where flowers that had been ironically planted by the hands of the violent, the addicted, the dishonest and the simply stupid were starting to show off their colourful innocent beauty. I spotted a signpost for 'Official Visitors' and made my way towards it.

I felt a clammy nervousness seeping uncomfortably from my armpits and onto my shirt. I had never been inside a prison before. I imagined that my very presence would spark some kind of full-scale riot. I imagined myself being held hostage by a Mr Big demanding Sky Sports in the recreational area in return for sparing my life. I tried to push my fears from my mind. I had to stay focussed. I had to pull myself together. I wiped the sweat that was now cascading over my eyebrows. I was a professional. This was a big case.

But...

What had Howard McPhee meant when he told me that Hawkins might make some unusual requests? Oh God.

At the door marked 'Official Visitors' was a gaggle of prison officers talking about football. I stood at the entrance and watched them ignore me. A huge man with a broad Scouse accent was holding court.

'I tell ya, for half, no for a quarter of the money that shite gets paid, I could go out there on a Sat'day afternoon and do fuck all.'

'But I can watch you do fuck all any day at work, Dave,' replied an equally huge colleague, as they continued to steadfastly ignore me.

I harrumphed loudly and a third male, of similar large proportions, turned towards me.

'Yes, sir. How can we help you?' he asked in a loud and sarcastic voice, as his mates looked on menacingly.

'I'm a solicitor,' I declared pompously, 'here to visit Terry Hawkins.' I continued in my least Liverpudlian, most head-up-my-own-arse accent. The hugest of the guards looked at me quizzically,

'Eh, mate, are you from the Wirral?'

'Yes,' I replied, astonished at being asked.

'You'd never tell,' he added, before breaking into a throaty laugh, lovingly created by Benson and Hedges. His mates laughed along. They probably got special training in how to prick the pomposity of lawyers - there was probably a course.

A female prisoner officer with a jaw like a rugby forward moved towards me.

'Did you say you were here for Terry Hawkins?'

I repeated that I was. She turned towards one of the enormous colleagues. 'Hawkins is Red Category, isn't he?' For some reason this prompted another even deeper throatier laugh from Benson and Hedges man. When he eventually found the power to stop laughing, he looked at me. 'You're going to love this, mate.'

I was confused.

A few minutes later I was no longer confused. I was however stark bollock naked behind a screen as the two burly security guards went through my clothes and the Benson and Hedges man started to put rubber gloves on.

Apparently 'Red Category' meant a full strip and cavity search for any visitors, including your solicitor. Fair play to the security staff though, at least now they had the decency to show embarrassment at my predicament.

'Sorry, sir, but these are the rules, I'm afraid,' said B&H man as I bent over and he slid his gloved hands down the groove of my arse. 'I can tell you, I'm enjoying this even less than you are.'

I was too stunned to think of any answer other than a rather poncey, 'Don't worry, it's okay.'

Once dressed again, but with my pride in absolute tatters, I was led through various prison yards and in and out of countless gates and heavy doors until I reached a set of windowed rooms in one of which, I was told, I would find Terry Hawkins. The guard showed me which one and I knocked nervously. The guard looked at me like I was mad.

'This is the nick, mate. Just go in.' I blushed, realising that I looked like the bloke hopping off the last boat to arrive at the dock.

I took a deep breath and entered. Hawkins had his back to me. He sat upright, his arms stretched out across the table. He was wearing a prison-issue high-visibility bib. Underneath he was wearing some kind of vest. From his uncovered arms I could make out every sinew and muscle. He wasn't a large man, but I knew that each muscle was taut and potentially lethal.

I introduced myself.

'Good morning, Mr Hawkins. My name's Richard Strafe from McPhee, Fox and Phillips.' He looked up at me and said nothing. I sat down opposite and put my notebook on the table. I couldn't think of what next to say so I took my biro out of my inside pocket and placed that on my notebook. Still no words came to me, so I took my pencil and my red marker pen from the same pocket and placed them neatly by my biro. I then opened up my notebook and looked at an empty page as though reading something significant. At least this presented me with the power of speech.

'Ah, yes. Here we are, Mr Hawkins,' I stuttered nervously as I tried to convey the impression that he was the type of person I came across each day. 'I just wanted to come and introduce myself and let you know about your new barristers. Then I just wanted to take down some notes for a proof of evidence.'

I looked up at this point just as he looked at me. For a split second we made eye contact. His eyes were sharp and pale, filled with hate and menace. He looked as though he would kill me in an instant if he had the chance. I looked away as his stare reached my already wobbly sphincter.

'Who the fuck are you?' His accent was unmistakably South London, spikey and defiant, his voice quiet and brimming with contempt.

'As I said, Mr Hawkins, I'm Richard Strafe from McPhee, Fox....'

'I know what you said, Mr Strife.'

'Strafe.'

'What the fuck ever. I know what you said, but what I want to know is, who the fuck are you?'

This was turning out to be a difficult day

I took a deep breath and continued, 'I'm your solicitor. Mr McPhee sent me.'

He looked at me for a few seconds, sizing me up. I tried to hold his gaze.

'Stand up,' he ordered. I felt compelled to comply with his order and stood. He continued to look at me, his cold eyes passing over every part of my body. I didn't know if he was going to kill me or shag me. Suddenly he stood up himself and came towards me. I instinctively backed away. He laughed menacingly. 'Don't be frightened, Mr Strife.'

My arms went to protect my face, as Hawkins started to pat my chest and back. I wondered what he was doing.

'Open your legs,' he barked, and again I immediately did as he asked. He continued to pat my body, moving around my groin and the inside of my legs.

'What are you doing?' I asked nervously.

He turned towards me. 'I'm finding out if you're friend or foe.'

'I'm friend,' I stammered, 'definitely friend.'

His hands continued down my legs towards my ankles and shoes before he eventually seemed satisfied and sat back in his seat. He motioned for me to do the same. I did.

His gaze warmed from arctic cold to simply icy as he continued to stare at me from his side of the table.

'You could be anyone, Mr Strife,' he said by way of explanation, and I nodded enthusiastically. 'For all I know you could be Old Bill.'

'Old Bill?' I exclaimed. 'Don't be daft, do I look like a copper?'

He shrugged. 'You look like a twat, so you're halfway there.'

I started to long for my usual clientèle, the trippers and slippers, the neckbrace wearing victims of rear-end shunts hoping to make a few quid. I didn't have the first clue how to deal with someone facing a triple murder charge.

He started to show signs of being bored.

'Look,' I said, taking my wallet out of my inside pocket and producing my card. 'Here's my card.' I enthusiastically produced my card, complete with its own personal logo:

RICHARD STRAFE BA (HONS)
SOLICITOR
Specialist in Civil Litigation
'Had an accident? Call Richard Strafe'
McPhee, Fox and Phillips

He looked at the card and snorted out a rather sinister laugh as though something was amusing.

'Well, now I know you're not police,' he said. I looked quizzically at him, 'because not even the fucking police would be stupid enough to send a pretend solicitor with a card that says he specialises in Civil Litigation.'

I hadn't thought of that.

'Had an accident?' he mimicked. 'Fucking hell, I'm supposed to have chopped three geezers' heads off. That's hardly an accident, is it?'

He had a point. We were surely fucked now. Hawkins would sack us and McPhee would blame me. I could do without that.

I thought about spinning him some kind of yarn: tell him that as well as Civil Litigation, I had done a thesis in University on decapitation or something. Strangely however, Hawkins' attitude changed.

'Who's the bird?' he asked, referring to the picture of Angela that was also in my wallet. 'The bird?' I repeated unnecessarily. 'That's Angela, my eh, girlfriend. Well, I think she's my girlfriend.' My nerves were making me indiscreet. I added, 'Things haven't been great.'

Bizarrely, Hawkins, this alleged perpetrator of the Wavertree Massacre, was interested in my love life.

'What's gone wrong then?' he asked gently as though we sitting in a pub with a couple of foaming pints and bag of ready salted McCoys being shared between us.

My own response was even weirder. I found myself opening up to him.

'She thinks I'm an arsehole,' I told him, before adding, 'and I have been.'

Suddenly, I was telling him all about Danny Cappaldi and the CD at Lucy and Byron's dinner party, I was telling him about how I'd never wanted to be a solicitor in the first place, how all I ever wanted to do was play in a band and write a song that would be played forever. I think I even mentioned Ellie bleeding Smith.

Hawkins seemed to understand this. He seemed to empathise. 'All I wanted to be,' he told me, 'was the most feared motherfucker on my estate.'

I beamed at him. 'Well, you've accomplished that.' I said, far too enthusiastically. 'You're the most feared motherfucker in the bloody country.'

For the next minute or so we sat in silence. I had overstepped the mark. I tried to get us back on track.

'We've got you a great barrister, Mr Hawkins,' I said, consciously sounding like an overexcited schoolboy. Hawkins didn't seem too impressed. He looked away from me, then looked up around the small room. A look of resignation came across his face. He leaned towards me across the table and motioned for me to put my face closer to his.

'This room,' he whispered and pointed his finger towards the ceiling, before continuing, 'It's got....' He didn't finish his sentence, but instead moved away from me and tugged at his right ear. I didn't understand.

'What, big ears?' He shot me a look of exasperation.

'No,' he snapped, before tugging his ear again.

'Oh,' I said, the penny having dropped, 'you mean...'

'Yes!' he shouted before I could finish my own sentence.

I assumed that Hawkins was totally paranoid and put it down to years of drug abuse. This was the UK, we didn't bug prison cells. Did we?

He turned to me again.

'I know all about being a solicitor,' he said.

'That's nice,' I replied, inadvertently sounding sarcastic.

'I know that you expect me to sack you now I know that you're not even a criminal solicitor.'

I started to stutter an answer, but he stopped me.

'It's alright,' he said, 'I quite like you. I'm happy for you to carry on.'

I felt a swelling of my ego as this convicted drug dealer and violent thug told me he liked me.

'But there are things I expect,' he added, a tone of menace

creeping once again into his voice.

'Of course,' I answered.

'The most important thing for me is client confidentiality. I expect nothing I tell you to go further. Not even to McPhee. Do you understand?'

I nodded.

'You're going to be my special solicitor. Is that alright?'

'Yes,' I said. Now there was definitely a tone of menace in his voice.

'We're going to look after each other.'

I nodded again.

'Now, Richard, I don't want to have to threaten you or the lovely Angela, but you do know that a grass gets dealt with in a particular way, don't you?' I knew what he meant by this alright. He was watching me carefully now, as though he was assessing me for something.

'Good,' he repeated. 'Now we all know where we stand.'

'Yes, yes, we all know where we stand.'

He leant over again and picked up my pad and my red marker. He then started to write something in it. As he wrote he started asking me questions about his barrister, which I answered. Eventually he tore the page on which he had been writing from my book, looked furtively towards the guards outside the window, and handed it to me.

I read it. It said,

Go to the Anglesey Arms in Liverpool, any afternoon, and you'll find a man by the name of Maurice Hunter. Tell him to sort Rutland - usual terms.

He looked at me, his eyes narrowing slightly. I nodded, letting him know I had finished reading it.

'You understand all I've said, don't you, Richard?'

I nodded again.

'You've understood my instructions, yes?'

'Yes,' I murmured.

'I've enjoyed our little chat about Angela and you. And

you've enjoyed our little chat about confidentiality?'

I intimated, unenthusiastically, that I had.

'Good.'

With that he took back the page, rolled it into a ball and put it into his mouth.

'Now,' he said through a mouthful of paper, 'fuck off. You'll be well rewarded.'

I got up to go.

As I reached the door, he spoke to me again, 'Oh and Richard,' I turned towards him, 'I think Danny Cappaldi's a cunt as well.'

13

That night I lay in bed and stared at the ceiling, just as I had done throughout my life. I remembered being a little boy and being scared of the giant black shadow created by the wardrobe and its eerie smaller mate, the dressing table. I remember convincing myself that the outline of my Superman dressing gown hanging up behind the door was in fact the evil black nun, a phantom popular at the time with children under ten.

Then I remember being older and lying here considering my own mortality, the reason for my existence, the unbearable mystery of the unknown, life and death, eternal life and the enormity of the universe. Well, it was that and wanking.

Now I had real fears, real things to be concerned about. I was about to turn thirty-six and things were not good. In fact they were worse than that, they were totally and utterly fucked up.

I lay in the silent darkness and considered each of my problems.

First, there was my girlfriend - she had left me. There had been no contact for weeks. I guess, if I was honest, she had pretty much kicked me into touch.

Then there was my dad and his 'lump'. He had looked a bit peaky over the last few days, even I could see that.

Then, if that wasn't enough, I had become the 'special solicitor' to a homicidal maniac and I had been ordered upon pain of death to find some other homicidal maniac to help 'sort out' the Crown's star witness. I couldn't even begin to count how many criminal offences I would be committing if I carried out Hawkins' orders. I started with conspiracy to murder and the life sentence that would bring.

Hawkins was like no one else I'd ever met in my life. I couldn't deny that I had felt a strange empathy with him - after all, I had opened up to *him*. I couldn't believe that I'd done that. I couldn't believe that I'd told him all about Angela. I had wanted to, though. I had wanted him to care about me and my problems. He was, as the tabloids would have it, the famous Wavertree Executioner, and I had wanted him to be concerned about me. He sensed that; that was why he chose me to carry out his instructions. He knew how to play with my emotions. He had probably done the same routine with loads of others. There were probably dozens of people who would carry out his work for him, even if he personally was inside.

He scared me totally and utterly shitless.

I knew that if I didn't do what he asked - deliver his message to this Maurice Hunter character - he would deliver some kind of exacting revenge upon me or Angela. Angela didn't deserve to have revenge exacted on her. She had suffered enough just by going out with me.

I could always go to the police. I supposed that they would put me and Angela into some kind of witness protection scheme. God, poor Angela, one minute she's simply trying to get away from a shitty relationship, the next, she's being comforted by some kindly WPC who's telling her that she won't be able to see her family again and from now on she has to live in Carlisle, work in a florist's, and go by the name of Ruth. She'd bloody kill me.

Mind you, I didn't fancy it much either: the idea of being anonymous, the idea of always living in fear of being recognised. I wanted immortality, not invisibility. I wanted fame, not a life being provided for by the state and living in a nice brand new home on one of those new estates where everything is brick orange.

I had no choice. I had to simply deliver the message to Maurice Hunter. Anyway, it wasn't like *I* was going to kill Colin Rutland. It wasn't like *I* was going to pull the trigger. And anyway, Rutland was probably as big a bastard as Hawkins. They deserved each other. Oh no, I was now trying to convince myself that it was morally acceptable; next, I would be telling myself it was my duty.

I lay in the same bed in which my mother had innocently tucked me in and kissed me, the same bed in which my dad had read me stories about talking animals and good pixies and evil goblins, and considered all these things. But the thing that pissed me off most, the thing that gnawed excruciatingly at the very fibre of my soul was the fact that the next day I would find myself again alone on the corridor of death, whilst Danny Cappaldi was probably in some recording studio or on a film set, or on a beach, or holed up in a penthouse apartment with some glamorous bird.

I didn't sleep well that night. At about midnight I was completely awake. By half one, I was moodily stomping across the corridor to the khazi for my third piss of the night. After that I must have dropped off because I woke up around four, panting and hot with sweat. I'd had one of my Nazi versus Cliff Richard dreams again. Only this time Cliff was in an open-top car with Angela, giving a salute to legions of storm troopers. Angela was wearing some kind of military uniform, but any kinky thoughts I might have considered having were destroyed by the image of Cliff goose-stepping out of his Mercedes.

I needed some kind of liquid and went downstairs.

I didn't expect my dad to be sitting quietly in the kitchen. It was dark, except for the half-light coming in from the utility room. The sight of him in his dressing gown surprised me. I had never seen him in his nightclothes before. I'd never seen him downstairs in the kitchen in the middle of the night before.

For a few seconds I watched him. He looked so sad. So old.

The bleak light made him look drawn.

'Can't sleep?' I proffered.

'Oh,' he said, his face looking up and catching the light as he instinctively drew his dressing gown around him. He smiled at me and in that instant I felt like everything was completely lost.

I opened the fridge and got out a bottle of milk which I poured into my 'Kenny Dalglish Super Reds 1988' mug.

'Are you alright, Rich?' my dad asked me.

'I should be asking you that,' I answered.

He smiled at me again. A quick, thin-lipped smile.

'I'm fine,' he added. I didn't believe him.

'You don't look fine, Dad.'

He tried to laugh it off, just as he would have done when I was a kid. 'I just can't sleep, that's all. It's your mother's snoring - you'd think I'd be used to it by now.'

Now it was my turn to give him the quick, thin-lipped smile.

'Anyhow,' he continued, 'what's keeping you awake?'

I contemplated telling him. I contemplated asking him if he thought that I should deliver my message to Maurice Hunter, but he spoke before I did.

'Listen, Rich,' he said, 'we know you haven't had much time to get home over the last couple of years. We know you're very busy, son. But, well, me and your mother, we're just pleased....' Before he could finish his sentence, he grimaced in pain and his hand shot to his stomach.

'Dad, are you alright?' I asked stupidly, half getting up, though with no idea what I could do or should try to do to help.

He continued to grimace. 'Yes,' he managed, through clenched teeth, 'it's these pills they're giving me. I'll be alright in a minute.'

I sat down again and watched as he held his stomach for a few seconds, inhaled through his gritted teeth and screwed his eyes closed. Then, as he had predicted, the pain appeared to subside and he unclenched his teeth, opened his eyes, and moved his hand away from his stomach.

'You alright?' I asked him again. It was easier to ask after the pain was gone.

'Yes,' he said, 'fine.' I knew that now the greater pain was being caused by my being a witness to it.

'You get off back to bed, lad,' he advised. And I nodded.

I had made up my mind. There was no way I could add to my dad's problems, there was no way I could add to Angela's problems. The easiest way was to deliver my simple straightforward message to Maurice Hunter.

14

It took me a whole afternoon to find the Anglesey Arms. Having eventually discovered from an old phone book (funny, it was missing from the up-to-date phone books) that it was situated in a tiny back alley called Cuff Street off Bold Street in the centre of Liverpool, I couldn't find bloody Cuff Street. I walked the entire length of Liverpool city centre, to no avail. I asked five different taxi drivers and each of them gave me a different set of directions: 'I think it's on the left up by the old Radio City building, mate.'

'If you go to the end of the road here, turn left and left again, then take the next left, you'll be nearly there.'

What?

Eventually, I spoke to an ancient-looking newspaper seller, a man who clearly once shouted *'Get your Echo! Beatles make it big in America.'* In fact it wouldn't have surprised me if he had once shouted, *'Get your Echo! British forces come unstuck in Rourke's Drift.'* Mind you, fair play to the old codger, he knew where Cuff Street was, and indeed where the Anglesey Arms was. He pointed to a tiny opening in between a couple of high street boutiques.

'Go through there and you'll be in Cuff Street.'

I took his advice. He was spot on. Why hadn't I seen it before?

Cuff Street was narrow and untouched by fancy new city-of-culture development. Cuff Street had bins and back gates that led into mysterious buildings. Cuff Street had corners and damp walls, fire escapes and places to run to. Cuff Street had a dark history to it.

The Anglesey Arms was the only easily discernible building in Cuff Street. It was a pub from a different age. The windows were dark and forbidding, the front door was heavy and closed. There were no signs advertising karaoke or Sky Sports at the front of this pub. You weren't supposed to be enticed into a pub like the Anglesey Arms; you came here to disappear, away from the wife, from the boss, from the docks. You came here to drink with other men and declare your love for your Saturday afternoon heroes Bill Shankly or Alex Young.

Inside, I was struck by the smell of empty pub, of hops, and yeast, of stale nicotine and cleaning fluids. The smell was so thick, you felt that if you swung an axe you could open a scar and count the rings telling the pub's entire history.

It was some boozer. The front bar was long and ornate, with shining beer taps and pumps standing like sentinels along the oak splendour. It was well stocked with optics in different shades of greens and browns. Real drinks - whisky and rum; there were no alcopops here. In the middle - guarding the bar like a large dog - was a large barman. He glanced at me as I walked in, his hands flat on the bar either side of a copy of the Racing Post.

I nodded. 'Alright?'

He nodded back to me.

Suddenly I felt extremely stupid. What the fuck was I doing here? How would I find Maurice Hunter? What would I say to him? What would he say to me? Would he shop me to the police? Fucking hell. Say I was being set up?

I approached the bar and ordered a pint of bitter, which the barman poured with an air of reluctance. He quite clearly wasn't expecting any customers on this particular afternoon.

As he poured, I looked around for anyone who might possibly be Maurice Hunter. There was no one. I felt uncomfortable. I felt like the intruder I clearly was. I tried to engage the barman in conversation. 'Any luck with the gee-gees then, mate?' I proffered, reckoning that was probably a better start than a casual comment about the plight of the Tribesmen of the Indus.

'Yes,' he replied. Then silence.

I knew that was my lot and looked around the pub. It really was a beautiful old building. I wondered why I had never been here before. The ceilings were high and decorated with ornate chandeliers, friezes of trumpet-blowing seraphim and cherubim and gilt roses.

In the corner was a jukebox. I could never resist a jukebox and went over to it. As I ambled over, I prepared myself for the usual rubbish I find on jukeboxes. The usual collection of dodgy compilations, American soul singers, awful 80s soft rock. And, of course, the ubiquitous Cappaldi's Greatest Hits: The First Chapter. Fucking Cappaldi's Greatest Hits: The First Chapter. What a twat. What a twat to allow a Greatest Hits album to go out when you are still playing; what a twat to allow a Greatest Hits album to go out when you've only had four proper albums; but what a huge, carbuncular (is there such a word), fucking twat to call it 'The First Chapter'.

'The First Chapter' - what a twat.

Normally, when faced with jukeboxes such as this, I gain my revenge by choosing the most obnoxious track I can find and putting it on fifteen times in a row. I tell you, by the time Prodigy's Smack My Bitch Up is playing for the fifteenth time, the pub with a jukebox like that is a far emptier place.

To my great surprise, the jukebox in the Anglesey Arms wasn't at all like the usual. Instead of the calamitous mixture of 'Now 147s' and Kylie, there was a cracking collection of old Ska bands, The Selector, Booker T and MGs and The Shadows. There were rock'n'roll bands from the 1950s and 1960s that I confess I hadn't heard of. The Continentals, Davie and the Dynamics, the Carvelles. Then there was a good collection of British bands from the 60s and 70s: Cream, The Who, Led Zeppelin. This was good stuff; there wasn't a

Danny twatting Cappaldi track near it. I turned to the barman to congratulate him on his jukebox - but before I could utter a word, he told me gruffly that it wasn't to be switched on until 7pm. It was about 6.40.

I was inspired though. My imagination had kicked into gear. Perhaps I was in some kind of underground drinking establishment only frequented by the most notorious of Liverpool's criminals: the type of place where, as a homage to the good old days when the streets where safe, you never grassed and you always looked after your mam. In this establishment the only music allowed on the jukebox was authentic 1960s rock'n'roll, rare Ska and British Rock.

I could dig that. The clientèle here would hate Danny Cappaldi. He didn't fit at all.

I had visions of me sitting down with a group of middle-aged Scouse gangsters and telling them the story of how I was treated by Britain's favourite pop pin-up. I imagined them listening carefully through a fug of cigarette smoke, before one of them, probably called something like Billy Big Bollocks McNeil, or Jack The Mad Carter, would turn to his mates and say sagely, *'Not only has this Danny Cappaldi character contributed to the downfall of the greatest type of music known to mankind - Rock and Roll - he has also treated our friend Richard here in a manner that can only be described as unacceptable and unsound. Gentlemen, there is only one language the likes of Cappaldi understand.'*

At this the gang would nod. The writing was on the wall.

I smelt Dr Costa's cologne before I saw him, or heard him. It must have been some brand to overpower the smell of hops and yeast.

'Ah,' he said, staring over my shoulder at the jukebox, 'Buddy Holly.' His voice had a note of faraway pride. 'One of the greatest stories of all. People will always be singing the songs of Buddy Holly. People will always know that he died in a plane crash.' He then uttered a word in a language I didn't understand that sounded like 'fantastic'.

I turned to him. Dr Costas was wearing a beige suit with a yellow shirt open at the collar. Things had definitely improved for Costas in the fashion department since his evil golfing gear of our first meeting. He still wore his beige slip-ons though, but I found that comforting.

'Shall we sit down?' I said.

He nodded and took a seat by the jukebox. The bar was silent and empty. The barman still stood motionless behind the bar, his mind filled with the possibility of horse racing. A ray of bright evening springtime sunlight found its way through a chink in the opaque windows, streaming across the bar and illuminating the ancient dust that danced around the room.

Costas sat opposite me, his legs crossed. A cigarette held nonchalantly in one hand, a glass of some kind of spirit in the other. I was glad to see him. He seemed to know that.

'So, how have you enjoyed Liverpool?' I asked him.

He wrinkled up his face. For a few seconds he seemed to be searching for an appropriate answer.

'I expected more,' he said finally.

'Why?'

'You wouldn't remember the sixties,' he said, the same faraway look flickering across his face that every old bastard seems to have when they talk about the sixties.

I tutted. 'Oh, please, you'll be telling me about The Cavern Club next.'

'Richie, if I offered you one night at The Cavern Club in 1964 you, my friend, would give me just about anything in return.' He paused. 'Wouldn't you?'

He was probably right.

I shrugged. 'We just get sick of hearing about the party everyone else was at, that's all.'

'You have to have your own party.'

I didn't want to get into this psycho bollocks.

'You must have known though, you, the Keeper of Myths and Legends, that the Liverpool of the sixties is long, long gone. So why did you bother coming?' I made little sarcastic inverted comma signs with my fingers when I said 'Keeper of Myths and Legends.' I regret that.

He took a sip of his drink, looked at his glass as the light caught it and took a long tug on his cigarette before answering me.

'You are always so angry, Richard, aren't you?'

'Yes, I bloody well am. And you're so bloody evasive and enigmatic and, quite frankly, ridiculous.'

He gave a little chortle.

'I am here partly on business,' he said, 'and partly to see a few old haunts and a few old friends.'

'Ah,' I said, 'I was right. Don't tell me, the Cavern Club and Ringo, eh?' I regret saying that as well.

He ignored my facetiousness.

'There is no point in hiring a hit man to kill Danny Cappaldi.'

Once again he had managed with a single sentence to deliver a hearty blow to my solar plexus.

I put my hands up to my head. How the hell...? I decided to simply accept it. After all, I was indeed thinking that very thought. I took a deep breath.

'I wouldn't do that,' I said quietly.

'Good, because there would be no point, would there? Because the whole point, Richard, is that you gain your immortality by carrying out the act yourself.'

For a second I considered the possibility of Dr Costas actually being an undercover police officer. I contemplated frisking him in the style of Terry Hawkins, but concluded that the sight of me rubbing the legs of a slightly effete fellow wearing a beige suit would be a sure-fire way of getting the barman away from the form for the 2.15 at Haydock Park to throw us both out.

I didn't know what to say. I was utterly confused. I suddenly thought about Mr Hetherington who got knocked over by a flying cow on the way to meet his mates. I thought about his little purple bag and I wanted to cry.

Dr Costas seemed to sense this. 'Listen, Richard,' he said, 'part of my business here in Liverpool is you.' He turned his head slightly towards me.

'Me? Why me?' I asked desperately.

He took another sip from his glass, another hit from his fag and crossed his legs. I knew that the speech was on its way.

'Today,' he started, 'everyone worries about global warming, disease, war, terrorism. But they are not the real catastrophes facing mankind.'

I stopped myself from making a wisecrack about reality telly or something equally cynical. He continued, 'The real disaster facing mankind is tedium. If we are not careful, we will just collectively lose the will to live.'

'What, all of us?'

'Yes.'

I thought about this.

'Think about it. The world is becoming utterly tedious. There are no more just wars, just mistakes by politicians leading to boring conflagration. Without just wars, there can be no military heroes. Will there ever be another Achilles? Another Leonidas, the Spartan? Even another Nelson or Wellington? No, of course not.'

As ever, he made a point that was as strikingly insightful as it was absolute bollocks.

'Then there is sport. Sporting heroes are a thing of the past. Real sporting heroes, I mean - not these overpaid prima donnas who whore themselves around the world.'

I wasn't sure I agreed with him here, but he was on a roll and I wasn't going to stop him.

'Then there is music and art. The people can no longer appreciate it because they have everything at their fingertips or else are too busy trying to earn money to keep up.' He paused for a second to find an example of what he was saying. 'How can you be impressed by the wonderful light and shade of a Caravaggio painting, when you can see a blockbuster movie any day of the week?'

I felt the need to interject. 'It's not all bad.' I said. 'Film and technology and the rest have done some wonderful things.'

He leant over to me. 'I did not say that it was all bad, Richard. I did not say that.' He stopped to allow the forceful look to fall from his face, before carrying on. 'What I said was that the greatest problem facing man is tedium.'

I was still confused. I considered it.

'Consider how important myths, stories and legends are. Consider the greatest story of them all.'

'What, Lord of the Rings?' I regretted saying that too.

'No. The story of Christ. Is there anything more powerful than that? Has there been anything more significant than that?'

I had to conclude that there wasn't.

'Our laws are based on it; our moral and ethical codes are based on it. Christopher Columbus travelled in search of America under the cross of Christ. Battles have been fought because of it. Discoveries made. Religion and the promise of eternal life have helped most humans live together in some kind of conviviality for two thousand years.'

'But what the fuck has that got to do with me?'

'You. Ah, you, Richard.' He looked at me in wonder, as though he was in some way proud of me. 'Yours is a simple story, Richard, isn't it?'

I couldn't disagree.

'Yours is the story of love and betrayal; of jealousy and...' he paused, 'perhaps revenge.'

I sat there looking at him. I still wasn't sure what that had to do with the discovery of America or God.

'You see, today, stories such as yours are rare. But without them, people don't interact. People don't talk to each other, relate to one another. They forget.'

'Forget what?'

'They forget that there is more to this life than the momentary ecstasy of television, of consumption, of prefabricated pop music, of going to work each day to a job you hate, to earn as much money as you can or to get a promotion you don't really want.'

He looked at me. His eyes were bright now, shining blue against his tanned leathery skin.

'Mankind will carry on progressing, Richard. Neither of us can do anything about that. Me, because I am not meant to; you, because you think too much about the demise of the top forty.'

I thought this was a bit harsh.

'Soon people will hardly speak to each other unless they are on a telephone, or the internet, or at work or drunk. Soon, technology will mean that we shall all be Caravaggios, so a real Caravaggio will remain undiscovered and wither and die. There will be no mysterious popstars, no alcoholic geniuses writing poetry, there will not even be religion for men to fight and die for. There will not even be love, just sex and pursuit of beauty, or what we are told is beautiful. It is what makes us different from worms or dogs or giraffes.'

He was quieter now.

'I still don't know what this has got to do with me.'

'I can't make you do anything, Richard. I am cleverer than you, of course, because I am Greek. I can guide you, but I can't compel you. But perhaps your story, if you let it happen, will be a small victory in the battle against tedium.'

'What will I get in return?'

'You may get the immortality you crave.'

With this we stared at each other. The evening sun had gone now, and the rays of sunshine that had awoken the streams of dust had disappeared. He finished his drink. A clock on the wall by the bar struck seven. Immediately, just as the barman had told me, the jukebox kicked in. It flashed a few lights, then cranked itself into gear. I looked over and saw a seven-inch single make its way out of its place and onto the old-fashioned turntable. It was Peggy Sue by Buddy Holly. Of course it was.

Dr Costas got up and made his way out of the pub.

There was too much in my head now to seek out Maurice Hunter. There was too much on my mind. I now had to save mankind from losing the will to live.

Fucking hell.

15

By the autumn of 1986 I was a sixth former. Buoyed by my outstandingly mediocre 'O' level results, and my inability to do Maths, Sciences and Languages, I had opted to study English, History and Economics. I wasn't too great at History and Economics, but I loved English. We did Keats and King Lear, Dickens and Donne. I can still quote them now. I had a good teacher - Binky Jones, a giant man, with a mop of curly hair and huge glasses. Why is it that influential teachers have to look like people off Care in the Community schemes?

I sat by Graham Hodges. I had steadfastly ignored Graham Hodges throughout school, but now, in the blossoming adulthood of sixth form, Hodgy, I realised, was quite a funny bloke. But I had a more cunning reason for sitting next to him than his ability to impersonate all the characters on the Harry Enfield show; I sat by him because he happened to be in the seat directly behind Ellie Smith. I could watch her now. I could stare at her hair, and the gently snipped ends of it where it had been cut. I could watch her lips moving when it was her turn to read Shakespeare out loud. I could see her chest rising slowly as she breathed in and out. I could do all of this until Hodgy disturbed me by suddenly shouting out his party piece of 'Ello peeps,' or 'Only me.'

Ellie had come to a few of our rehearsals. She never quite eulogised in the same way she had when she first heard us though. Now, more often than not, she would sit quietly cross-legged and listen. I was desperate for her to show us some appreciation again. I was desperate to hear her say how fantastic we were - but she was never quite so animated again. In fact sometimes she didn't even seem to be listening at all.

On a couple of occasions she brought her homework with her. We would play hell for leather, frenzied and loud, whilst she would quietly and indifferently read Keats' poems or Great Expectations or something by Camus she was reading for French. I was bowled over by this. I just wanted to read them with her, to her. I just wanted to watch her taking in Endymion, or Ode to Autumn, or the adventures of Pip and Estelle. I wanted to discuss existentialism with her, impress her with my own reading. I wanted to do all of this and more. Of course, most of all, I wanted to shag her.

But the reality was that I would hardly speak to her. I would leave that to Neddy, Pim and Danny. Sometimes Danny would pretend to sing to her. He was an outrageous flirt, an incorrigible show-off. She would be his audience whether she liked it or not. I always assumed that she liked the attention. I always assumed that every girl fancied him. But Ellie Smith, she was cooler than most girls. Sometimes she would just sit there reading her books, ignoring him. Ignoring all of us. I wondered why she came at all, but I was glad she did. My heart would leap every time the basement door opened and Mrs Cappaldi led her into our dim world.

Throughout that autumn we practised a lot, in preparation for our first gig. We could play twelve songs pretty well note-perfect: six of our own, and six cover versions. I was pleased that I had written three of our own songs. Danny had written the others.

As we got better, we started to try to develop our own style. Not consciously. It wasn't a thing we discussed. We were trying to be too cool for that, but I confess, I did a lot of gazing at my shoes, because that was what Johnny Marr did, and if it was good enough for him......

Pim would grin and play frantically. Sometimes he would grimace with the effort, his long hair tangling in sweat. I liked

Pim. He grinned at the end of each song, regardless of how we'd played it.

Ned had changed since we first played in my bedroom. He had become more confident and was developing into a bit of a showman. He had always been a little bit camp - though he seemed to have a bird on the go all the time - but as he turned seventeen he was becoming just a little bit camper. Not Larry Grayson camp, don't get me wrong, more Mark Lawrenson. I didn't mind that; what I minded were these small dance routines he had started doing. I didn't like those at all. I wasn't having dancing routines of any sort, so I let Ned know. I told him you wouldn't get Andy Rourke - the bassist in The Smiths - doing a dance routine; if he wanted dance routines, he should fuck off and join the amateur dramatics.

I couldn't tell Danny anything. I wouldn't have dared even if I'd wanted to. Danny had his own way of reacting to the music, of expressing the pure celebration of being young. He had this thing sometimes when he would dance crazily, uncontrollably, arms and legs whirling everywhere. He loved doing it. He normally did it during our song, 'Everything's Sensational'.

I'd written it.

It had a rise at the end where the guitars would slowly march up the fret board, gathering pace and volume. Pim would smash around his kit, hammering his snare and drums. As we were doing this, I would gaze even more intently at my shoes, but Danny, Danny went mental.

We were doing it once, a few weeks before our first gig at Jenny George's Christmas party. We'd finished the last verse. It had been a good, tight rendition. Then Danny went crazy.

Everything's sensational
It's gonna be sensational
Everything's sensational
It's gonna be sensational.

Then he started to ad lib, dancing close to where Ellie was sitting, cross-legged as usual.

You are sensational
You are sensational
You are sensational
You're fucking sensational

He repeated his reprise over and over, as we hammered the last chord, before eventually finishing with a huge unholy noise.

Ellie hadn't looked up once. She hadn't paid Danny any attention. I'd never seen Danny react to anything before. He was always so cool, so reassured. But Ellie's ambivalence annoyed him. In a fit of pique, clearly still buzzing from the song, he snatched her book, and started to read loudly through his microphone, in a whiny, piss-taking voice:

Ode to Melancholy
No, no, go not to Lethe, neither twist
Wolfs bane, tight-rooted for its poisonous wine

I felt my blood boil. I had never seen Danny act like such an arse before. He sounded so stupid, he had mispronounced the words; he didn't understand the rhythm of the poem. I was embarrassed for him. Ellie wasn't. Ellie didn't seem to mind, but I minded.

'Danny,' I shouted, 'stop being such a twat.'

He stopped quoting from Ellie's book, and dropped to his knees holding his microphone to his mouth. He started singing in an overtly dramatic way. 'Danny,' he screamed like Robert Plant in a particularly tight pair of slacks, 'stop being such a twat.' He was taking the piss out of me now. I tried to ignore him. Ellie was ignoring him. But he continued: 'Especially when Riiiiiichie,' he elongated my name, 'is the last virgin in the band.'

I could have killed him for that. I could have quite happily caved his head in with my guitar. Instead I decided to storm out.

That's what I decided to do. Unfortunately my attempt at storming out was absolutely crap. It would have been better if I had thrown my guitar to the ground, shouted an insult and left. It would have been a more effective 'storm out' if I hadn't had to unplug my guitar from my heavy metal pedal, my heavy metal pedal from my reverb pedal, my reverb pedal from my compression pedal, my compression pedal from my wah-wah pedal, then my wah-wah pedal from my amp. Then I had to put my guitar into my flight bag. By then, the moment for a good 'storm out' had passed. Instead it turned into a rather feeble clumsy, sulky flounce.

That night when I was at home watching Minder with my mum, dad and brother, I received three phone calls. Ned, I expected. I knew that Neddy would phone me out of some kind of solidarity. He told me that he thought Danny had acted like a twat, and that I shouldn't worry about it. I didn't really want to listen to Ned's sympathy though, because it would invariably lead to a conversation about sex and whether I had or hadn't popped my....... you know. I told him that I was sick of Danny being a twat and I'd leave the band if he continued to say things like that. I didn't mean it of course. I would never have left the band.

Then during the ad break Danny phoned. This was less expected. He asked me if I was alright.

'Yeah, why shouldn't I be?' I answered unhelpfully, when I should have said, 'No, I'm fucking not alright; you can't take the piss out of the thing that is currently more important to me than anything else in the whole universe - my status of virgo intactus.'

The conversation continued in a circle never going near the subject.

'We did a great Venus in Furs tonight,' he said referring to our high-octane version of The Velvet Underground song.

'Yes,' I said moodily, 'not bad.'

'I'm just feeling a little stressed, that's all. About the gig. And everything.' This I knew was about as close as I would get to an apology.

'Okay.' I added, 'Look, Minder's coming back on, so I'd better go. I'll see you Thursday.' I put the phone down feeling as though the great big grey cloud had cleared leaving a sunny blue sky.

A short while later the telephone rang again. My brother answered. He came into the living room where the rest of us were silently congregated around the box. 'It's for you, Jimi,' said my brother, who had recently taken to calling me Jimi, as in Hendrix.

'Who is it?' I asked, knowing that the only mates who ever called me had already called me.

'Someone called Ellie,' he added emphasising Ellie in a way that he knew would cause me to rouge.

I jumped to my feet, instantly forgetting the whacky antics of Terry and Arthur on the television and rushing into the hallway to speak to Ellie.

'Hi,' I said, my heart pounding like a pneumatic drill inside my ribcage.

'Hi, Rich,' she answered. This was a good start.

There was a pause as I struggled to stop myself from blurting out something stupid like 'What do you want?' Thankfully she spoke next.

'I got your number from Danny.'

'Yes,' I said, totally lost for words.

'I just wanted to ring to say thanks.'

'Thanks?' I repeated. 'Why?'

'Because Danny was being an arse and you stuck up for me. And you two had a row. And I know how much you like him. And I just wanted to say thanks.'

Like *him!* Like HIM? Had she no idea how much I liked *her?* Had she never received the thoughts that I telepathically sent her each English lesson? Had she never felt my eyes

140

boring into the back of her head, happy just to be looking at the back of her head? All I said was 'Stop being an arse'. If called upon I would have swum through the sulphurous waters of the river Styx for her.

'That's okay,' I said, feebly. 'I think we are all a bit nervous about Jenny George's party.'

'Oh, you shouldn't be,' she added, enthusiastically, 'you were brilliant tonight. Venus in Furs was fantastic.'

'Yeah?' I said,

'Yeah, really brilliant. You guys are going to go down so well at Jenny's.'

For some reason at this moment I decided to give her a blow-by-blow account of the plot of that night's episode of Minder. I wish I hadn't done that now. Nevertheless, she had phoned me. Ellie Smith had phoned me to say thanks and to tell me how brilliant we were.

I went back into the lounge to join my family. I put my feet up on the poof along with my dad and brother. I took a sip of tea out of my Liverpool Champions of Europe 1984 mug and silently carried on watching the telly. Inside though, happy songbirds were singing happy thigh-slapping show tunes and I was grinning the biggest grin the Wirral had ever seen.

16

After failing in my attempt to make contact with Maurice Hunter at the Anglesey Arms, I spent the next five days shacked up in the relative safety of the former office of the absent Butternorth LLB, on the corridor of The Disappeared at Linkbournes.

Each day I would park my dad's Vauxhall in a special free parking spot he told me he always used in Liverpool and skulk through the unfriendly corridors up to my desk. I was beginning to enjoy the anonymity of the decaying office. I felt comfortable and secure in the fact that the only person I saw all day was the limping office halfwit Tommy, who occasionally came up to retrieve photocopy paper, and the only person I spoke to was my corrupt sadist boss Howard McPhee, who would call me from time to time to remind me that my genitalia was trapped in some kind of contraption and that if I didn't carry out some kind of task, some extremely unpleasant thing would happen.

I wasn't scared of McPhee any more. I had come to the conclusion that he did not know the full extent of the demands that Hawkins had made upon me and that, if he had, even he would have drawn the line at arranging for a star prosecution witness to be killed.

After my initial decision to go along with Hawkins' request and seek out this Hunter fellow, I was now unsure. My decision changed almost as often as the fluorescent strip light in my office flickered. One minute, I decided that I would tell Angela that we had to move somewhere safe because a moron with a penchant for decapitation was after us; the next I would decide that they'll never think that I was involved, that Hawkins is hardly likely to grass me up, so I might as well pass the message on to Hunter and at least stay alive.

I was genuinely confused. I was confused and I hadn't even started to add my apparent mission to save mankind from oblivion into my thinking. Often when genuinely confused and unsure, the best course of action is inaction - doing everything to prevent yourself from thinking about the problem. I had been doing this for years. I was an Olympian at it. So I sat in my office and whiled away the days. It is amazing how many ways you can find to pass the time and prevent yourself from doing any work.

On my own in Butternorth's office, with no colleagues to annoy, and no view to look out on, I had to make do with the items at my disposal. The photocopying machine made a great toy. After cursing it for days whilst photocopying the contents of my files, I now spent hours having photocopying races to see which types of paper could be copied quickest. I tried to photocopy using only my left hand; I tried to photocopy blindfolded; then - and I'm not proud of this - I started to photocopy bits of myself. Before long, I had painstakingly photocopied my entire body, and tacked it up on the wall of Butternorth's office. It looked macabre. It looked like a weird perversion of the Turin shroud. But still, it took my mind off everything else.

It took my mind off murder.

After a couple of days I received the call I'd been dreading: it was McPhee. But this time rather than just rant at me, he was imparting some information.

'Strafe? It's Howard here.'

'Yes, hello, Howard, how are you all down there?'

'Never mind that, we're all fucked. Now look, tomorrow,

you'll be going to see Hawkins again with our two barristers, okay?'

'Great,' I lied.

He told me what time, and the names of the two barristers I would be meeting down there, a QC called William Golightly, and his junior Damien Parker-Manly. I hated them instantly.

I spent the rest of the day photocopying various items of stationery, managing a wonderful art nouveau series of copies of my stapler, which I entitled 'Stapler,' and put on the wall next to the copy of me.

At home that night I sat in the lounge with my mum and dad, watched television and ate pasta from a tray on my lap. We watched the two soaps, a programme about reformed burglars carrying out interior decorations in the houses of liberals, and then had a cup of tea before the nine o'clock detective mini-series about the gambling, hard-drinking, tough-talking, straight-thinking detective fighting the system and crime at the same time. Funny how he always shags either the victim, a female police officer or the perpetrator of the crime - yet never gets reprimanded by his boss.

As we sat there I occasionally glanced at my father. He sat quietly and comfortably in his armchair. I could see the colours of the TV reflecting in his face. He seemed content, but I wondered if he really was. I wondered if he was thinking about his mortality. I looked like him. I could see the shape of my face in him. I could see my mouth as I looked at him. It made me sad.

I got up to get a packet of biscuits on the go and the phone went. I was up on my feet so I went to get it.

I didn't expect Angela.

'Richard?' she asked. I had to think who it was. Her voice seemed different.

'Yes.'

'It's me, Angela.'

'Angela, fuck. Hi.'

I realised why her voice seemed different. The aggression

had gone. The edgy quality that suggested that we were minutes from a blazing row that had been in her voice for months was missing.

She continued nervously, 'I didn't expect to find you in.' I didn't know what she was getting at. She must have sensed that as she continued, 'You know, what with Liverpool being a party city, I thought you'd be out, eh, partying.'

'Oh, you know me, Ange,' I answered tentatively, 'my party days are well behind me.'

She laughed. This was excruciating. It got worse.

'So how are you?'

'Fine. You?'

'Yes. Fine.'

'How's your mum and dad?'

'They're..' I toyed with telling her about my dad, but decided against it, '..they're fine, yes. Great.'

We went through a whole list of questions: her job - fine; my job - fine; the flat - fine; the bastard smoke alarm that was faulty - fine. Everything was so bloody fine, you'd think that we were on drugs.

We both knew that she was ringing for a reason but neither of us wanted to confront it. There was a silence. It was a long silence. It was so long it felt that during it whole planets could have evolved from burning molten rock mindlessly cruising through space into lush and bounteous worlds complete with complicated life forms, language and entertainment that doesn't include TV programmes about decorating your house.

Eventually, she spoke. 'We need to talk, Rich.'

I didn't want to talk to her. I didn't want to have to engage in conversation about who should have what bloody books; who should have what CDs; where we went wrong, how we'll still be friends. I didn't want to have to listen to her telling me about some new bloke she'd met and how it was early days but she quite liked him. I didn't want any of that: I had other things to think about. I had other, more important things to talk about, to come to terms with. I would rather have put a fork in my own eyeball than talk about breaking up and moving on. I knew that if she mentioned the word 'closure', I wouldn't be responsible for my own actions.

That is what I thought. But, 'Yes, I suppose so, you're right,' is what I said.

'Why don't I come up this weekend and we can talk properly?'

Come up? This weekend? And see me? This couldn't happen. This was totally wrong. It wasn't safe for her to be with me. I didn't want her to be with me. At least I didn't think I did.

'This weekend? Shit, Ange, I don't know. I'm really busy.' I was prevaricating, and it didn't sound good.

The aggression seeped back into her voice. 'Well, don't you want to meet me to sort all this out? Rich, we *need* to talk.'

'Yes, of course. I know. Look, Angela, this weekend would be all wrong. I'm sorry. It's not you, it's not the possibility of us meeting up....'

She interjected before I could finish my bullshit, which was good because I didn't have a clue what I was about to say. 'Well, what is it then?'

I stopped and took a deep breath. I was going to have to come up with something better than, 'It's not you, it's me.'

'Listen, Ange, I'm sorry. You are just going to have to trust me. You can't come up here now. I can't explain. If you just give me a week or so, then I'll come back to London or something, and we can sort it all out then.'

She paused to consider this. 'Are you seeing someone else?'

'What? No, for fuck's sake, of course I'm not seeing anyone.'

She emitted a strange sound. I thought she might have been crying. That or wind. There was another silence.

'Please,' I repeated as gently and rationally as I could, 'just trust me on this.'

Her voice was soft and vulnerable. 'Okay,' she answered.

I took a deep breath after I had put the phone down. My

147

heart was beating as if I'd just run for the bus. I didn't fancy the chocolate Hobnobs anymore and went back into the lounge, where my parents didn't appeared to have moved any part of their bodies during my absence. I wondered if they were actually breathing.

'Was that Angela?' asked my mum.

'Yes,' I replied as nonchalantly as I could.

'How is she?'

'She's fine,' I said meaninglessly, before adding, 'She wants to come up in a week or so.'

'That'll be nice,' added my dad.

And the three of us went back to watching the telly.

I couldn't sleep that night. Millions of thoughts had been kaleidoscoping through my mind. My dad, Angela, my mission, Hawkins - eventually they all merged into one. I tried to get to sleep by listing things, modern man's equivalent of counting sheep. I listed all the members of the Liverpool teams of the 1970s and 1980s but that was no use; by the time I had got onto John Aldridge I knew that wasn't going to get me to sleep. I tried to list my record collection. This worked better: I don't remember four o'clock.

But I woke up knowing that I was going to Liverpool prison and worrying about who I had given my Psychedelic Furs album to. I knew that Hawkins would want to know about my progress with Maurice Hunter. What I didn't know was how much he knew. I mean, did he have other people on the outside making sure that I was doing as I was told? Was my progress being monitored, my every move closely observed by one of his henchmen? I figured not. He had contacted me because I was the only person, other than the two barristers who he had sacked, who had seen him in prison. No one else was allowed. I guessed that if he had access to other people, then he wouldn't have had to come to me. There wouldn't have been all that malarkey about writing on, then eating, pieces of paper.

Still, I couldn't be sure. Someone who is capable of cutting the heads clean off three people is clearly capable of doing anything.

I dragged my feet all morning. I didn't want to get to the prison earlier than the other two. I didn't want to have to be alone with him. I got myself dressed slowly, like a thirteen-year-old who doesn't want to have to go to school. I adopted a surly and evasive demeanour at breakfast. My mum asked me why I was playing with my Frosties. I didn't want to tell her that I was pushing the cereal around my bowl because I didn't want to go and meet a man who would ask me how my part in a conspiracy to murder another man was coming along - so I just told her that I was tired. I knew that she would dismiss it as me worrying about Angela. I was happy to let her think that.

I drove as slowly as I could but on the one day when I could have done with a legitimate good old British traffic jam, the streets were like Monaco on Grand Prix day. I sailed through every bloody set of traffic lights and was barely detained at a junction. I arrived at Liverpool prison bang on time.

Thankfully, from the guffaws of the security staff, who were recounting the tale of strip-searching the two barristers, it appeared that William Golightly and Damian Parker-Manly were already there. I, who had washed every crevice in anticipation, presented myself willingly for the strip search. In fact I was more than happy to allow big Benson & Hedges man and his mates to linger as long as they liked. After all, every second spent with some big Scouse bloke's hand up my crack was a second less in the company of mad Terry Hawkins.

When I entered the conference cell Hawkins had yet to be produced. Instead Golightly and Parker-Manly were there on their own.

'Ah,' said the elder of the two, a grey-haired ramrod backed man, who I assumed was Golightly the Queen's Counsel.

'You must be from McPhee's?'

'Yes,' I said. I hate barristers. I hate some of them almost as much as I hate Cappaldi.

Well, perhaps not that much, but I wouldn't get tired of kicking a couple of them.

'Good, good,' he replied, in that pompous, arrogant, self-opinionated, self-important, twattish way barristers have.

The two of them then ignored me and continued to talk about Liverpool in sheepish tones that suggested they were embarrassed about their adventures with the security staff.

'What I like most of all is the girls,' said Parker-Manly. 'Liverpool must be the only place in the world with a temperate northern climate, yet has a population of young females who are continually suntanned.'

Wanker. He was right, but that wasn't the point. That cliché should only be uttered by locals; it's the same law that says Woody Allen is the only person who can make jokes about Jewish people.

Golightly put his head back and laughed falsely. Parker-Manly looked back at me and I bared my teeth.

The door opening and arrival of Hawkins interrupted their amusement. I sat on a chair in the corner at the back. I willed the chair to become invisible as Hawkins entered the room. He ignored the two barristers and looked at me. I offered him a nervous glance in return.

Hawkins sat down and stretched out his sinewy arms across the table. It was an exhibition of his manhood. He might not be an educated man, but he was letting everyone in the room know who was the Alpha male.

Golightly began by introducing Parker-Manly and me, who he described as the 'young man' from McPhee's. Double wanker.

Then he continued to talk to the alleged triple murderer.

'Mr Hawkins, in simple terms, the Crown's case is this....'

He spoke in a patronising, unnecessarily loud voice, as if he was talking to a Spanish waiter. I couldn't believe he told Hawkins that he was using simple terms. It made me smile.

How stupid were these men? Didn't they realise that Hawkins was a match for them in every way? He was at the top of his profession as well, and he hadn't reached that by having to have everything put to him in simple terms.

Golightly continued, 'They say that you were involved in a business arrangement with De Voos, O'Kane and Avro, and that they were skimming money from you.'

Hawkins interrupted him, 'They were. Three million quid, they *skimmed.*' Hawkins' interjection took Golightly by surprise.

'Yes, quite, well, they say that because of this you decided to take matters into your own hands and, eh,' Golightly stuttered, unable to finish his sentence, so Hawkins finished it for him.

'So I chopped their heads off.' He pulled his hand across his throat as he said it, and grinned.

'Yes,' said Golightly.

Hawkins looked bored. Occasionally he looked beyond his barristers towards me. At one point our eyes met, or rather, his eyes marched up to mine and headbutted them. After that I put my head down and wrote furiously in my notebook. I had never taken such detailed notes. I wrote down every word that was uttered.

Golightly continued to outline the case to Hawkins. He asked Hawkins to explain how he knew the three dead men.

'Business acquaintances,' Hawkins informed him.

'What businesses were you involved in?'

'Nightclubs,' Hawkins said, adding cryptically, 'and a bit of buying and selling.'

Golightly ignored that.

We then went painstakingly through all of Terry Hawkins' accounts. It appeared that in the last year, Hawkins had made - from various ventures - over fifteen million pounds. Hawkins listened with a look of disinterest as Golightly asked him questions about his business. Occasionally he would sigh with exasperation as Golightly got something wrong, before correcting him in terse tones.

Eventually Golightly asked the question that was on all our minds.

'Mr Hawkins, I've got to ask you this,' he said by way of preamble, taking his glasses off and sitting back for effect. 'Were you selling drugs?'

Hawkins looked over at me at this point and I quickly averted my gaze. He seemed to take an age to contemplate the question, before looking Golightly directly in the eye.

'No, I wasn't.' I knew he was lying. Golightly and Parker-Manly knew he was lying as well.

I wondered what Golightly would say next.

'You realise that it will be suggested to you that you were selling drugs and the only way you could have made this amount of money was by selling drugs?'

Hawkins stared at the old barrister, looking straight at him, beyond his eyes, deep into his brain.

'Mr Golightly, even if I was selling drugs, even if I was pissed off that these three wankers had stolen my money, even if I am glad that they met their unfortunate ends, and would buy whoever did it a large drink, it does not prove beyond reasonable doubt that I had anything to do with it. You're a QC, you know that.'

Golightly looked for a second at Parker-Manly, nodded at Hawkins and moved on.

'You will be aware, Mr Hawkins, that the entirety of the case against you lies with the evidence of a Mr Colin Rutland.'

'Lying bastard,' interjected Hawkins immediately.

'Quite,' said Golightly, 'but why would he lie? Tell me, have you fallen out with him?'

Fallen out with him. It sounded so funny. Here we were with a man accused of triple murder, torture and decapitation, a man whose criminal activities had made him a multi-millionaire, being asked if he had 'fallen out' with the man whose evidence would send him to prison for life, like two schoolboys having a tiff in the school yard. Hawkins thought it was funny as well - he smiled. He was a good-looking man when he smiled; his teeth had survived crack cocaine.

'No, we didn't fall out,' he said emphatically. 'He couldn't hack it, so I moved him on.' The words had a chilling resonance to them.

'He says he saw you in Liverpool in a restaurant with De Voos, O'Kane and Avro on the day they disappeared, and watched the four of you get into a car.'

Hawkins wasn't smiling now.

'Well, he's wrong.'

'Well that's what he says, and if the jury believe him....' Golightly didn't bother to finish his warning; he didn't have to.

Golightly looked at Parker-Manly. He started to put his pen away and wrapped a pink ribbon around his brief and his notebook and asked Parker-Manly if he had anything else to say. Parker-Manly told him that he didn't. He didn't bother asking me. Twat.

Hawkins sat impassively. As they made to leave he spoke again.

'What if he doesn't give his evidence?'

I choked as Hawkins said this.

Golightly looked at him slightly confused. 'What do you mean?'

'What will happen if he doesn't turn up to court?'

Golightly adopted his patronising voice again. 'Mr Hawkins, let us assume that Mr Rutland will be in court.'

'Not if he's dead, Mr Golightly.'

I coughed audibly as Hawkins said this. Golightly smiled weakly at Hawkins as though he had made a lame joke.

I got up to leave, hoping that Hawkins wouldn't notice me. He did.

'Hold on, Richard,' he said as I scurried towards the door. Golightly and Parker-Manly looked round, surprised by his tone of voice which suggested that we were in fact close mates.'You two can go,' he told the barristers. 'I need to talk to my special solicitor.' They left and shut the door behind them.

Hawkins looked at me, pointed to the walls and pinched his ear to remind me that he thought the room was bugged. I didn't doubt him. I wasn't going to take any risks.

Just as before, he talked to me as though we were friends.

'I bet you were surprised when you found out how much money I made, hey?'

'No,' I said, 'I knew that already from the papers.' I indicated to the brief on the desk, then immediately wished that I hadn't contradicted him. He cooled slightly.

'I don't think I need to tell you any more about the instructions I gave you last time. The special instructions.'

I shook my head silently.

'Good.'

'You know, that amount of money buys me an awful lot of favours if I end up in prison for life,' he added.

My eyes narrowed. I knew what he was getting at.

'If I am behind bars for any length of time, I still employ people to carry out,' he paused, searching for the right words, ensuring that he didn't say anything that might be picked up, 'to carry out any unfinished business I might have with people who have let me down.' He smiled sweetly, casting an intense gaze at me as he did before adding menacingly, 'Give my love to Angela.'

I nodded. I was now officially shitting myself.

I telephoned Howard McPhee. I wasn't sure what I expected McPhee to do. I didn't really know what I wanted him to do. I suppose I was looking for a sign. I was looking for something that would tell me that McPhee knew what Hawkins was trying to get me to do and that it was alright: or that I should just ignore it, and not worry. Perhaps McPhee would laugh at me. 'Strafe, you really are a Scouse muppet. As if Hawkins is going to have you killed from behind bars.'

I dialled tentatively.

I was put through to McPhee by a receptionist whose

voice I didn't recognise.

'What is it, Richie?' boomed a voice I did recognise: McPhee's.

'Just thought I'd give you an update of our meeting with Golightly and Parker-Manly yesterday,' I said nervously.

I could tell by the pause on the other side of the phone that McPhee was trying to remember who Golightly and Parker-Manly were. Eventually the penny dropped for him.

'Ah, yes, our man Terry Hawkins. Yes. How was it? Is everything okay?'

'Oh yes,' I said brightly, 'everything's fine.'

I then proceeded to go over everything that Hawkins had told us about his accounts and his witnesses. I could tell that McPhee was bored, but disinterest was better than his usual bullying.

Occasionally he would chip in with, 'So everything's going well, then?'

To which I would repeat that everything was fine. After he asked if everything was going well for the third time I paused. 'Well, there is just one thing…'

I could sense his mood blacken as he contemplated what the 'one thing' might be.

Suddenly I was no longer Richie, I was Strafe.

'What's that, Strafe?'

I tried to find the right words. 'Well, it's like this. He's, er, asked me to take some messages to some of his colleagues on the outside.'

McPhee seemed relieved. 'Oh, is that all? There's nothing wrong with that, is there?'

'Well, I suppose not,' I whined reluctantly.

'Listen, Strafe, there are some clients who we have to go the extra mile for. As long as you're not acting in contempt of court. You're not acting in contempt of court, are you?'

'No,' I answered quickly, unsure if arranging to have a witness murdered was technically in contempt of court or not.

'Good, then in that case, just do as he says.'

'Okay,' I said, unconvinced.

McPhee must have sensed my lack of conviction.

'Richie,' he continued, 'did I ever tell you who my favourite ever lawyer was?'

I was amazed, McPhee sounded as though he was about to impart some special information to me, or some avuncular advice.

'No,' I said.

'Vito Corleone's lawyer in The Godfather. You remember, the Irish chap, Hagan. He's played by Robert Duvall. Do you remember him?'

I told him that I did.

'Now there was a real lawyer. Someone who would go the extra mile for his client. For him, the battle wasn't about justice. It was about ensuring that every time Marlon Brando's bollocks were on the line, he could come to the rescue. Each time James Caan's dick was on the chopping block, he'd pull it from the fire. Corleone might have been The Godfather, the main man, the big boss, but without his trusted and able Consigliere, he would have been nowhere. Now that's what I call a lawyer, a true professional.'

McPhee was getting carried away with his own passion. His analogies were all over the shop.

He stopped, seeming to realise that perhaps he had said a little too much.

'I don't normally tell people about that,' he added a little sheepishly.

'Anyway,' he continued, 'I'm pleased with the work you're doing up there, Richard, and so's Hawkins. I have to say you've surprised me.'

I was stunned. Not about McPhee's bizarre delusions of Godfatheresque grandeur. That was no surprise: McPhee was mad and that he should hero-worship a corrupt, unscrupulous lawyer who did all he could to get his guilty client off charges for murder and extortion didn't surprise me at all, but praising me, that was incredible. I had never heard him praise anyone, let alone me. Before I had chance to thank him, or even say anything, he had bidden me farewell and hung up.

I sat back in my chair. I looked at the photocopied pictures of various pieces of stationery. McPhee thought that I was doing a good job. Fair enough. He thought that I should just carry out my instructions. Fair enough. Hawkins was going to kill me. Fair enough. I didn't want to die.

I decided the next day I would return to the Anglesey Arms and seek out Mr Maurice Hunter.

17

After Ellie Smith had decimated an episode of Minder with her unexpected phone call, I expected our relationship to change. I had this notion that she would become my girlfriend, my soul mate, the person with whom she could read her English books before engaging in scintillating conversation about Keats and Dickens or whoever else she was reading. I had an image of us both in my bedroom, me strumming the new classic hits I had just composed as she listened, languidly stretched out on my bed, her beautiful face cupped in her hands. Perhaps we would go away together, have wonderful adventures and discover the fantastic world that lay untouched by our teenage hands, unseen by our innocent eyes.

A part of me, though, was a bit daunted by Ellie's sudden phone call. She was, after all, more Danny's friend than mine. We knew that by the way in which she would stay at Danny's after our practices had finished. Danny flirted with her. Danny made jokes about her. I didn't. I worried that if Ellie and I suddenly became an item it would be a bit, well, weird. I worried that Danny might not like it. I worried it might spoil the band. I worried if Danny would in some way be jealous. I worried that I was wrong and really she didn't fancy me at all. I didn't want to be rejected by Ellie.

I decided to try to put Ellie out of my mind as best I could.

But it was difficult.

I wrote my songs. I wrote songs about her. I wrote *The Girl With The Long Brown Hair.* It was about her. I remember it, of course I do.

There's nothing special about me
That's what they say anyway
And if I dream out loud, it's because my dreams are loud,
And in them I fly away
With the girl with the long brown hair.

I wrote it on an acoustic guitar in the old music room just behind the bogs in school. I remember I was trying to sing it. I was in a world of my own. Eyes closed, mouth full open belting out this song, when I noticed the whole of class 4G were stood at the door, mouths agape. I stopped singing and they started to piss themselves. The bastards.

I did my homework. I actually got some good results. But most of all I dreamt. I dreamt about Ellie, and I dreamt about The Sensationals.

Our rehearsals grew more intense as we approached our début at Jenny George's party. The change started after I had stormed out. It was just a subtle change and Danny started it. He started taking our music seriously. Suddenly he was no longer content just to sing and do his crazy dancing. He would listen intently during the songs. He would stop the band and make suggestions to each of us. In the past it had almost always been me who had stopped and informed someone that they were out of tune, or out of rhythm. It had been me who would make us play a song again because we hadn't got it quite right the first time. Now Danny started doing it more and more. He would introduce extra parts into the songs. He would urge Pim to do little drum rolls here and there or use different parts of his kit. He would urge Ned to slide up and down his bass fret board. He would invite me to use a different effects pedal or try a little trill here and there. I didn't mind because I could tell that he was being utterly serious. He wasn't just trying to piss us off. I didn't mind because with nearly every suggestion he made, we sounded a lot better.

It wasn't just the music that Danny was taking more seriously. He started to ignore the people who came to sit in on our rehearsals rather than play up to them. Even when his university girlfriend Kathy turned up with a group of friends who stood in a row and danced and giggled, I could tell that his main priority was the band. I liked that.

In the week before our début we practised furiously. We went through our set each night. We worked out our intros and our endings. We polished our middle eights and our backing vocals. After we had finished we talked excitedly about how brilliant we were and how brilliant we were going to be. We discussed our first album and our tour. I had us touring Britain. We would play all the universities and the best venues in the big towns. Pim had us shagging undergraduates, five at once; whilst Ned, if I remember correctly, talked animatedly about the clothes we would have to buy.

Danny was aiming higher though. After the first album he said we'd break the States. No messing about, straight to New York, Seattle and Los Angeles. You can stick your Middlesbrough Poly, he said, I'm playing the Madison Square Garden. We all laughed in a demented fever of excitement.

Danny telephoned me on the Thursday before the party. It was just before the ten o'clock news. He didn't wait to exchange pleasantries. He never did.

'Guess who fancies you, Richie boy?'

My pulse accelerated from its restful pace of evening slumber in front of the telly with my parents to Olympic sprint. I tried to maintain some semblance of cool. Someone 'fancied me'. Who? It could only be one person. He didn't know anyone else who would be vaguely interested in me. I had to keep cool. It wasn't easy.

I had to make out that I didn't care that Ellie Smith fancied me, that I didn't care that the girl who I was deeply in love with felt the same. I didn't consider for a second that it might not be Ellie he was referring to. I didn't consider for a second that there might be other possibilities. 'Don't tell me,' I said, 'the lead singer from the Bangles.'

'Yeah,' he replied continuing with the joke. 'She wants you, man, in a threes up with the other members of the band.'

'Fantastic,' I said. I was so cool. But not so cool that I didn't want to know.

'Go on then,' I said, 'who wants a piece of Richie Strafe?'

'Mandy,' he replied with an excited quiver in his voice as though he had actually said Linda Lusardi.

Mandy! Who the fuck was Mandy? I tried to rack my brain. Mandy? I didn't know a Mandy. Who was Mandy? Did I hear him right? Didn't he really say Ellie?

'Mandy?' I said. 'Who's Mandy?'

Danny was still excited. 'Mandy. You know, Mandy.'

'No, I don't know Mandy.'

'Kathy's friend. You know, with the blonde hair.'

I did know. Mandy with the blonde hair. Kathy's mate. Fucking hell, she was eighteen.

She was gorgeous.

'Mandy!' I exclaimed in a boy soprano voice. 'Mandy. Kathy's friend?'

'Yes, with the blonde hair.'

I tried to be cool again. He must be messing about. She was eighteen. What would she want with me? I'd never even spoken to her. She'd never even spoken to me. How could she fancy me?

'Oh, Mandy,' I said, bringing my voice back down an octave, 'she's not bad.'

'Not bad!' Danny shouted back at me, 'Richie, she's the one. She's *the* one, man. I tell you, this is it. And she's coming to the gig.'

I knew what he meant by *the* one. I knew he was referring to my intact cherry. The bongs on Ten O'Clock News started. Thatcher was talking in the House of Commons, bong; Princess Diana and Prince Charles were unveiling some new building, bong; Gorbachev and Ronnie Reagan were talking about something called Star Wars, bong; everyone was being told to wear a condom. Bong bong bloody bong. It was Thursday. By Saturday, I would be a fully-fledged, all singing, all shagging, guitar-wielding superstar.

I tried to maintain my cool.

'She's coming to the party?'

By now though, Danny was already bored with talking about me; he wanted to move on.

'Richie,' he said, with a note of concern in his voice that informed me that the conversation about Mandy was over. 'What are you going to wear on Saturday?'

'I don't know,' I lied. I had thought about my outfit a lot. In fact I had tried on at least three potential sets of clothes that night.

'Wear your Dead Kennedys T-shirt, and your leather jacket.'

Bastard. He'd got it absolutely right.

That night I hardly slept and Friday dragged. We were doing the Hundred Years War in History, and I swear it seemed to take a hundred years for the lesson to end. I'm just glad we weren't studying One Hundred Years of Solitude in English. I could think only about the gig and the infinite possibilities of my first sexual encounter.

I pictured The Sensationals on stage, about to play our first song, and my heart pounded as my mind clouded over in a fug of crisis - what if we were shite? What if everyone laughed at us? What if I couldn't play? If my fingers seized up? I tried to stop myself from thinking about it. I tried to calm myself down. But each time I stopped thinking about our gig, I would start to think about having my first shag which I had convinced myself was to be with eighteen-year-old Mandy. I assumed that she wanted to shag me. I assumed that as a university undergraduate who had reached the age of majority she would be interested in nothing else other than sex.

It brought me out in a hot sweat. How would I know what to do? Would she laugh at me? What if it went wrong and I couldn't perform? What the fuck did I know about performing?

It was dreadful. I sat as Specsy Morgan, my History teacher, laboriously went through the Hundred Years bloody War and in turn fretted about my band and my entry into the world of sex.

Eventually the school bell rang. Friday school bell. That brilliant Friday school bell feeling that stays with you forever.

I skulked out of class and into the school yard. Kids kicked balls and shouted. Boys fought and swore. Teenagers smoked and snogged and basked in the glow of not having to go back to school for at least two days. At the gates I spotted Ellie and Danny. Their school bags were on the ground in front of them. I felt the usual sense of expectation as I saw Ellie, but this time it was tinged with a strange feeling of confusion - I had, after all, been set up with someone else. I didn't want her to know.

I hadn't seen Danny since his telephone call the previous night. He grinned at me as I approached. I knew that he had told Ellie about Mandy.

'Hey, it's Richie Strafe,' he shouted.

I smiled back. Ellie looked in a different direction, the wind blowing her hair.

'Listen, tomorrow,' he added excitedly, 'Ellie wants to meet us by the Old Lighthouse to take some photographs.'

Ellie smiled at me. 'I just thought it might be a good memento of the occasion,' she said.

'Yeah,' I concurred, 'brilliant.'

I liked the idea of that. I liked the idea of Ellie taking some atmospheric pictures of the band. The swirling sexuality of Jim Morrison came to my mind, or the cool of The Smiths outside Salford Lads' Club. I liked the idea of Ellie looking at me. Capturing me forever. I would definitely wear my Dead Kennedys T-shirt and leather biking jacket now.

We walked towards the bus stop and made arrangements. We would meet at six and, on account of him going through a cycling shorts phase which didn't really fit in, Ellie would tell Neddy herself how he should dress and do his hair. This was good; this was taking my mind off all thoughts of sex and guitars. By the time we reached the bus stop I had almost forgotten about the stress of the gig and all other stressful débuts I was about to embark upon. Once again, I was confident about my own elevation towards immortality.

18

Howard McPhee's recent conversation had had a strange effect upon me: after his manic monologue about the lawyers he really respected, I found myself rooting around in an old cupboard for my dad's copy of the Godfather Boxed Set, a present I had got him for some long ago Christmas. I eventually located it, hidden behind videos of my brother's wedding, my brother's first kid's christening, a video of Whatevertheotheronesnameis' first birthday party and a video of my brother moving into his new home. Bloody hell, all the events that I had been told about but either not attended, or was too pissed to remember, recorded in VHS form forever. For a few seconds I was tempted to settle down and watch them, but then the unmistakeable cover of The Godfather emerged from behind a video collection of episodes of Casualty and I remembered the job in hand.

I watched it. Of course I'd seen The Godfather before; I even watched all three from start to finish once, in one epic sitting. But this time, I watched with a keen interest in Hagan - the lawyer who would go the extra mile. It's a great performance from Duvall. McPhee was right: without him, Brando would have been fucked.

McPhee saw it as a game, as one big exciting Hollywood adventure. He probably saw life as a game with defeats and victories. In that respect, McPhee wasn't too different from my dad, only difference was my dad saw getting two for the price of one at Tescos as a victory whereas McPhee prized getting the clearly guilty acquitted. And, it seemed, the more guilty they were, and the more serious the crime, the sweeter the victory. I watched Duvall, I thought about McPhee and decided that I would get it done.

The next day I dressed in my best suit with a dark tie. I polished my shoes for the first time since my grandad's funeral. I pulled out a raincoat from my dad's wardrobe and hunted around for a pair of sunglasses. I was going to look the part.

Unfortunately, I struggled with sunglasses. The only ones I found were a pair of wrap around shades with the word 'Sunbeam' emblazoned across one of the lenses that I had purchased on a holiday to Ibiza with Angela when we were first together. I tried them on with my suit and my dad's raincoat. It wasn't right; I looked more like some kind of weird paedophile on a trip to Rhyl than a lawyer to the mob. I searched around in my brother's old room and came across a pair of cheap fake Ray-Bans he had worn during his Velvet Underground phase. I still looked a bit strange and was immediately hot in my dad's mac, but at least I didn't look like I should be arrested on the spot.

By the time I reached the back alley leading to the Anglesey Arms I was boiling hot and suffering from a serious lack of confidence. I had to get focussed. I stopped for a few seconds in the alley and tried to compose myself. I took deep breaths and wondered if I would see Dr Costas in the pub again.

He had told me of my mission to help stop the world from losing the will to live. It was an interesting mission. It was what I was doing now, wasn't it? I was doing something exciting. I was about to embark upon something out of the ordinary, wasn't I? After I had done this, I would concentrate on the rest of my mission, which I assumed had something to do with Cappaldi.

I gripped my briefcase, opened the doors confidently and walked in towards the bar. As before, the pub was quite empty, apart from the same barman who appeared to be standing in exactly the same position. This time though, he didn't ignore me in favour of the Racing Post. He looked up and stared intently as I walked purposefully towards him. I fought the temptation to take my sunglasses off even though the gloom of the bar combined with my brother's cheap Ray-Ban copies was rendering me almost blind. A bead of sweat formed on my brow and I cursed my father for having his raincoat lined with wool that, judging by the intense heat given off, must have been donated by some kind of Arctic sheep.

'What can I get you?' The barman's tone was completely different from the other day. I concluded that Hagan would not have been tempted by the lager. 'Nothing, I'm looking for Maurice Hunter.'

The barman looked at me suspiciously.

'And who are you?'

'An old friend he's never met.'

An old friend he's never met! I couldn't believe that I'd actually said that - what the fuck did *that* mean? Thankfully it was such nonsense that it took the barman by surprise.

'If he's here, who shall I *say* is looking for him?'

'If he's here I'd like to speak to him myself.'

The bead of sweat had now been joined by a number of its mates on my brow and I ran my hand through my hair to stop them dripping down my face. The barman eyed me for a few seconds. I tried to meet his stare, but through the gloom of my sunglasses, in order to see anything I was forced to contort my face into a moronic grimace. Incredibly, this seemed to do the trick.

'Wait here,' he ordered, before disappearing round the side of the bar. I waited for ages. I fidgeted. I put my hand down my collar and felt the sweat cascading down the back of my shirt. I took my sunglasses off and rubbed them with my arm, not realising that that simply made the lenses even worse. I was now almost completely blind.

The barman returned.

'Alright, go through the door there. He's in the back room.'

Back room! This was scary. No one mentioned going into a back room. What was in the back room? What would Hagan have done? He'd have gone. I went. I walked through a door into another bar. This one was long and equally dark and empty. I strained my eyes to see if anyone was there. There wasn't; just empty tables and chairs, an echo of what might be a loud and busy room. At the end of the bar was a light; an archway led into what appeared to be another large room. I made my way towards the light. As I reached the archway I could see four figures sitting around a table. Smoke drifted upwards like Indian semaphore from their table. As I approached they stopped whatever they were doing and looked at me.

I walked closer.

A voice rang out. 'Who the fuck are you? Roy bleedin' Orbison?'

It was a Scouse accent and came from a small man who appeared to be in his sixties, dressed in a blue Teddy Boy suit complete with velvet lapels and bushy chops straggling down from his wilting hairline. I didn't know what to do - nowhere in The Godfather is Hagan confronted by an ageing Scouse Teddy Boy.

I peered at the other three men around the table, trying to guess which one was Maurice Hunter. To the Teddy Boy's right was an uncomfortable-looking fat man of a similar age. He wore a suit that was clearly made for a smaller man. He stared at me, a curious smirk dancing over his fat jowls. Next to him was a slightly tarnished-looking bloke with a weatherbeaten complexion and thick grey hair. He wore a shabby old jumper that in better days might have been worn by a sports commentator or a game show host. The quartet was completed by a gormless-looking younger man wearing a pastel shirt and thick chunky chain that was de rigueur for men under thirty in Liverpool. He grinned at me, a vacant, open-mouthed grin. Quite clearly he hadn't a thought in his head. What was he grinning at? Hadn't he ever seen a bloke in sunglasses and a mac before?

I approached the table. I thought of Hagan. He would have pulled up a chair, opened up his briefcase and made them an offer they couldn't refuse.

'I'm looking for Maurice Hunter,' I said affecting my deepest, most forthright voice. The Teddy Boy, the Fat Bloke and the Young Gormless Chap in the shirt just continued to stare at me, grinning. The Weatherbeaten Fellah looked away, seemingly in total disinterest.

'I didn't know that his membership of the Roy Orbison fan club had lapsed,' rasped the Teddy Boy. (The first Roy Orbison joke was quite funny, the second was quite unnecessary). I tried to remain calm and expressionless.

'Is one of you Mr Hunter?' I asked.

'Who wants to know?' It was the Fat Man. He had a surprisingly gentle voice, it suggested that his vocal chords were as soft and fat as he was, like a balloon. I had anticipated his question though; I had rehearsed my answer.

'I am of no importance, but the message I bring will be of importance to Mr Hunter.' I liked that, I was proud of that, it was cool. Even Hagan would have been pleased with that. Unfortunately as I delivered it my glasses completely steamed up, so instead of delivering it with a nonchalant and enigmatic force, I delivered it through gritted teeth as I tried to see.

The four men exchanged glances. The Teddy Boy spoke next.

'I don't mean to be ungrateful, Roy, but we don't know who the fuck you are. I mean for all we know, you could be one of Her Majesty's glorious Constabulary.'

I had anticipated this line of questioning as well. Of course they were going to consider the possibility that I was a police officer. What I had planned to say was, 'As far as I am aware, there's no law against listening to a message, but if you don't listen then you'll never find out what it was all about.'

I should have rehearsed something simpler; there were far too many clauses in my response. In my blind, sweaty panic

171

what emerged from my mouth was something like, 'If you don't listen to my message, there's no law, as far as I'm concerned, so you might as well, you know what I mean.' It sounded like the English language in a didactic car crash - a combination of John Prescott meets Wayne Rooney. Thankfully it seemed to have some effect, because the four of them stopped grinning at me and looked again at each other.

Finally the Weatherbeaten Fellah spoke for the first time, his voice deep and gravelly, as if he had spent his whole life eating tar. 'Just let him speak, for fuck's sake.'

I wanted to thank him, but I didn't think he'd be too impressed by my gratitude. 'Alright, Roy,' said Teddy Boy, 'let's have it.'

'No,' I replied, braver now, 'not until I know exactly which one of you gentlemen is Maurice Hunter.'

The Fat Man sighed heavily. 'I am. Now what is it you've got to tell me?'

This was a bit easier than I had anticipated. I turned towards the four of them. Now all four were turned towards me. I was surprised that Maurice Hunter was the fat bloke - I would have put money on it being the weatherbeaten one.

'Alright,' I started, composing myself, aware that I was about to commit the crime of conspiracy to murder, 'I am here on behalf of Terry Hawkins.' I paused to see what effect that name would have on my audience. It was profound. The young lad reacted immediately. 'Terry Hawkins? That cockney fellah who wasted....' He didn't finish his question. 'Be quiet, Gary,' interjected the Teddy Boy. 'Let Roy speak.'

I continued, looking directly at the portly Maurice Hunter now. 'He wants a man called Colin Rutland,' I paused for effect, 'sorting out, and he thinks that you can help, Mr Hunter.'

They exchanged more anxious glances.

I have to concede that I was starting to enjoy myself now. This was the stuff of legend. This was the stuff of gangsters and the mob. I had found myself in a world of seedy pubs frequented by a strange criminal underworld where they wore 1960s suits, listened to Rock and Roll and immediately thought that any stranger was a police officer or a rival.

Maurice Hunter looked at me for a second and considered the message I had imparted. He started to make a chewing motion with his huge face. He continued to meet my gaze. Eventually he asked, 'What are the terms?'

'The usual terms,' I responded, hoping that he would understand this, because I hadn't the faintest idea what the usual terms were for knocking off a witness.

He continued to chew as his friends occasionally shot glances at him as though they were all considering the purchase of a second-hand van and I had just quoted them a price. 'Listen,' I said, 'I'm going to sit in the front bar. As I said, I have just come to deliver a message. If you are interested in Mr Hawkins' offer, send someone out, put some money in the jukebox and select the tune Al Capone by the Hotknives. If you want me to walk away and never disturb you again, then select Kashmir by Led Zeppelin.'

Teddy Boy looked at me. 'Al Capone by the Hotknives?'

'Yes,' I repeated.

He nodded. 'That's a Ska classic.'

The Fat Man looked at me again. 'Give us a few minutes.'

I nodded, turned around and made my way back through gloom towards the front bar. As I emerged the barman stared intently at me. I sensed that now I was more interesting than the Racing Post. I took my sunglasses off and rubbed the sweaty lenses with my thumb and forefinger. I made my way to the bar. I needed a drink.

'Scotch,' I said to the barman, 'with ice.' I never drank Scotch. In my life, I had progressed from cider to beer to red wine and never drank spirits, but now, as I stood by the bar, playing the rôle of lawyer to the mob with a layer of sticky warm sweat between my shirt and my jacket, I felt that Scotch was the most appropriate drink.

I sipped the Scotch. The barman stared at me. I asked him if he could put the jukebox on. He didn't say anything, but moodily shuffled towards a set of switches behind the bar and switched one on, causing the jukebox to spark into life with a whirr and sparkle of colour.

A group of young men came into the bar and ordered beers. Their laughing entrance dimmed immediately as they spotted the surly barman and a bloke wearing a raincoat and sunglasses stood at the bar. They waited for their beer.

The clock ticked on the wall as light from the opaque glass windows danced against the optics rack. The barman poured four pints, watching silently as the brown liquid filled the four glasses. Eventually, the Young Gormless Bloke came into the bar. He strode up to the jukebox and started to search carefully through the catalogue of discs. I watched him, my heart pounding against my ribcage. He had probably never seen a proper seven-inch vinyl jukebox before. He looked back at me, with a look of utter confusion on his face. In between us the group of young men drinking beer were exchanging interested glances as they looked at the Gormless Bloke looking at me, then looked back at me.

The Gormless Bloke went back to searching the jukebox, running his fingers across the screen as he read the titles of the discs. He turned towards me again and opened his mouth as though about to say something, thought better of it, then stopped.

I didn't know how much more of it I could stand. I was sick of looking like a flasher who had just nipped out for a pint; I was sick of being looked at with increasing suspicion by a group of young blokes and a surly barman; but most of all I was sick of waiting for the Gormless Scally to remember how to read and select the track that would say whether I was guilty of a conspiring to knock off the star witness in a murder trial.

The young blokes started to whisper. I yearned for the oak bar to wrap itself around me in glorious camouflage. Gormless Bloke turned to me. This time he spoke.

'Hey, mate,' he shouted at me from across the bar, 'was it Led Zeppelin for no, we won't take the job, and The Hotwhatsits for yes, we will take the job, or the other way around?'

I wanted to kill him. I looked up in exasperation. The blokes at the bar and the barman all stood and looked at me waiting for me to answer the question. I looked to my side and considered just ignoring him. His voice rang out again, 'Eh? What was that, mate?'

'The Hotknives,' I corrected him quietly.

He didn't hear me. 'You what?'

'The Hotknives,' I repeated, shouting this time, 'the Hotknives for yes.'

He gave me a thumbs up. 'Cheers, mate,' then went back to considering the jukebox.

My heart was in my mouth. The blokes at the bar turned back towards Gormless - a whole collection of witnesses. Would I have to have all of them killed as well?

The music kicked in. It wasn't Jimmy Page and the crew, it was a Ska beat. It was Al Capone by the Hotknives. Maurice Hunter would 'sort out' Colin Rutland.

19

I lay naked on my old single bed in my old room at home. I was still sweating. Thoughts bubbled up to the surface of my mind. What had I done? What the fuck had I done? This was mad.

After Gormless had selected the Ska track, I had coolly gone back into the bar room and sat down with Maurice Hunter. I then told him who Colin Rutland was and gave him a picture that I had been sent by one of Hawkins' associates. I gave him the last known address and told him the days when Rutland would be going to court to give evidence. Hunter had calmly nodded, then asked me when he would get his money. I told him I would sort this out.

I would sort this out!

How the fuck was I going to do that?

I didn't know how to sort out the payment for a mob killing. It wasn't like sorting out the payment on a second-hand Volvo estate. I would have to ask McPhee. No, I couldn't ask McPhee, I would have to ask bloody Hawkins. We would have to go through the rigmarole again of him searching me for a wire, then him being all friendly, then the daft, coded conversation which could see him eating bits of paper, followed by him gently but firmly threatening to kill my family.

I know he had given money on account to McPhee. I would have to take money out of the account to pay Hunter. I would have to tell McPhee it was for some serious matter. An expert. That was it. Yes, I would tell McPhee that I needed to take half a million quid out of Hawkins' account to pay for an expert. Yeah, right. Like McPhee is going to buy that. What expert costs half a million quid and wants his money upfront? I couldn't believe that I was considering it. I felt like a man hanging onto a cliff by his fingernails who is slowly, finger by finger, losing his grip.

Downstairs I could hear my mum fossicking about in the kitchen. She was making tea. I could hear her slicing potatoes. That meant home-made chips. Marvellous. Egg and chips probably.

I listened to her as I lay on my bed. It reminded me of childhood. It reminded me of a time when everything seemed possible. When I seemed to be protected from everything.

I thought about playing some music. But every movement I made seemed to dislodge a dark scary thought from inside me. This was all going to end badly.

My mum called me down for tea. Fantastic. I put some clean clothes on that she had left in a neat, fragrant, ironed pile on a chair and went downstairs. My egg and chips were already on the table. I didn't deserve this. I didn't deserve home-made chips and ironed clothes. I was a liar now. A liar and a conspirator and probably a killer too. Well, practically.

We sat and ate together. I asked her where my dad was and she thinned her lips and told me he wasn't hungry and had gone out for a walk by the marshy grasslands of the estuary. She was wretched. Worry had left big black bags under her eyes. She had lost weight. She smiled at me.

'You know, Richard, it's been great for me and your dad having you around the last couple of weeks.'

I smiled. If only she knew.

I couldn't talk. I couldn't even make small talk. We tried valiantly, both of us. She assumed that my silence was due to my concern about my father's condition. She told me not to worry. I nodded, my own lips made thin by my forced concern. Of course I was worried about my dad - but it was just one in a long list of worries.

We had custard and pie for afters. Me, the conspirator. Me, the lying bastard. And my poor knackered mother with her lines and her bags.

I left the house and went to look for my dad. I told myself that I would have to sort this out. I couldn't continue with this. I needed to talk to him.

I found him sitting on a bench looking out towards the Welsh hills on the other side of the water. He smiled as he saw me approach.

'Hi,' I said.

'Just looking at some of the cormorants over there,' he said. 'They've found something and they've been worrying it for ages.'

'Oh,' I replied, barely concealing my disinterest.

'Angela phoned for you before,' he added.

'Did she? What did she say?'

'Nothing much, just asking for you.'

'I'll call her later.'

That was interesting. Why hadn't Mum told me about that? I chased thoughts of Angela away. In the grand scheme of things, she was of little importance. The less she knew, the less contact she had with me, the better.

By now both of us were sitting side by side watching the cormorants taking off and landing, squawking and flapping amongst the thick marsh grass. I was poised to tell him everything. I wanted to. I was desperate to tell someone. I decided that I would try to mask what I had done in some kind of complex legal conundrum. I'd suggest to him that organising hit men was something all solicitors had to do from time to time. Play it down a bit. Make a joke out of it. Perhaps I'd laughingly blurt it out, 'God, Dad, you'll never guess what I had to do today...bloody well hire a killer to help my mass murderer get off scot-free. I dunno, us crazy lawyers, eh? It's just mad, mad, mad.'

Before I could say anything, he spoke first. 'The date for my operation has come through.'

'Oh,' I said unhelpfully. I wouldn't mention my problem. No way, not now.

'When?' I added.

'Two weeks' time.'

'Well that's good, isn't it?' I was looking at him now. 'I mean, if they thought it was really serious they'd have you in straightaway, wouldn't they?'

He smiled at me. 'Yes, that's what I keep telling your mother.'

'She's just worried about you, that's all, Dad.'

He turned away. 'There's no need. What will be will be.'

What will be will be. Fucking hell. I wanted to shake him now. What did he mean 'What will be will fucking be?' Didn't he want to take control? Didn't he want to fight for his miniscule amount of time on this planet?

'Listen, Rich,' he was looking at me again now, and his voice had developed that 'I am about to say something important' quality.

'It's been great having you around for the last couple of weeks.'

Christ, not him as well. Between them my parents should just get a huge great barrel of hot sticky guilt and pour it over my head. I shrugged.

'If anything happens to me, you will look after your mum, won't you?'

I didn't want to hear this. 'Dad, don't be stupid, you're going to be fine. It's just a routine operation to remove a minor growth.'

He smiled in a manner that suggested I was being cute in my naivety. 'Yes, son, I know that, *but,* if anything does happen...'

'Yes,' I said, fighting off a desire to grab his arm, or hug him or something, 'of course I will.'

We both turned back to the view. The sun was setting now. The sky turned milky tired and struggled to hold up the layer of thin clouds and shafts of orange setting sun. The shadows on the Welsh hills grew longer. The cries of the cormorants and sea gulls seemed weary as they settled down for the evening. I didn't know what to say to my dad.

'What really bloody annoys me,' he said finally, chewing his words through gritted teeth. 'What really bloody pisses me off,' he added, 'was that,' he stopped, choking back emotion, 'was that we've only had one year since I bloody retired.'

This time I did grab his arm.

'Dad, hey, don't worry now. It's going to be alright.'

He looked upwards towards the heavens. I could tell that he was stifling tears. I knew that there was nothing, absolutely nothing I could say.

His voice regained its usual composure. 'Do you know, I was in the chemist's today, and they tried to charge me full price for a prescription.'

'Yeah?'

'Oh yes, but I wasn't having that. I told her, once you're over sixty-five, love, it's free.'

His words evaporated into the evening. Here he was, facing his mortality with his son - one of the things he'll leave behind - and all he could talk about was a bloody free prescription. I loved him. I really did. But I still didn't want to be him. Ever.

We talked for a few minutes. He asked me if I was still using that free parking slot he had found in Liverpool. He asked me every other day. I said that I was. We agreed that it was great to get one over on the bloody Council sometimes.

I told him I was going to walk back up the hill. He didn't want to leave yet though. He wanted to face things here. Consider everything here, under the beautiful evening sky.

I got up and made my way forlornly up the hill.

All the awful thoughts had now risen to the surface of my consciousness and formed a horrible thick scum. I considered going somewhere to get pissed. I thought about going up to the Old Swanny for 'Showtunes Karaoke Night', but decided I wasn't really in the mood for a gang of young gay fellas singing Andrew Lloyd Webber numbers.

Cars passed by. Lights started to appear in the windows of houses. I wondered about their lives. Eastenders would be starting on the TV. A soap opera that would outlive them all. Oven chips, fish fingers and frozen peas on a tray washed down with a cup of tea made during the adverts.

As I approached my parents' house a car passed me, then slowed down, then reversed. I peered at it. A head popped out of a wound down window. A female voice rang through the night.

'Richie.'

Ellie Smith was the last person on earth I expected to see.

20

Ellie's eyes were on me. They had to be. I loved it. I wanted her to be watching me all the time. I wanted her to be recording me in her mind. I wanted her to be judging me and approving of me.

She clicked her camera and I posed. Me and the other Sensationals. She clicked her camera and we all pissed ourselves. This was brilliant. This was what being a popstar was all about.

We had met up at 6.30pm at the Old Lighthouse. We had spent the afternoon setting up our equipment at Jenny George's parents' hotel and now we were having our photo shoot with Ellie. It was brilliant.

We were standing by some rocks with the Old Lighthouse behind us. Ellie came towards us with the camera.

'Right, when I count three, I want you all to look in different directions,' she told us.

Fantastic, we all knew this one. This was the standard album cover band shot - the one where the four members of the band all look moodily in different directions. In the eighties every band was doing it.

'One, two, three....'

We all looked in exactly the same direction, then fell about laughing. Even Ellie was laughing.

She walked towards us and crouched down, taking us from below. Then she told Danny to walk slowly towards her. He did. He walked towards her and turned his face to an angle -

he looked intensely at her, his simmering youth caught forever by Ellie's camera. I wasn't jealous, though. Not then. It was all part of the laugh, the party, The Sensationals. As Ellie clicked her camera recording Danny, his confidence grew. He started to lunge towards the camera as though it was a rival male that he was showing off to. He put his hands out towards it, beckoning it, almost touching it, toying with it. He laughed. He grimaced. He tried to look hard. Danny loved it. And the camera loved Danny.

After a while Ellie came and took photos of each of us.

'I want you to look seductive,' she laughed at Pim and he pouted at her.

'I want you to look butch,' she said to Neddy and he sucked his cheeks in and ran his hands through his hair. Then it was my turn.

'I want you to look intense,' she said to me.

Intense.

Why was I intense whilst Pim was seductive and Neddy was butch? Is that what Ellie Smith thought of me - intense? The others had laughed at the camera but I scowled at it. I'd give her intense. 'Good', she said, 'that's it, Richie.'

Danny said we had to get going. We all looked at each other. This was it. Photo shoot over. Now we were going to have to go and pick up our instruments. There was a frightened reluctance. It was all very well playing the rock star, but actually performing, that was a different matter.

Pim, as ever sensing the mood, brought out a quarter bottle of cheap whisky. 'Here we are, lads,' he said, 'for medicinal purposes.' He opened the whisky and took a giant gulp, then wiped his jacket across his mouth and handed it to Danny, who did the same. Danny handed it to Ellie, who, to my surprise took an equally thirsty gulp before handing it over to me. I couldn't refuse, even though I hated whisky. Bloody Pim, why hadn't he brought something that wasn't going to make me hurl up my tea? I took a swig, gasped back the desire to retch and passed the bottle on.

After a second round the bottle was finished.

By now we were standing in close circle.

Danny looked around the circle.

'Right, who feels pissed?'

We all shook our heads and laughed.

'I know,' said Ned, 'if we all run, the alcohol will course through our veins quicker and we'll be pissed.'

It seemed plausible.

'Right,' said Danny, 'last one back to the car's a poof.'

We ran and hoped that the booze would seep through our systems and into our brains. We ran and laughed and looked at one another as we did. We got to the car red-faced and just as sober as we had been minutes earlier.

21

Cross Foxes Pub

I sat opposite Ellie Smith in the Cross Foxes Pub.

I hadn't seen her in eleven years,

I had thought about her every day.

For a few seconds we just smiled at each other.

Then we lied about how we were both fine and our lives were great.

Then we started talking properly.

22

Click, click, click, click.

Pim counted me in and I struck the first chords of Boys Don't Cry: our tribute to The Cure, our careful and faithful rendition of Robert Smith's masterpiece of masculinity and adolescence. My fingers felt like they had been dipped in a jar of Vaseline. I heard myself strike a bum note. I grimaced, but just carried on. By now Danny had grabbed the microphone and faced his audience of about seventy teenagers who were lucky enough to have been invited to Jenny George's party. He started to sing.

I could say I'm sorry if I thought that it would change your mind,
But I know that this time I've said too much been too unkind.

Danny started with his eyes closed, mouth gripping the mike stand, his lips practically touching it as he sang the opening lines. But when he got to the bridge he opened them and thrust his head forward, daring the crowd to take the piss out of us. It was brilliant. Danny was totally at home. It was as though every cell in his body had been created for this. There were no nerves, no gradual understanding of what he was trying to do: he just did it. The switch was flicked and Danny Cappaldi went from schoolboy to a singer who people couldn't help but want to watch.

The audience, who were packed up quite close to the tiny

stage, started to move and sway. Girls dressed in bat-winged jumpers and rah-rah skirts bobbed their perms and moved to the beat we were creating. It was brilliant. It was like the crap dancing you see on Top of The Pops and we were making it happen. We were making people move. I could see a group of pretty girls dancing with that look of ambivalent and vacant defiance that they strike when they are dancing in a pack in a disco. I could see it, and my guitar was helping to cause it.

We finished Boys Don't Cry. It wasn't great. We'd played it better a hundred times during our rehearsals. But the audience clapped and cheered. I suppose that they were always going to. It was a Christmas party, they knew the song and most of them were off their tits on Dry Blackthorn Cider.

We went straight into another cover. This time Billy Idol's White Wedding. This was a good song for me: plenty of opportunity to strut and show off my skills with big guitar chords. I was starting to relax now. I stood behind Danny and affected a look of cool disinterest as I played my riffs with exaggerated use of my arms and hands. I had practised this moment and fantasised about it so often in my bedroom at home.

When I looked up, Danny was right at the front of the stage. He was crouching, singing to a group of girls who were grinning like fools and trying to touch his hands. Danny pouted at them, teased them and pushed his groin at them. It was a perfect song for him.

I looked at the crowd again. True, some - boys mainly - were just standing there like statues staring at us, but most were dancing, jumping up and down to the music. They were smiling, laughing; they couldn't believe that the kids they knew at school were creating something that they recognised as music - pop music, their music.

We finished White Wedding, and Danny thanked the audience and welcomed everyone to the greatest party of the 80s. Next we tried to challenge them with one of our own numbers. It was one Danny had written called *Look Out World*

Here Comes The Kid. It started with me playing a furious guitar riff, before Ned and Pim came in. We played it brilliantly. We had never played it so well. It was a great song. It was difficult for the room full of sixteen- and seventeen-year-olds though. They didn't quite get it; they wanted to hear us playing the hits. Some of them stopped dancing.

It didn't bother Danny though. Danny just challenged them even more. This was his song. He looked at them as though they should be grateful for the fact that he was sharing it with them. He screamed the title at them, which was also the hook line of the song. He didn't care if they didn't get it. He didn't care if they would rather dance along to the songs they knew. He knew that he would win. And he did. By the second chorus, the girls were bobbing along again and some of the boys were starting to pogo and mosh into each other closer to the stage. Danny was no longer the crooner appealing to the fledgling sexuality of teenage girls, now he was a leader, empathising with the violent masculine emotion that guitar music can invoke. He knew it. He made the transition seamlessly. I took his lead and played my guitar hard, and the room responded to us.

We played that song at breakneck speed. We played the next two tracks just as fast. It was more energy and adrenalin than skilled musicianship. But no one cared. When we played the fuzzy tape recording my brother John made on his beat box back to ourselves later, we couldn't believe the speed we'd played these songs. Our version of Venus in Furs was two minutes of pure vigorous noise. We enjoyed this. We enjoyed it more than most of the crowd, but still they couldn't help but react to Danny's dancing and singing. As he manically chanted Lou Reed's lyrics about bondage and sado-masochism, no one in the room had a clue what it meant, but the boys at the front continued to push each other and mock fight. Their eyes bulging, their best copping off shirts drenched in sweat.

We played some more of our songs now, starting with 'Billy

Don't', the first song I had played to Danny. Then we tried another of our own straight afterwards: 'At the Bus Stop', a slow lilting love lament of a teenage boy waiting at the bus stop watching the world go by - or at least, watching the world going on its way to Birkenhead.

It was a risk, playing two of our songs one after the other, especially when one was slow. The boys did stop pogoing. The girls did stop dancing. But, incredibly, everyone started to listen and people watched us playing. I wanted to be doing this forever. I wanted to be on stage playing my guitar with people listening for all eternity.

Danny sang this song with his head slightly bowed and one hand behind his back in an enigmatic pose. He sang it wonderfully.

Softly sang the raindrops in the evening air,
Softly like the shadows playing on your hair,
And all the world goes by and I just watch it pass,
And all the world goes by and I just hope it's gonna last,
So meet me at the bus stop baby,
Where everyone is going somewhere, and we'll just watch
and wait.

I strummed, Pim kept time with his understated rim-shots, and Ned played the cleverest of all his bass lines. In fact, Ned would never play a cleverer bass line than this. But it was Danny who the audience were mesmerised by, it was Danny they watched. By now, they were no longer seeing him as the cocky kid from school but as a singer entertaining them.

After this, we played our souped-up version of West End Girls by the Pet Shop Boys. It took them one or two bars to get it, but they went suitably mad. Then we played another of our own called 'Blonde Girlfriend', followed by a rather dull version of 'Don't You Forget About Me', before finishing with a rousing, tumultuous rendition of 'Teenage Kicks'. By now, the crowd loved The Sensationals. By now, as I hammered the two essential chords required for this song, I was playing instinctively, and my appreciation of what I was playing had become secondary to the reaction I was getting from the crowd. The more they cheered, the more I thrashed my guitar. The more they danced, the faster we seemed to play. We played the last chorus three times, the band seeming to know that we couldn't stop at the point we had rehearsed. We had to let the moment go on for longer.

As we played the last chord, Danny left the stage. Jenny's guests cheered and clapped their hands above their heads. We hadn't planned this. It was something Danny did spontaneously, he wanted to make his own exit and take the applause of the crowd on his own.

We carried on as three - Pim smashing his sticks around his drum kit, Neddy breaking a string on his bass as he thrashed his last line, and me churning out feedback as I thrust my guitar against my amp for maximum noise. They cheered. We finished, smiled and left the stage walking through some swing doors into the kitchen off Jenny's parents' hotel dining room.

The sound of cheering died a bit as we stood in the kitchen.

Danny was grinning, waiting for us. 'Fucking hell, fucking hell,' was all he could say; it was all any of us could say. 'We were fucking brilliant.'

Outside there was a shout for more as the clapping continued.

We looked at each other. We had hoped for this. We had kept one song in reserve. We jumped up and down. Ned went to walk back out of the kitchen, but Pim stopped him. 'Wait,' he said, as though he had been doing this all his life. He looked at the kitchen doors, his head cocked to one side, listening to the claps and cheers. After a little while, as though reacting to some particular signal, he beckoned to us to walk back on the stage.

We followed him.

We picked up our instruments again and the crowd cheered.

This was it, this *was it*.

Pim clicked his sticks again and we exploded into our encore: 'Everything's Sensational'.

When it was over, I just wanted to talk to everyone about it. I wanted everyone to tell me how fantastic we were. I wanted everyone to clap me on the back and tell me how I was going to be famous. I couldn't stop talking. I spoke gibberish and used words and phrases I had never used before. 'Did you cats dig us?' was a question I asked not once, but three or four times to different people. I should have been shot for that.

They did love us, though. That night, they loved The Sensationals. That night, we made the music and they sang and danced along, they clapped and cheered.

I pushed in the cork and drank a bottle of Bulgarian red wine that someone had thrust into my hand. I didn't even know where I'd put my guitar.

I could see Ned sitting down, surrounded by the lads from his Physics class. He was sitting back in his chair like a king as they all sat up and worshipped him. They would let him copy their homework now.

I couldn't see Pim. I assumed he was doing what he had promised us he would - enjoying his first groupy. (It turned out I was wrong about that, and Pim actually spent most of the first three hours after the gig trying to retrieve his cymbals from a couple of scallies who'd stolen them from the van out the back).

Danny was in the dining room dancing, surrounded by girls. The lads from school didn't go up to Danny; even then you had to be invited to go and speak to Danny. I could see that Ellie was standing on her own by the wall. I started to go over to her. As I crossed the dance floor, hands slapped me on the back, people stopped me to say how great we were. Daz Evans, the school psycho who had crashed the party, asked me how much my guitar had cost; Jason O'Connor, the school's supplier of all things herbal, told me we were brilliant and invited me to find him later for a smoke; Colin Thompson told me we were brilliant, much better than Billy Idol, who he'd recently seen at the Royal Court and was shite compared to us. I laughed and smiled at all of them. I shook hands and made high fives, and talked my gibberish, but now I wanted to speak to Ellie.

Just as I approached her, I felt another slap on the back. This time it was Danny, his face beaming at me.

'Shame about Teenage Kicks,' he said.

'What?' I didn't understand.

As ever Danny didn't carry on, his power was subtle, its effect upon me mighty.

'Katherine was saying you were out of tune for the last verse.'

He continued to smile at me, but the words that came from his smiling mouth reached deep into my throat and scratched my insides.

I went to remonstrate. 'No, I fucking wasn't.'

He ignored me; he had made his point. In fact he had jabbed his point into my soul.

'Fuck that for now, we'll get you one of those machines. Come and meet Mandy.'

I hadn't forgotten about Mandy. My plan was to meet Mandy as Richie Strafe, popstar in waiting, ace guitar axe man. Suddenly, I was meeting her as Richie Strafe, the bloke whose guitar was out of tune.

Danny led me to the group of girls he was with.

'Ladies,' he said, 'I'd like to introduce you to Richie Strafe.'

I was happy again now as he said this. He had made me sad, now he had made me happy. That was Danny Cappaldi.

He introduced me in turn to each of the group, finishing with Mandy.

I smiled coyly. I couldn't compete with his personality. My star was like a pocket torch to his massive sun.

Fair play to the girls though; they said all the right things. They giggled and asked us if they could come on tour with us. We all laughed. They told us that we could get gigs at their student union and we all nodded enthusiastically.

I looked around for Ellie. She was still there but now she had been joined by a group of the girls from her French class. One of them was clearly upset at something and the others were trying to console her. I could see one of them mouth to the others, 'She's a right bitch, that one,' and they all nodded.

We went into the kitchen. It was lighter. Danny jumped up and sat on the stainless steel worktop. His girlfriend Katherine stood by him. He tapped some of the pans that were arranged on hooks above him, to the beat of the song playing in the background. I drank my Bulgarian wine. Dexys Midnight Runners' Geno came through the swing doors. The girls yelped with excitement and ran back into the dining room. I thought about following them, but suddenly the Bulgarian red wine had decided to make friends with the whisky Pim had given us before and was starting to taste a little strange. I sat up on the work surface next to Danny.

I thought about taking issue with him about my out of tune guitar. I thought about the red wine and the whisky that were now terrorising the bangers and mash me mam had given me for tea hours before, in the time before I was famous.

'So?' said Danny, as he and Katherine stared at me with big grins on their faces.

'I wasn't fucking out of tune,' I replied moodily.

'No, not that. So, do you fancy Mandy or what?'

It was a stupid question. Mandy was eighteen years of age, I was just seventeen. She was at university; I was still tied to school with its homework and green V-neck jumper and array of fascists who have to be called Sir or Miss. She was wearing a skintight mini skirt that covered her arse like clingfilm around a particularly perfect chicken fillet. She was blonde and, probably, I'd guess, at a time in her life when her body and face were without any discernible flaw. If she had been a rose she would have been picked and stuck in the most elegant of vases; if she had been a panda, they would have sent her off to some zoo in Peking so that other lucky bastard male pandas could shag her senseless.

Of course I fancied her.

'She's alright,' I replied nonchalantly, when - as if by magic - she walked through the kitchen doors armed with a bottle and smile that I could feel in my underpants.

'Who wants some of this Hungarian Riesling?' she asked.

I feared the worst.

23

Cross Foxes (continued)

She looked at her drink. She looked at the small pool of spilt liquid that had formed on the table. She looked at the gang of kids laughing at the table opposite. Occasionally she looked up at me. She was older now, of course. Her hair, though, was still long and thick and autumnal. Her eyes still flashed with intelligence, wit and understanding. Just looking at her face I could remember everything.

After the most rudimentary of conversations about our current lives - jobs okay, partners not discussed, parents all still alive, location not around here - we moved on down memory lane.

She smiled as a memory came to her and moved her eyes from her drink to me as she recounted it.

'What was the name of that girl Danny had set you up with at Jenny George's party?'

There: one of us had mentioned his name. One of us had ventured the word Danny. It was out there and was sitting shivering in between us just as it fucking always had.

I smiled back with an intake of breath. 'Ah, that was Mandy.'

24

Mandy passed the bottle of Hungarian Riesling between us. I watched as Danny and then Katherine drank some, then she passed it to me. I couldn't refuse. I swallowed as much as I could without regurgitating me mam's sausages all over her.

Danny and the girls laughed about how cheap it was. I laughed along as well, though I didn't know cheap wine from Vimto.

I asked Mandy what she thought of The Sensationals. She smiled fondly at me without answering. That really fucked me off. But before I could figure out how much it fucked me off, Danny and Katherine started to snog, a full-on, hand-travelling snog.

I knew that this was my cue. Danny was in control. He knew that I would have to act. I looked at Mandy, who was staring at me, a peculiar half smile on her perfect lips. No girl had ever looked at me like that before. Up to then my experience of snogging had consisted of a hopeful lunge with very little in the way of romantic or erotic overture. I looked around Jenny George's parents' kitchen. Stuck on a fridge with a Snoopy and Woodstock magnet was a smiling family photograph. Mr George appeared to be wearing a chef's whites and had his arms around his wife. In front of them was Jenny and a younger girl I assumed was her sister. They all had exactly the same smile, all of them exactly the same. White teeth with a gap in the middle and wrinkled noses. For a second my mind registered the fact that it was a bit weird that both Jenny's parents should have the same facial characteristics - but the thought did not ferment any further.

Mandy and I kissed. I could taste white wine and perfume and cigarettes. Initially I thought about my sausages and the awfulness of unceremoniously hurling them all over her. It put me off my stride. Then as her tongue searched in my mouth, I involved myself more and more. She pressed herself against me and I reciprocated. My teenage erection had no idea what to do, it was like an escaping prisoner who realises that he is very close to freedom, but isn't quite sure which key will open the final gate.

She stood back, laughed and shook her head.

'I can't believe I'm doing this,' she said.

'What?' I said.

'Come on,' she continued and led me out of the kitchen past the smiling Mr and Mrs George and into the dining room where people were now in a big circle dancing to Frank Sinatra singing New York New York.

I noticed that Ellie was with them. The girl who had been crying was on one side, Ned was on the other. They were laughing. Nothing mattered. They were oblivious to the adventure I was about to embark on.

Mandy led me up the stairs to a room. Clearly she and her friends had staked this out earlier. 'Come on,' she said again.

I felt a taste of wine and potato fill my mouth but swallowed it back hard.

She switched the light on in a room. Within seconds we were grappling on the bed. I was up for it now. She moved her hands over my body. She touched my stomach. My body reacted, my imagination moved on apace. I realised that in a few seconds she was going to touch my penis. Oh my god, she was inches away from my big pink flute, my stick and berries, my old fellah, my cock, my mighty pork sword. I felt a great surge of energy shoot through my body towards my genitals. I realised that I had to control this or it was going to be a disappointment to all concerned. I tried to think about things that would take my mind off sex: England's Spain 1982 World Cup Squad; geography lessons with our dwarf teacher 'Quasi' Thomas; trees; Jenny George's smiling fucking interbred parents, anything.

Just as I was about to give in, Mandy stopped and looked at me and repeated what she had said earlier. 'I can't believe I'm doing this.'

'Yeah?' I said. 'Neither can I.'

She shot me a look that she might usually have reserved for kittens or puppies. 'You're so cute.' I felt myself bridle. I felt my 'mighty warrior' soften in my jeans.

'I mean,' I added tersely, 'it's not every day I get to shag my first groupy.'

To this day I am not quite sure why I said that. In my defence, I blame wine, nerves, a surge of excessive egotistical bravado, and the fact that my thought processes were a bit addled after concentrating so hard on naming Ron's entire World Cup 22 in an effort to stop myself from coming.

She could have slapped me. She could have become overwhelmed with earthy passion, turned on by my confident defiance. I didn't expect her to piss herself laughing.

'Oh, Richard, you are so funny,' she said.

Suddenly I thought of Ellie dancing with everyone else downstairs. I wanted to be there with them. I didn't want to be here. This wasn't good. She didn't want to shag the person I wanted to be. Tonight I was Richard Strafe, lead guitarist and co-songwriter with The Sensationals, not some kid who's trying to lose his cherry.

I got up.

'Look,' I said, 'I'm just going to the toilet.'

She pissed herself laughing again and I knew that I was doing the right thing.

I walked out of the room leaving Mandy lying on the bed propped up on her elbows.

I never saw her again.

I found a toilet and threw up a huge great spew of red

semi-digested sausages, mushy stuff I assumed was potato and some kind of mystery stringy stuff that I couldn't account for.

It had the desired effect. I was now ready for the world again.

I went back downstairs, back to the backslapping and the well-meaning comments from my school friends. Back to the sweaty dancing, the different concoctions of alcohol, the crying girls and their consoling mates. I went back downstairs to Ellie.

25

Ellie was there too.

Her eyes sparkled as she remembered sitting on a chair in Jenny George's parents' dining room.

'Mandy, that was right.' Behind her eyes, I could tell the scene was forming again, memories were returning. A quiver of excitement entered her voice. 'Christ, weren't you sick on her?'

'No,' I said, remembering vaguely that at some point that rumour had spread itself around the sixth form and that I had done nothing to correct it.

I wondered if she remembered what she had been wearing that night. I did. I would never forget. It would be one of the last things that left my consciousness: her purple Doc Marten boots and short purple tie-dyed skirt. I wondered if she could remember smiling at me as I walked up to her and sat down. I wondered if she remembered my Dead Kennedys T-shirt and leather jacket.

I could tell that she was thinking about the same thing. Her gaze moved away from me, back to the table of kids who were trying to balance glasses in a tower, then to her drink, and back to the small puddle of spilt lager that had now snaked like an estuary towards the edge of the table.

I knew that she remembered.

26

Still picking bits of sick out of my teeth, I walked up to Ellie. She was sitting next to Ned and Hodgy, my History classmate. Hodgy was doing one of his impressions. They were laughing. As I approached, Ellie smiled at me.

I sat next to her.

'Here comes the future of rock and roll,' she said.

'Oh gee, thanks,' I replied, adding, 'Don't worry, I'll still talk to you lot.'

Hodgy started to conduct a mock interview with me in his Terry Wogan voice.

I cracked open a bottle of beer, played along, and told them my world fame wouldn't change me.

I wanted to talk to Ellie. I felt that she wanted to talk to me. Not to me and Danny. Not to me about English homework or school or any of that; I felt that she wanted to talk to me.

'Danny thinks we're going to get some gigs in Liverpool,' I said to her. I had to mention him. It was like a strange force always brought him back into my conversations with her. 'That's brilliant,' she said.

'Yeah, then, when we're at university, we're going to reform down in London and see if we can get some kind of record deal.'

'Uh-huh.'

I told her all my plans. I told her how Danny was going to Art College at St Martin in the Field, and I was going to study at University College, London, and we were all going to get a flat together.

I told her about how my big dream was to come back and play a huge open-air gig in New Brighton. I told her we wouldn't be playing covers for much longer, but we had to play them at the moment. I told her that in future my music would be a way of expressing how I felt about the world. I told her that we would be signing to an independent record label, because that was the only way to retain artistic integrity. I told her that the world was so phoney and that we were all promised so much and that everything afterwards was just a disappointment.

I talked to her until Hodgy and Ned moved away. I talked to her through the entire contents of a box of Blue Nun white wine. I told her all the things that I had wanted to tell her in school. I told her all the things I wanted to tell Danny but hadn't quite got round to it yet. She listened.

She told me she was going to apply to university in London as well.

We kissed for the first time just after the Blue Nun was emptied of its last saccharine drop. We kissed just as the DJ played Holding Back the Years by Simply Red. I have always hated Mick Hucknall, I can't remember why, but I owe him for providing the incidental music to that one moment which in a small part of me will go on forever.

I walked home that night. Pissed and with sick on my shoes. In my mind the night's events replayed themselves like a video fast-forwarding itself. The photo shoot and Pim's whisky; picking up my guitar with sweaty fingers and watching Danny standing at the front of the stage, arms outstretched, reassuring the crowd that everything was going to be sensational. Laughing Mandy; and finally touching Ellie's face and making a date to see her the next day as she disappeared into her dad's car.

Ellie became my girlfriend. We started going steady.

The Sensationals had to wait another two months for their next gig. After that they came thick and fast. We played

Stairways and the Iron Door in Birkenhead, we played the school summer disco and entered a 'battle of the bands' competition at Pontins in Rhyl. We played ropey pubs in Liverpool, Wallasey, Southport and Runcorn. We were booed as often as we were cheered, although polite indifference was the usual response - apart from the Cadbury's Working Men's Social Club in Morton where the landlord turned us off halfway through White Wedding because we were too loud.

We had some great nights and some shite nights, but nothing would ever compare with Jenny George's party.

Me and Ellie did all the things that teenage couples do. We found ingenious places to snog and grope each other. We wrote long intense letters declaring our total disinterest in all things commercial and establishment. We vowed to save the whale, save the rainforests, save the fucking panda bears - bloody hell, life was going to be busy. We went to gigs in Manchester and discussed the experience all the way home. Some bands had sold out, some bands were seminal.

We read the same books. She usually read them first. Margaret Atwood, Erica Jong, Angela Carter were all devoured by her and read by me.

Sometimes I thought I was more intensely into it all than she was. Sometimes I thought that I was suffering for our love whereas she was just mildly affected.

She appeared to be able to travel by train to Salford Uni Students' Union on a Thursday night, see The Wedding Present live, dance like a loony, drink six or seven bottles of Newcastle Brown Ale, get the last train home with me, read Jeanette Winterston voraciously all night, and still deliver her 'A' grade essay on the use of slapstick in Shakespeare's Twelfth Night by the next morning. Whilst I, shagged out and hopelessly behind, would have to proffer some dire excuse about having to go to university open days as our thin-lipped teacher Miss Eggerton earnestly reminded me that this was the most important year of my life.

She was right about that. This was the most important year

of my life, and as far as I was concerned I was living it, I was experiencing it. Not just in school, but everywhere. I was awake to everything. Things bothered me. The world bothered me; politicians who wore pinstriped suits and spoke bollocks bothered me; my parents who told me how I had to go to university to get a job and why didn't I become a lawyer or a teacher bothered me. Lawyer. Ugh. No chance.

I had decided I was going to study English, applied to and was accepted by University College, London. The only problem was that they wanted me to obtain 3 'B' grades in my 'A' levels. Judging by my mock exams, I wasn't even close.

I was confident though. I felt that I could pull my finger out and get my grades.

I felt that fate would somehow prevail on my behalf. I simply had to go to London. My future depended on it. The future of Rock and Roll depended upon it. The Sensationals would have to reform in London. I assumed that this would happen. I assumed that my university career would be fairly short. A bit like Mick Jagger's ten minutes at the LSE, before the Rolling Stones released 'I Wanna Be Your Man' and exploded upon the world. That would be me. I liked the idea that people should know that I could go to university if I wanted. I liked the idea that in future people would say, 'Richie Strafe, guitar legend, your life could have been so very different if you'd decided to stay at university,' and I'd say, 'Yes, but fate dealt me a different hand.'

By the spring of 1988 the only hand fate was dealing me was night after night in my bedroom trying to make sense of the scribbled gibberish that passed for my school notes. My essays were all crap. My notes were indecipherable and a couple of my books were missing. I would phone Ellie, who was going to King's College London to study Social Anthropology and French (she liked the idea of the artistic expression of French literature coupled with the socially responsible pursuit of anthropological study), but she wouldn't talk to me for more than five minutes as she had too much studying to do.

I would phone Danny, who only needed one 'C' grade in Art to get into his fancy Art College, but he would show absolutely no empathy with my plight.

I would allow myself to watch TV from 7.30pm to 8pm, but invariably found myself still watching TV at 8.10pm as my parents shouted at me to go upstairs and study. I would sulkily make my way up to my bedroom and strum my guitar for another twenty minutes, tidy my sock drawer for half an hour before embarking upon an hour of crisis-ridden revision.

It wasn't good. I struggled with the exams. I sat there in our school bloody gym painfully watching my contemporaries writing reams and reams as I fiddled with my pencil and my novelty pencil case.

And so when I arrived at school on a rather bleak August morning to collect my results, there was a certain inevitability about how I had fared.

In my own way I had prepared myself for failure. I had decided that abject failure at school would be no real bad thing. I had revised my romantic view of a popstar who rejects academia and replaced it with a misunderstood genius for whom school was far too prescribed and authoritarian to allow full vent to his tortured gift.

What I wasn't prepared for was abject mediocrity. I got all grade 'C's.

I didn't know whether to laugh or cry.

I can still remember my English teacher Binky Jones' disappointed face as he consoled me. 'I have to say, Richard, all you needed was a little bit more application and they could have been all "B"s.'

I noted the big weird bastard didn't say all 'A's. I shrugged.

'Anyway, with a bit of luck you'll still get into one of your second or third choice universities.'

Now I knew whether I wanted to laugh or cry; I wanted to cry.

So confident had I been that I would get the grades to go to

London that my other choices had been made in the sixth-form common room using the University Guide Book, a blindfold and a pin and had seen - to whoops of delight from my friends - me apply to Swansea University to study Sport Science, Keele (wherever the fuck that was), to study Anthropology, Glasgow to study Medicine, and Southampton to study Law. Not surprisingly, Swansea and Glasgow rejected me, which left me with an escape route comprising of two places: Keele and Southampton.

Ellie got two 'A's and a 'B'.

Danny got the 'C' he needed.

They would be going to London.

I definitely wanted to cry.

I was faced with three choices. I could stay at school and have another go; I could drop out altogether and get a job in London and concentrate on the band; or I could go to Keele or Southampton and pursue anthropology or law.

I knew which idea appealed to me.

I sat by the school gates with Ellie, Danny and Ned.

I felt like a twat. I felt like a twat for doing so, so bloody ordinary. And I felt like a twat for making Ellie and Danny - who just wanted to celebrate their results - listen to my dilemma.

'You can't just give up university,' she said.

I sulked.

'Three "C"s are brilliant.'

I sulked.

'Yeah,' said Danny, 'I would have given my right arm for three "C"s.'

Right, I thought, but you didn't need three of the bastard 'C's. You only needed one and one of my mum's steak and kidney pies could have got a 'C' in Art, for fuck's sake.

They weren't helping. They were hindering. They were trying their best. But it was never going to work.

I needed to be away from them. I limped home to tell my mum and dad. I knew I had to. I knew they'd be home, as my dad had taken a suspiciously fortuitous day off, though he told me it had nothing to do with my results.

My mum and dad were thrilled with my results. Genuinely, lovingly, touchingly thrilled. They didn't react as if I'd got three average grades in the most important exams I'd ever take. They reacted as though I'd been awarded the Nobel Prize for Science, Literature and Peace all in one go.

'Three "C"s!' my dad exclaimed. 'That's brilliant!' I tried to put things into perspective.

I tried to instil a little bit of reality into their reaction. 'Mr Jones says I won't get into London University with those grades, but I've got to phone them tomorrow and I've got to phone the other places today.'

Even that didn't bring them down. In fact it seemed to make them more excited. 'So my little boy going off to university…that's fantastic. I'm so proud.'

They were smart, my parents. They were smart and scheming and clever. They weren't born yesterday. They knew that if I had half a chance I'd go off to play my guitar somewhere, or work in a fast food store or just fuck off to live in a caravan and make mandolins or something and kick education firmly into the long grass. They knew this, and they knew that they had to start a momentum going in which I would somehow end up going somewhere, anywhere.

I got out a map and found that Keele was off some obscure junction of the M6 and could be reached in an uncomfortably short time from my house.

I chose Southampton. The pin had chosen law. I would study law in Southampton.

That night all the spotty sixth-formers, failures and geeks went to the same pub to celebrate, commiserate and get predictably pissed on as little money as they could.

Ellie told me that Southampton wasn't far from London and we could see each other most weekends.

Danny told me that Southampton wasn't far from London, and anyway, students had hardly any lectures and we could easily form the band in London. Ned, who was going off to Brighton to study some kind of science type thing, was keen. Pim, unfortunately, had managed to knock one of the waitresses up in his dad's restaurant and wouldn't be going anywhere for eighteen years. But drummers were ten a penny. The Sensationals would miss him, but they would start a new chapter in London.

27

Ellie gave me a lift home. She still knew the way to my mum and dad's house. She was, she had told me, about to move to start a new career teaching primary school children on an island off the western coast of Africa. She was genuinely excited.

'You should see their faces,' she said. 'They just want to learn; they just want an opportunity. Some of them have to walk miles to get to school. They take it seriously. They've got no money for books, or pens and pencils. Some of them haven't even got any food. Can you imagine that? Remember what we were like? We used to moan like hell if we had to share a textbook or if chips were off the menu in the school canteen.'

She would be living in a house by the beach. She told me she could see the fishermen from her window going off with their nets each morning.

I was glad for her. I was glad to see that her passion had been undimmed.

She seemed happy and it seemed the right thing for her to be doing. I would have somehow been sad if she had been trapped working for the Department of Works and Pensions answering queries about Working Tax Credit. I would have been even sadder if she had been working for some City firm earning millions and wearing power stilettos.

She was home for two days to say goodbye to her folks.

That was nice.

I felt a need to tell her about me. Confide in her in some way. Give her something from myself that she could take away.

'Ellie,' I said tentatively, 'have you ever heard of something called the Great Library of Myths and Legends?'

She broke into a smile. 'No,' she said, 'it sounds like something out of 1984. Perhaps Eurypides was taken before the Great Library of Myths and Legends and severely chastised for trying to bring back the original copy of Homer's Odyssey three hundred years out of date.'

I chuckled along. 'Funny you should think of the Greeks,' I said.

She looked puzzled.

'I've met a person who works in this library and he's Greek.'

I could tell that she was thinking all manner of things.

'He's a client,' I lied, trying to think up a story. 'He's suing them.'

'Oh,' she said, 'what for?'

'There's asbestos in the roof. Terrible business. He's very ill now. Might not make Christmas.'

'I'm sorry,' she added, her concern making me feel guilty about my lie.

'I've never heard of it though. Where is it?'

'Eh, Athens,' I said tentatively.

'Athens!' she exclaimed. 'Why is he using your company?'

'They've got a branch in Streatham. They're a very new organisation. They operate mostly over the internet - you know getting people to submit their stories and things online.'

My lie was going from bad to worse; I had to change the subject. She quite clearly had never heard of the Great Library of Myths and Legends. Mind you, I suppose that if everyone knew about it, it wouldn't be able to carry out its work.

I told her about my dad. She made all the right noises.

I told her a bit about my case with Terry Hawkins. She made all the right noises. She even asked me how I could defend someone who was a complete bastard, so giving me the opportunity to go into my pompous recital about 'the golden thread of British justice is that everyone is innocent until proven guilty.'

I didn't want to talk about these things though. There was only one thing I wanted to talk to her about. She knew it. I knew it. She looked at the road. The rain was falling steadily now and I could see her face concentrating on driving safely through the rain.

I had to ask.

'So,' I said, 'I don't suppose you've seen much of Danny over the last few years?'

There was a silence.

I didn't expect a silence.

'Not for a while,' she said.

Not for a while! Not for a while? What did that mean? Did that mean she had seen him a few weeks ago? How long was a while? A while wasn't long. Fourteen fucking years, that was long.

'Oh,' I said, surprised, 'when *did* you see him last?'

There was another silence.

'He sends me tickets to his shows occasionally.'

Fucking cunt. Fucking bollocking wanking cunt. Tickets to his shows! The bastard. I am definitely going to kill him now. I don't care how I do it.

She turned her eyes away from the road.

'Richie,' she said softly. Then stopped. She didn't know what to say next. She didn't know whether to apologise for him or tell me something about him.

I helped her out. 'Don't worry,' I lied. 'All that business is a long time ago now. I haven't thought about it for years.' I was convincing.

We drove on. She turned into my road. Time was running.

'Look,' she said, 'I think that Danny and you should get together and have a chat. I think he'd love to see you.'

'Why?' I interjected sharply. 'Has he mentioned me?'

'Well,' she stalled bravely, 'he always talks about the old

days. About life up here and school and things.' She was diplomatically telling me that the two-faced, evil bastard had never mentioned me.

We pulled up to my house. A lifetime ago we would have snogged passionately at this point, hating the moment when we had to leave one another. I didn't want to kiss her now though.

'He sent me a ticket to his concert in Manchester next Tuesday. I can't use it. Why don't you have it?'

'I don't know. I mean, I don't really like.....'

'Please,' she said smiling at me, 'you might enjoy it. It's got a backstage pass and everything.'

'Has it?' I said. 'Okay. Why not?'

I skulked silently back into my parents' house and went into the kitchen to make a cup of coffee. I tried to be quiet and not wake my parents. My mum heard me though, just as she had heard me skulking around throughout my life.

'Richard, is that you?' she shouted from the upstairs bedroom.

'Yes,' I whispered in an unnecessarily loud whisper, adding gently, 'Go to sleep.'

'Angela called,' she replied.

My heart sank; I could do without that.

28

The next morning I couldn't settle at all. I sat in my room up in the corridor of death and found myself tapping a pencil against the desk. There was much to be done. There was much to be considered.

At about half eleven, the big lummox Tommy stomped up to the room brandishing a fax from Howard McPhee. He handed it to me smiling manically as he did so. He had clearly read it.

Strafe,

What the fuck's going on? Are we ready for the trial next week? Your silence is causing me concern.

McPhee.

Good old Howard.

'You in trouble then, eh?' asked Tommy, barely concealing a laugh.

'Tommy,' I said adopting a tone of resignation, before adding, 'you couldn't even begin to guess the trouble I'm in,' in a serious tone that made him realise that I wasn't taking the piss.

'Tell me, Tommy,' I said, 'if you were going to kill someone, how would you do it?'

He looked at me stunned, not sure if I was joking. Then a different look crossed his face, which I realised meant that the vast expanse of nothing which passed as his brain was conjuring up a thought. After some not inconsiderable time he answered sagely, 'It depends if you want to get away with it or not.'

'Go on,' I said, interested now. 'Say I want to get away with it.'

'Then that's easy, you club him to death with a huge icicle or a leg of frozen lamb.'

I looked confused.

'Then there'll be no evidence, 'cause the ice will melt. Or you can eat the lamb, then there's no murder weapon.'

I considered this. I wasn't sure if I could face eating the object that I had used to club Danny Cappaldi to death. And the icicle idea might go tits up in summer with ice's tendency to return to its natural state of water, thereby leaving me to attempt to kill the bastard with something the size of an ice lolly.

'What if you don't care if you are found out or not?'

'How spectacular do you wanna be?' I could tell that Tommy was warming to this theme, whilst I was beginning to think that I had underestimated him.

'Pretty spectacular.'

'You kidnap them, then take them to some kind of seriously big event, I dunno, something like the cup final, or Big Brother grand finale or something, then you shoot them to the head, once, bang, goodnight Vienna.'

Tommy made the face of a madman and carried out the execution using his fingers as a gun. It was a scary sight. It was far too realistic.

I considered him for a second.

'Tommy, have you been giving this serious thought?'

He cocked his halfwit face at me, adding excitedly 'Oh, yeah.'

He left and I continued with the job of tapping my pencil against the desk.

Eventually I started to annoy myself. I had to consider my options; I had to weigh up my alternatives. The way I looked at it, my problems were these:

First, but in no particular order of shiteness, I had arranged to have a man killed, and had promised to pay the hit man, but didn't know how I was going to arrange that, and thus would probably end up with both the psychopath who wanted the killing and the psychopath who would do the killing seriously upset with me - that wasn't good and would almost certainly lead to my early demise;

Second, I had my mission to save the world from losing the will to live. I wasn't sure how I was going to do this, but realised that it had something to do with killing an internationally famous rock star;

Third, I had my girlfriend or ex-girlfriend or whatever she was desperate to get in touch with me to formally put an end to our dying relationship;

Fourth, I had my mad boss trying to get in touch with me to bollock me about God knows what;

Finally, my dad was ill.

There was only one thing for me to do. I decided to succumb to the temptation of Sloppy Joe's Lap Dance Emporium. I looked out of the window. Yes, I could just about see that it was reassuringly open for business: it's never too early for naked women and gratuitous masturbatory indulgence.

I was surprised to find two other sad bastards already in Sloppy Joe's. The three of us were outnumbered though by the half dozen or so scantily clad women who stood at one side of the bar, bored and drinking tea. It was a strange sight - a gaggle of half dressed orange women in naughty nurse outfits, spangly bikinis and negligées, drinking mugs of steaming tea.

I went to the bar and was served by the campest man I have ever met in my life.

'Hiya,' he bellowed at me, before adding, 'It's a bit early for you, isn't it?'

'I have never been here before in my life,' I replied, affronted by the suggestion that I was some kind of regular.

'Course you haven't, love,' minced the barman. 'Now, what can I get ya?'

I looked forlornly at the row of optics and the beer taps - I didn't fancy a drink much.

I looked at the camp guy and gestured towards the girls. 'Is there any chance of a cup of tea?'

The barman reached across the bar and gently touched my hand in a gesture of compassionate understanding. 'Of course there is.'

I paid eight bloody pounds for the tea as it came with a free dance from one of the girls. It arrived in a mug with the words Happy Easter on it. I took it gratefully and sat down.

Within seconds a rather tubby girl dressed in a Union Jack bikini with peroxide hair and a body the colour of baked beans sauntered over. She had an unfortunately deep voice with a North Lancastrian accent.

'Hi, I'm Amber,' she said, before adding, 'the first dance is free, love, after that it's five quid a track.'

I didn't know what to do. I had never been into an establishment like this before. I didn't particularly want to see this girl dance, nor indeed was I curious as to what she had under her Union Jack bikini, but on the other hand I was totally petrified of her. Not only was she heavily built, but, I assumed, would probably have some sort of unwritten code of ethics with her fellow dancers which meant that rejecting one would be rejecting all. I had visions of being set upon and beaten shitless by a gang of lap dancers dressed in nurses' uniforms and underwear - there would be fake tan everywhere.

I decided to take the dance. 'That would be lovely,' I said, and handed over the token I had been given by mincing boy, which she somehow managed to secrete about her body.

'How long do I get?' I asked innocently.

'As long as track lasts,' she answered.

'But there isn't any music,' I proffered tentatively.

'Oh aye,' she said, before shouting across to the barman at a volume that could have split concrete. 'Dave, could you put music on?'

Dave took a while to react, during which I sat with my legs open. In between them stood Amber, who chewed voraciously and scratched her G-string.

The music came on at a volume to rival Amber's voice. The track, predictably, was the latest chart-busting bloody number one by Cappaldi.

This was terrible. This was perhaps a new low. Here I was at half eleven in the morning, drinking an eight-pound cup of tea with a gyrating overweight lap dancer between my legs, listening to Danny Cappaldi's latest smash hit.

Fair play to Amber though, she pulled out all her best moves. Her tits were thrust in my face, her arse was pushed up against my crotch whilst periodically bits of her, which should have forever remained a mystery to me, were revealed with a certain amount of forced enthusiasm.

I didn't know where to look. I tried to look her in the eye, but this unnerved us both, so I concentrated over her shoulder on the back wall. I felt a need to make conversation.

'So,' I said jovially, 'where are *you* from?'

'Wigan,' she replied without breaking her rhythm.

'That's nice,' I lied.

'No, it's not,' she continued 'it's shite,' before adding, 'I'm only doing this to fund my studies.'

'Oh,' I said, 'what are you studying?'

'Theology,' she said, before bursting into great guffaws of laughter.

The dance finished. I shook her hand. Why did I do that? Then I sauntered off to the toilets.

When I returned I was surprised to see a familiar face in the seat next to mine.

'I thought I saw you heading to the lavatory,' said Dr Costas.

I looked incredulously at him.

'What is a keeper from the Great Library of Myths and Legends doing here?'

'I could ask the same question about a hotshot solicitor who has been entrusted with the task of saving mankind,' he replied, running a hand over his perfectly ironed cream slacks.

'No,' I said, 'that's not fair. *I* never held myself out to be culturally superior.'

'No,' he said, 'you just held yourself out to be immortal.' He smiled at me, before adding, 'But anyway, is there anything wrong with watching a beautiful woman dance? Surely men have been mesmerised by such an experience since the dawn of time? Think of Salome, think of the Mata Hari. The list is endless.'

'Beautiful women,' I said. 'I doubt Salome danced for King Herod wearing fake tan and a schoolgirl outfit.'

Despite his pomposity I was pleased to see Dr Costas. I had things I needed explaining to me.

'Seriously though,' I said to him, 'why are you here?'

'Business,' he said curtly. 'My work rarely ends.'

'Business?' I replied. 'In here?'

'Oh, yes,' he said, leaning slightly towards me and pointing to a young girl who was currently upside down halfway up a pole. 'You see her over there?'

I looked over. 'What, blonde hair, gold knickers?'

'Yes.'

'What about her?'

'She is about to become immortal.'

'Has that pole got anything to do with it?' I asked.

As ever Dr Costas either didn't understand, or chose to ignore my quip.

'She is beautiful, isn't she?' said Dr Costas, staring far too intently for a man at the wrong end of middle age wearing cream slacks and a white chunky wool V-neck sweater.

I had to agree, though. She had a certain innocent beauty about her, a wholesome prettiness that was not unappealing.

Costas continued, 'If she wants - and I can't make her do anything against her will - she will meet a senior politician in the next few weeks. A politician with a particular fondness for a certain type of sex.'

'No,' I said, sounding a bit like the barman. 'Who? Please. Is it Anne Widdecombe? Let it be Ann Widdecombe.'

'I can't tell you that, Richard,' said Costas. 'That will be her story. Her chance at immortality.'

I looked at her. She couldn't be more than seventeen. She smiled as she danced. She looked innocent. I wondered what she was doing here. I wondered what her fate would be.

'Is her task to save mankind from losing the will to live as well?' I asked.

'Like you, Richard, she has the chance to become immortal. Like you, Richard, she can take it or reject it.'

'Remind me,' I said. 'What do I get if I take my chance? If I kill Cappaldi?'

'That's obvious, isn't it?'

'No, no riddles, Doctor. Tell me straight.'

Costas sipped his drink which - as usual - had been served to him in a cut glass receptacle, and smiled creepily at one of the girls who had started to come over.

'You get two things, Richard.'

'Which are?'

'You have the instant but, let's admit it, transient emotion of watching the man you hate more than any in your power. I know that you realise that this will only give you a certain short-lived satisfaction, but it will be an intense satisfaction.'

I sort of understood that. I would enjoy seeing Cappaldi squirm as I brought my revenge upon him. But, I supposed, Costas was right in that once it was done, that feeling wouldn't last for long.

'What is the second?' I asked.

'The second, Richard,' he said, looking at me intently in the eye, 'is what you have always craved: to have your name immortalised forever.'

I thought about this and my head spun. What about morality? Surely it was wrong to kill popstars? If it wasn't, then everyone would be at it, wouldn't they?

Costas seemed to read my thoughts. I hated it when he did that.

'It is not absolutely wrong to kill,' he said, 'otherwise humankind would have ceased to exist long ago, brought to a crushing halt by its own immorality. It is, though, wrong to kill without justification.'

'But who justified Cappaldi's death?' I asked. 'Who authorised it?'

'In your case, your actions have been sanctioned by the Department of Myths and Legends.'

'So if I am brought to trial, you'll provide my defence.'

He laughed.

'Of course not, Richard, your actions are going to make you immortal. The only judge and jury you must be concerned about is the greatest judge of all.'

'What's that, then?' I asked.

Costas flashed me a look of smug satisfaction. 'History, Richard. History is the greatest judge of all. And we, Richard, at the Library of Myths and Legends, will make sure that your story is always kept in the consciousness of humankind.'

I thought about this. It made sense. It was absolute gibberish. It made sense. It was gibberish.

'I have to go,' I said and made my way out of the gloomy, depressing establishment that was Sloppy Joe's Lap Dancing Emporium. This was the first time I had left him. As I got to the door, a big mincy voice cut through the room. 'Bye!' I turned around to acknowledge the barman, and as I did I could see that Costas was no longer there in his seat.

29

As I walked back up the corridor of death towards my office, I was surprised to hear voices emanating from the room of Butternorth Bsc Hons. Initially I was quite pleased.

After all, I had spent the previous couple of weeks craving company. I wondered if it might be Tommy and a couple of his weird geeky mates wishing to continue our conversation from before.

I entered and saw Mr Truss, Tommy and a third bloke I had not met before. They were surveying my strange collage of various photocopied objects. Their interest, not surprisingly, appeared to have been taken by the full size photocopy of my body.

Their conversation stopped when they saw me. Truss shot me a furtive glance then appeared to look away, though with his eye problems, he could have been looking anywhere. Tommy stood a little away from them, grinning in his usual sadistic way. The third man, dressed in a blue pinstriped shirt and crimson braces, immediately and confidently addressed me,

'Mr Strange?' he asked.

'Strafe,' I replied.

'I'm Harry McCardle, Senior Partner at Linkbournes,' he boomed.

I looked at him, incredulous. It was weird, eerie almost. Harry McCardle was a bizarre northern clone of Howard

227

McPhee. They had the same air of bullying superiority, and they looked the same, with their glasses perched towards the end of their nose in some kind of masculine defiance to the onset of myopia.

'Listen, Mr Strafe,' continued McCardle, 'I'm not going to beat around the bush. We've become concerned about one or two things.'

I looked at him in innocent incomprehension.

'What things?' My mind started to compute: bloody hell, what if somehow, they had got wind of the plot to get rid of Colin Rutland? What if they had followed me to the Anglesey Arms?

'Well, first,' continued McCardle, 'these strange...' he paused, gesturing to a rather strange photocopy of my wallet next to my socks, 'images, they are really odd. But that isn't our main concern, and anyway Howard McPhee will have to pay for the paper you've used since you've been here.'

I started to feel my heart sink. How could I explain to McPhee the fact that I had photocopied my entire body and pinned it up on the wall? Come to think of it, I couldn't really explain it to myself.

'But that is not what is really bothering us, Mr Strange.' He flashed a look at Mr Truss, whose lazy eye was all over the shop. They both momentarily looked uncomfortable. 'We have a policy here, Mr Strife, that any member of staff who goes into that strip club across the road during working hours is immediately and summarily dismissed.'

Oh fuck.

'Quite frankly it looks terrible for a solicitor - or anyone from here for that matter - being seen to enter there. What are clients supposed to think? It's bad enough having the bloody thing on our doorstep in the first place.'

I felt my head drop. I felt the blood surge to my cheeks as I realised how embarrassing it was. I felt like a twelve-year-old caught by his dad grappling through a copy of Tits and Ass Monthly, and being told nicely but firmly that there is plenty of time for that in the future.

I tried to think of some kind of defence. I considered making up some client who had to meet me in there. I considered a blatant denial of being in there. But in the end no words, truth or otherwise, would form in my mouth.

McCardle softened, something that made me feel like crying. 'Now, we can't sack you, Mr Rife, because you're not one of our staff. But I'm afraid that we can no longer let you use these offices. I'm sorry, it's too embarrassing.'

I nodded silently. I might as well have said, 'It won't happen again, sir.'

He continued, 'I am afraid I have had to ask Mr Truss to inform your Mr McPhee about this.'

Oh great. The bastards. There was no need to do that. It all fell into place now. The big twat Tommy had seen me, and squealed to Truss, who in turn chirruped to his boss McCardle. Fucking bastards. Now I looked like a prize knobhead. There was no need to tell McPhee.

'Tommy's going to help you with your boxes,' concluded McCardle, before exiting the room and slithering back down the corridor of death.

We silently moved the fucking boxes back to my dad's Vauxhall that I had parked in the side street. Ironically, I parked next to Sloppy Joe's. As we loaded the boxes my cause wasn't helped by the girls who stood at the door in their full rude regalia with the camp barman and wolf-whistled at me.

I drove the car away and parked up in a disabled space a few streets away. I needed a plan. No, I had my plan; all I needed was the bollocks to carry it out. I needed to decide, was I going to spend my life in perpetual humiliation or was I going to do something completely different?

I put on the radio. There was a news programme. The newsreader sanguinely told of war and death, of bombs and terrorists. There were clips of politicians very forcibly saying nothing. There was a business news section telling of huge profits for new stores and the death of old ones, then a sports bulletin that informed us that another huge club bankrolled by another millionaire chairman had bought another bland striker to kiss the badge and disappoint supporters. I looked up the road. This was Liverpool, but I could be in any city in the world. The shoppers milled around the same shops, wearing the same clothes and being entertained by the same things: listening to the same music and talking about the same godforsaken, sad, self-indulgent, overpaid, talentless knobheads who all strive to appear on the same shite magazines. Costas' words came back to me. 'Mankind is losing the will to live.'

I made a decision. I would become immortal after all. Fuck McPhee and McCardle, fuck Angela and Cappaldi and Ellie Smith. Fuck them all. Things had to be done.

I drove towards the prison. I phoned McPhee from my car. Apparently he had been trying to contact me. He sounded psychotic, even for him. 'Fucking hell, Strife. What the fuck has been going on? I've just had that Truss on the phone, saying that you've been frequenting titty bars and they've had to turf you out of your office. For Christ's sake, Strafe, what are you playing at? I always assumed that you were a wanker, but I had hoped that you kept that out of office hours.'

He wanted to continue, but I butted in. 'Listen, McPhee,' I said defiantly, 'shut the fuck up. I've got my cock well and truly in the vice over this Hawkins thing. That business with the titty bar was a front.'

There was silence on the other end of the line as McPhee tried to recover from the fact that I had sworn at him.

'Now,' I continued, my voice low and measured, 'you were the one who told me that the best lawyers are the ones who go the extra mile, yeah?'

'Well, yeah, but not if that extra mile leads to a bloody lap dancing bar.'

'Howard,' I said calmly, 'Tom Hagan would have done just the same if he had found himself in my position. You're just going to have to trust me. I'm on my way to see Hawkins now.' I paused for effect. 'There is going to be a bit of progress in the case. I can't tell you anymore until after it's all happened. I just need you to trust me on this.'

I knew that McPhee would be manically swinging on his chair, his face contorting into various unhappy guises as he considered placing his trust, blindly, in me.

'Fucking hell, Strife, we've all got our meat and two veg in the grinder here.' He paused again. 'I mean, if you fuck up here....'

'I know, Howard. It will be very messy, there will be veg everywhere. Now, I'll be back in London by the end of next week. We'll talk again.'

'End of next week!' exclaimed McPhee. 'But that's impossible, that's in the middle of the trial.'

'Believe me, Howard, it'll all be over by then, trust me.'

Rarely have I enjoyed a conversation more.

I had information that McPhee didn't have. I had managed to completely perplex him. He was in the dark over this. He was in the dark with his dick in the socket and he didn't know what would happen if someone flicked the switch.

I had to drive on before all my metaphors, which were crashing into one another, had an accident of their own.

I smiled a mad toothy open-mouthed smile to myself as I put the car in gear. I needed some music and pushed the button on my dad's car CD player. At this point, of course, what should have happened is that some entirely appropriate adrenalin-punching guitars should have filled the car: perhaps something demonically energetic like *Rock the Casbah* by Clash, or deeply cynical like *Bring On the Dancing Horses* by Echo and The Bunnymen. I needed something poignantly relevant like The Cure, or anarchic like the Dead Kennedys. I needed some good driving music that would match my defiant sneering attitude.

Unfortunately, the only CD my dad appeared to have in his car was something called *Eezy Drivin'* that he had got free from the Mail on Sunday. Thus I drove to the prison to confront an axe-wielding psychopath with the tune of *Blame it on the Boogie* by The Jacksons ringing in my ear. Strangely though, it did the trick.

I walked up to the windowed cell where Hawkins was waiting with a steely determination. I had entered almost enthusiastically into the ignominy of the strip search. I had silenced the stroppy security guards with my new purposeful walk and the cold-eyed look of destiny I had etched across my face. I was Richard Strafe. I had a mission. I was not going to be undermined by a bunch of oversized piss-takers. Nor was I going to be frightened by Terry Hawkins. I didn't care what threats he made. I didn't care how many people he had killed. I, after all, had written at least ten original songs that had been played live, and I had a degree from Southampton University. I had a brain and I was going to use it.

Hawkins was waiting for me. He had a scratch along his face. He was in handcuffs. A security guard stood in the corner of the room.

'I'm afraid that Mr Hawkins cannot be released from the handcuffs today, sir,' said the security guard.

'What?' I answered snappily. 'Why?'

'There's been an incident, I am afraid.'

I looked at Hawkins, whose face had formed into a naughty boyish smile, as if he had taken his chum's conkers and he frankly didn't care who knew. His handcuffed wrists were held out on the table in front of him.

'What kind of incident?'

'Mr Hawkins has been involved in assault.'

Hawkins turned towards the security guard. 'Allegedly been involved in an assault,' he corrected him. 'No one has proved that I have done nothing.'

I looked at the security guard. This was tricky. I didn't want anyone to hear our conversation. I had to get rid of the guard.

I drew back in stunned indignation.

'How dare you handcuff this man when he is talking to his

lawyer?' I don't know who was more surprised by my outburst - me, the security guard, or Hawkins.

'Listen here, Mr Hawkins is an innocent man until and unless a jury say otherwise - not when you or your governor say.'

The security guard went to interrupt me.

'No,' I shouted, 'this just isn't good enough. It's bad enough that every time his lawyers arrive to see him so that he can conduct his defence they are strip-searched. My God, you guys felt behind the ball sac of an eminent Queen's Counsel. So far I've let that go. I mean, it's just not on.' I was starting to waffle, I needed to get back on track.

'The European Convention on Human Rights,' I said, waggling a finger at the hapless guard, 'the European Convention on Humans Rights says quite clearly that no man should be denied the right to speak unmolested with his lawyers.' I had no idea if the Human Rights Act said anything of the sort, but I was in my stride now. 'I want these handcuffs removed immediately. And then, sir, I want you removed so that I can talk to my client in peace.'

The security guard thought about it for a second. He looked at me. His gaze was met full on by my steely man-of-destiny look. There was no contest. It was a bus hitting a Vespa. He had to back down.

'It's for your own safety, sir,' he added in the last whimpering tone of a man who had met his match.

'I, sir, will be the judge of what is good or bad for my safety, thank you very much.' I said the last four words slowly and with emphasis. Game, set, and match. Grumbling, the security man undid the cuffs and slouched out of the cell.

At this point I sat down. Hawkins looked at me afresh, a look of astonishment on his face. 'Fair play to my solicitor,' he said.

I tried not to smile or blush. After all, he was a psycho. I had to keep control.

'What happened?' I asked touching my own face on the spot

where his scratch was.

'Someone was taking the piss,' he responded nonchalantly.

'And?'

'And I *might* have bitten his ears off.'

'His ear off,' I echoed for no particular reason.

'No, not his ear, his *ears*,' Hawkins corrected me, emphasising the plural, before adding, 'Well, that is what they are saying, anyway. But no one appears to have seen it.'

I cleared my throat. An image of big Tommy without any ears slipped momentarily into my mind. Ouch.

'Now,' I said, gesturing nervously to my ear to remind him of the bugs that may or may not have existed. I cleared my throat again. I had to get back into the zone. The ears thing had thrown me a little.

'Now, I have instructed an expert to deal with the evidence of Colin Rutland, just as you requested.'

He nodded.

'That will be carried out when we have placed him in funds.'

His face dropped slightly. He knew that all his accounts had been frozen.

'I've thought this through, Mr Hawkins,' I said, whilst starting to write on my pad. 'Our firm will foot this cost until after the trial. Then we'll have it back as part of your overall bill.' He nodded as I showed him a piece of paper on which I had written,

CAN YOUR WIFE GET £2MILL IN CASH? HUNTER WON'T DO IT FOR LESS.

He exhaled loudly and emphatically. His mind computed everything - his finances, his wife, me, his fate. He stayed silent for some time.

'Alright, then,' he said slowly, the menace returning to his face.

'Good.'

I showed him the next piece of paper:

GET SOMEONE TO MEET ME AT WATFORD GAP

SERVICES TOMORROW MORNING AT 9AM. TELL
THEM TO WEAR A RED BASEBALL CAP.

He fixed his gaze upon me. My heart was bursting. It was
pumping against my ribcage. Sweat poured down my back. I
could tell that he was contemplating not whether he could
deliver two million quid, but whether he could trust me or not.
I fixed my gaze back on him. I willed myself to keep calm. I
hoped that the sweat I could feel developing on my hairline
would not drop down my face.

He said nothing, just nodded.

'Good,' I said. 'There is nothing more to be said.' I nodded
at him. 'I'll see you at your trial on Monday then.'

He nodded again.

I decided that at this point I would place the pieces of paper
in my mouth and eat them. I suppose I felt that it was a macho
thing to do. A sort of 'anything you can do..' gesture. I had
never tried to eat two pieces of A4 paper before. It isn't easy.
Your whole digestive system – no, your whole body - knows
that it shouldn't be eating paper. It takes ages. When I had said
'I'll see you at your trial,' I had hoped to walk confidently out
of the room. Unfortunately, I was now stuck chewing this
bloody paper. I sat down again and chewed vigorously. The
fucking evil white pulp wouldn't go down. How the fuck had
he done it last time? He looked away, embarrassed at what a
twat I was. I looked away myself. I tried to smile in a 'silly
me' kind of way.

It took the best part of ten minutes for me to finish the
blessed paper. Ten minutes of silence. Ten minutes of me
occasionally spewing out bits of semi-masticated paper. Ten
minutes in which Terry Hawkins, by general acclamation the
most evil bloke in the country, became increasingly
exasperated. God knows what the watching security guard
must have thought we were doing.

As I eventually left, trying desperately to stop myself from
being sick, Hawkins grabbed my wrist. His face was
thunderous.

'If you fuck up or if you screw me....' He didn't need to finish the sentence.

I almost shat the paper out the other end.

30

I arrived at the Watford Gap Services paranoid with fear, blind from my brother's cheap sunglasses and soft with the happy sounds of *Eezy Drivin'* bouncing around my head like toddlers on speed.

I sat down with an overpriced cup of tea (this one, thankfully, did not come with a free dance from the menopausal woman in overalls who served it to me), and twitchily looked around for the CI5 or MI5 or FBI officers I was sure would be following me. I took off my sunglasses. I had to see what was going on.

I was expecting to be met by Terry Hawkins' missus. In my mind I had built her up to be a statuesque blonde model, who in her desire to help her husband would find me devastatingly attractive and probably wish to fulfil any of my sexual desires. She would speak to me in an Eastern European accent - which was a bit unlikely, as I knew that she came from Tooting. In my fantasy, though she would arrive in dark Gucci sunglasses and a fur coat, carrying a calfskin attaché case in which was held the two million quid. I hadn't quite reckoned on the red baseball cap I had ordered her to wear with the fur coat and Gucci.

There was no sign of anyone matching that description. Indeed there was no sign of anyone wearing a red baseball cap at all. Instead there were just the usual people who frequent motorway service stations: the great gangs of Asian families journeying to weddings in the North, carloads of students nursing hangovers with buckets of Coca Cola, and homicidal fathers with beer guts, harbouring thoughts about killing their increasingly irritating children.

I looked at my watch - 09.10. I tried to pour my tea in my cup and spilt it all over my lap. I swore loudly and sprang to my feet, reacting to the scalding water hitting my groin. Everyone turned to me. Fucking hell - I was trying to look inconspicuous. Tom Hagan wouldn't have burnt his cobblers pouring himself a cup of tea.

I tried to regain my composure. I unfolded my copy of The Guardian and sank into my plastic seat. I looked for a red baseball cap - nothing. I looked for the men from Special Branch - fucking everywhere. The bloke mopping up behind the cakes counter - he was one, I was sure of it: he'd been mopping for hours now. The fellah in the denim jacket sitting alone - he had to be CIA: he kept twitching his lapel, and, fuck, that was surely a gun-shaped bulge in his coat. Oh my God, they were going to shoot me. That was it, they were going to wait until Mrs Hawkins had handed over the attaché case and then they were going to shoot me. They'd shoot me and say that I was reaching for a gun in my overcoat. That's what they'd say. I was going to be the victim of a big cover-up. I'd be dead and the last fucking piece of music I'd heard before death was *More than a Feeling* by Boston, as featured on *Eezy* bloody *Drivin'*.

I had to regain my composure. Perhaps I wasn't being followed. Perhaps no one had overheard my conversation with Hawkins at prison yesterday. Perhaps everything was going to work out.

A young couple entered, talking loudly and touching each other unnecessarily. They were dressed like students. I was suspicious. I had seen the TV programmes. They would be the diversion - they couldn't fool me. I knew that as soon as the bloke with the mop made his move, they'd be the first to pull out semi-automatic weapons and shout, 'On your knees, don't make a sound or we'll shoot!' Just as long as no one called me motherfucker or anything like that, I didn't want any profanity or excessive high drama. I wanted my fate to be executed in a traditional tidy, well-mannered, British way: 'On your knees, thank you very much.'

The glass doors swung open and I caught sight of a red splodge: a red baseball hat? I leant forward and strained my eyes. God, I was the most conspicuous person in the whole bloody room - and saw that it was indeed a red baseball cap. It wasn't being worn by a tall, model-like picture of femininity though. It was being worn by a dumpy woman in a cheap cardigan. And she wasn't carrying an expensive attaché case; she was carrying two enormous bulging black bin bags.

I watched her as she stopped in front of the glass doors and looked around searching the room. I knew that she was looking for me. I could tell. It was instinct. I knew that in those black bags would be two million quid.

A kid ran past her and bumped into the bin bags which bounced against her hip. A mum ran, picked up the kid and apologised. The small dumpy woman in the red baseball cap didn't even notice; her eyes were sweeping the room.

What should I do? I knew that if she came to me and handed over the money, and I really was being watched, then I was trapped, stuffed, there would be no going back. I looked at her. But she didn't see me.

I looked at the bloke with the mop. He was still mopping, indifferent to all that was going on. I looked at the bloke in the denim jacket. He was staring into space, the steam from his coffee meandering up towards his face. I looked at the young couple. They were snogging vigorously by the hot foods.

Dumpy started to walk purposefully away from the door. She wasn't walking to me, though. She was walking towards the bloke in the denim jacket. Fuck, say she was going to give the money to the wrong bloke? What would I do then?

As she got closer, I could see that she was foreign - perhaps Spanish or Italian. She was clearly in her sixties and judging from her complexion, hands and distinct lack of jewellery, wasn't a member of the Hawkins' family or one of his lackeys. She also looked very silly in a bright red baseball cap bearing the word 'Gooner' emblazoned along the front.

She walked up to the man in the denim jacket, her balloon-like bin bags slapping her legs. I looked around the room; no one had moved, nothing was happening. She bent over to speak to him. Still no one stirred. I saw her aged lips move. What did she say? I could have sworn I heard the word Strafe. The man in denim jacket hunched his shoulders and shook his head. She moved away.

I stood up and stared at her. She turned to me. Our eyes met and I moved my head ever so slightly to indicate to her that she should come towards me. Tinker Tailor Soldier Spy this was not. If anyone had been looking for any people acting strangely in a motorway service station, they would have looked no further than the bloke in the dark suit, tie and overcoat motioning to the middle-aged Mediterranean woman wearing an Arsenal baseball cap and struggling with two bin bags.

She understood my sign, though, and moved towards me. As she got closer she bent her head towards me and whispered, in the loudest whisper known to man, 'Are you Mr Strafe?'

'Yes,' I said, and motioned her to sit down.

I was right: judging by her accent and her pronunciation of Mr as 'Meester', she was foreign.

'I have the money for you, Meester Strafe.'

I was confused. This was too weird. Where was the sexy Mrs Hawkins? I wasn't going to rip off Señora Gooner's dirty cardigan for a bit of insatiable lust in the car park.

'Hold on, hold on,' I said. 'Who *are you?*'

'I am Mrs Hawkins' cleaner,' she said, her face breaking into a proud smile that revealed a set of brown broken teeth. 'Mrs Hawkins send me as much safer.'

I got it now. Of course Mrs Hawkins was under surveillance. But Dumpy here could go as she liked, especially with a couple of bin bags under her arm. No one would know any different. It was clever. Thank fuck one of us knew what we were doing.

I looked at the bags. I could see wads of money-shaped objects sticking through the plastic. Mrs Hawkins' cleaner knew what I was thinking. 'Everything is in here,' she said, tapping them firmly. I nodded and a wave of exhilaration passed through me.

'Okay,' I said.

We then sat there in silence. I didn't know what to do. Was I supposed to pay her? Was I supposed to simply stand up and walk out of the room carrying the bags? I looked around the room. No one seemed remotely interested in the small dumpy foreign woman with the two bin bags talking to the bloke in the suit. I relaxed slightly.

'Would you like a cup of tea and a bun?'

I quite liked Mrs Savola. We had quite a nice chat as she ate her bun. She told me that Mrs Hawkins was very nice, but Mr Hawkins, 'He not so nice.' Which was as pertinent and insightful as it was a statement of the bleeding obvious.

She told me that he beat Mrs Hawkins, but that they lived in a lovely place so, she shrugged, that wasn't so bad. She told me she was helping Mrs Hawkins, not Mr Hawkins. I nodded. I was just glad that I wasn't being shot at.

I tell you one thing, though. She was as strong as an ox, because when I picked up those bloody bin bags, it was like picking up a dead weight. I never realised that two million quid could be so heavy. I dragged them to my car. I slipped on *Eezy Drivin'* and I made my way back up the M1. Fucking hell, there I was sitting with two million quid in my car. *Albatross* by *Fleetwood Mac* had never sounded so good.

31

I drove straight to Liverpool. I bought a calfskin attaché case, returned to my car and extracted £500,000 from one of the bin bags. I then spent half a bleeding hour trying to arrange the wads of money in a way that would fit neatly in the case. How do they do it in the films? How is it that whenever some gangster opens up a case with money, it always looks bloody perfect? In the end, I packed them in as best I could and made my way to the Anglesey Arms.

The barman knew me now. He looked up and disengaged himself from the Racing Post when I entered. He moved off immediately to the back room when I requested an audience with Maurice Hunter.

Hunter was at exactly the same table with the same people: the ageing Teddy Boy, the Weatherbeaten Man and the Young Gormless Scallie. As I neared their table, Teddy Boy greeted me.

'Here he is: Roy Orbison. Where's your glasses today, Roy?' His tone was friendlier, much less menacing than before.

I smiled.

Maurice Hunter rearranged his bulk on his chair and looked at me with purpose. He motioned to the Scallie, who immediately got up and frisked me. I was getting used to this now. I was now probably one of the few people who could endure to be frisked without automatically clinching their buttock cheeks.

Scallie nodded to Maurice Hunter, who upon hearing that I was not wearing a wire or carrying anything resembling an offensive weapon, beamed at me and beckoned me to sit down.

'Would you like a drink, Mr....?'

I ignored his request for my name and asked for a Scotch with ice. I was dying for a pint of lager, but thought that Scotch with ice was more consistent with the rôle I was playing.

'Wayne,' said Hunter motioning to the Scallie. 'Get,' he paused, 'get Roy a Scotch with ice and tell Billy none of the usual shite either.'

He turned to me, a lascivious look on his face. 'So, Roy, what's in your case?'

I opened the case. I have to concede that I really enjoyed this: the flick of the two locks and the slow unveiling of the wads of money that emerged like sunlight from within. The only downside was that the money was strewn all over the shop. But still, it was money, and loads of it, too.

Hunter turned to Weatherbeaten Man, who nodded.

'Good.' He turned to me and held out a huge flabby hand. 'Roy, your Mr Hawkins has a deal.'

I shook his hand, hoping that the sweat that was cascading from my palms would be soaked in by the fat from his hands.

'When does the job have to be done by?' asked Weatherbeaten Man.

'It has to be done on Wednesday. The target, Colin Rutland, is giving evidence on that day. It can't be done before or after.'

'Why?' asked Teddy Boy.

'Because that is the way Mr Hawkins wants it,' I said, adding, 'and he is after all paying all our wages.'

They were content with this. They were no longer worried that I was either Old Bill or a bullshitter. I'd just handed them half a million quid and that meant I was a player. I liked this. Of course I did.

Wayne returned with the drinks.

I sipped my Scotch. I let the ice rattle against my teeth. I let the hard sour of the alcohol hit the back of my throat and slowly burn its way down to my stomach.

Teddy Boy wanted to know more about me.

'So, Roy, how long have you been working for Hawkins?'

'I'm what we call his consigliere,' I lied. 'It's not so much how long I have been working for him, but how long he has trusted me.'

Teddy seemed to accept this gibberish. 'Oh,' he nodded, as though I was making perfect sense, 'but you're not a cockney, are you?'

'No,' I said.

Weatherbeaten, who I learned was actually called Ronnie, interrupted. 'He's from the Wirral,' turning to me, 'aren't you, Roy?'

I smiled at him. 'I was once, Ronnie,' I said, before repeating myself with a faraway look in my eye, in an attempt at appearing enigmatic. 'I was once.'

We spent the next two hours drinking whisky and talking. I embellished my story more and more, as the double Scotches became trebles. I became Hawkins' envoy for his Far East operations. I became the man who he sent to do his work in Pakistan and Afghanistan. I hinted that I had worked with the Taliban and Al'Quaida in bringing over 'gear'.

Wayne was the most impressed.

'Fucking hell, mate,' he said, 'so have you met that Osama Bin Whatshisname fella?'

'No,' I said, 'no one sees Osama.' I called him by his first name, indicating that I might in some way be familiar with him.

I realised though that Hunter and Ronnie would only take so much bullshit. I moved the conversation on.

We had a few more drinks. Tongues were loosened. They started to laugh about previous 'jobs' they had done.

The one where they had caught another local gangland operator who they were supposed to 'take out' shagging a

Man United footballer and had pissed themselves laughing so much, they forgot to kill him. That was still worthy of a ten minute head-in-hands, backslapping guffaw.

Not all stories were as funny. They had been paid by a residents' group to take out a known paedophile. They had carried out that execution with aplomb and gratuitous violence.

They boasted about the beatings they had given, the faces they had scarred, the men who had shat themselves, the men who had begged for mercy, the men they had killed.

I listened and nodded. All I ever wanted to do was play my guitar. I was starting to feel the need to leave. I didn't want to be Tom Hagan anymore. The whisky was no longer sitting happily in my stomach, but was starting to grumble.

I went for a slash. Wayne was in there with Teddy Boy. The three of us stood looking at the wall, cocks in hand, relieving ourselves. I felt the need to say something.

'So,' I said, 'how will you sort out Mr Rutland?'

Teddy turned to me. He was a little fella, old now, but still obviously a dangerous violent bastard when riled. He was the type of bloke who could endure the biggest beating, but would never give up. I was glad that he had taken a liking to me.

'Rutland,' he boasted, 'will be a piece of piss.'

'Oh yeah,' said Wayne nodding to himself like a fool, 'a piece of piss.'

'How?' I said attempting to sound as cool as I could.

'A motorbike job,' said Wayne.

I nodded sagely as if I knew what he was talking about.

'Of course, a motorbike job.'

'It's the best way,' added Teddy.

'Oh aye,' nodded Wayne, 'quick, no mess, no dodgy long shots.'

'Yes,' I said, 'always the best.'

I went back and left Wayne and Teddy talking in the toilets. 'I suppose,' I said to Hunter, 'that you'll be using a motorbike job to sort this one?' Hunter didn't answer and looked unsure, but Ronnie the Weatherbeaten Man immediately told me that there was no other way for a short notice job like this. Hunter nodded in assent as Ronnie spoke.

The other two returned from the toilet. I looked at my watch in the time old manner of 'I must be getting on,' but this wasn't one of Angela's dinner parties. These four wanted to carry on drinking, and wanted my company. Before I knew it another Scotch was sitting by my side of the table. Torturing me with the notion that I had to drink the bastard.

The conversation turned. Football was discussed, and the plight of Everton. Then, to my delight, music. The Teddy Boy was by now completely pissed and had moved his face up close to mine. I had asked who was responsible for the jukebox.

'Do you know,' he said to me, his breath tearing through the space between us and hitting me in the back of the throat, 'do you know that music and beating the shite out of people has been my life?' He wagged a finger at me for emphasis, before continuing, 'You know the Sting character out of Quadraphenia?' I told him that I did, but he didn't appear to have heard me properly. 'You know the one who has got the biggest bike and that?'

'Yes,' I repeated.

'Well, they based that character on me,' he said emphatically.

By now one of Teddy's arms was draped around me and he was talking directly to the side of my face.

He pointed his fag to the assembled group. 'That's true, isn't it?' he said to them.

Ronnie answered for them all. 'Oh aye. Yes, everyone knows that around here,' he said, as though he was simply informing me of one of life's greatest and simplest of truths.

'Yeah, New Brighton 1963, May Bank Holiday, that was where it really kicked off. Not Brighton on the South Bleeding Coast, where all those Southern poofters were, but New Brighton up here.' He was on his Vespa and on his way down

Memory Lane. 'I thought I had the world at my feet in them days. I thought that everything was going to be one great big continuous fight.' His eyes were starry - that or glazed - as he recounted his youth.

'Fantastic,' I said, pissed now.

'So what kind of music were you listening to then, Teddy?' I said.

He told me of his love for the Dakotas, The Detroit City Five, The Meteors and other authentic Rock and Roll bands from the fifties and sixties that have long faded into obscurity for everyone but for aficionados like Teddy.

'These people were pioneers,' he snarled, his fist clenched with pride as he recounted the groups. 'We were the first real teenagers and they were important.'

I nodded. I couldn't disagree.

Hunter liked his music British and from the late sixties and seventies: Pink Floyd, Led Zeppelin, Captain Beefheart, Procul Harem, he told us, before recounting a tale about a roadie from Deep Purple who had to be whacked for some spurious crime against humanity.

'We took him backstage as the band played,' he told us, a faraway look in his eye. 'I'll never quite hear *Smoke on Water* in the same way again.'

'What about you, Ronnie?' I said, turning to the Weatherbeaten Fella.

'No,' he said gruffly, 'doesn't mean anything to me.'

'No,' I exclaimed. 'Music is the food of love. Without music, what is the point of life?' I didn't think I was getting my point across. I became more excited. 'This is how important music is,' I said, scrabbling for words in my desire to prove my point. 'You know the song *Cecelia* by Simon and Garfunkel?' I indicated big hair as I mentioned the name of Art Garfunkel. They nodded, and Wayne sang what appeared to be the first bars of the song, albeit with all the wrong words.

'That song,' I continued 'was once used by rebels in an African country to show opposition to the ruling dictator who had a mistress called Cecelia.' They looked at me like I was mad.

'Not particularly rebellious that, is it, Roy?' said Ronnie laconically.

I was exasperated now. 'Do you know I'd rather be a piece of music than a person,' I said, travelling further into my surreal world. 'Yes, and if I could be, do you know what piece of music I'd choose?'

They looked at me, then looked blankly at each other.

'Cecelia,' said Wayne, 'after the African bird the dictator was shagging?'

I ignored that and continued along my own illogical diatribe. 'I'd be Johnny Marr's guitar riff in Heaven Knows I'm Miserable Now, by The Smiths.'

I closed my eyes and my fingers instinctively formed the shapes necessary to make the chords Johnny Marr uses for the opening bars.

For a few seconds I forgot that I was in the back room of a pub having just handed over half a million quid to a gang of people who were going to kill an innocent man. I stopped just before Morrissey joined in.

Teddy had a faraway look in his eye, as though he was trying to think what piece of music he would be. Wayne also had a faraway look in his eye, as though he was trying to remember what his name was.

I stood up, picked up my drink, finished it, and blew the wind out of my cheeks.

'Look, there's just one other thing," I said, 'then I've got to go.'

'Go on,' said Hunter.

'I need a gun.'

They looked at each other again.

'Not a big gun, or a fancy gun, just a gun.' I made my hand into a gun with my fingers. 'Just something that will fire bullets.'

'Why do you want a gun?' asked Hunter.

I was half tempted to tell them about my mission to save the world - it was after all a less stupid reason to kill than a million quid - but I decided not to.

'I've got a bit of business to address myself, when all this is done,' I stammered. 'You know how things are.'

Hunter thought about it for a few seconds before his face broke into a big fat grin. 'Sure,' he said, 'follow me.'

I followed him down to a small door, which he opened, then down some dark steps into a cellar. He flicked the light switch to reveal a kind of underground firing range and arsenal. On the wall were mounted racks of rifles and shotguns. At the far end of the range were targets in the shape of men, some of which bore the scars of bullet holes.

'This is where we practise,' he said, a certain amount of pride in his voice.

I was taken aback. Fucking hell, these maniacs actually practised killing people.

He opened a drawer and picked out from what must have been twenty dull metallic handguns a small one, with a barrel that would contain six bullets. It was the type of gun you didn't want as a toy when you were a kid, because your mates had a Colt 45.

'This is an old Webley,' he told me. He picked it up, looked through the nozzle, spun the barrel, stood at the range.

'It should be enough for what you want. Unless, that is, you want to enter Baghdad.' He laughed at his own joke, his jowls vibrating as he did.

He unleashed a volley of shots. It was incredible. There was this fat man with his great wobbling arse and belly, a huge giant blancmange of a man who had drunk solidly all afternoon, but as soon as he had this gun in his hand he was absolutely still, like a rock. I had to squint to focus on the target, but it appeared that he had hit the bullseye with each shot.

He filled the gun with bullets again and handed it to me. I hit the wall, narrowly missed the light, and sent one fluke into the outer rim of the target. I turned to him. 'This gun'll be fine,' I slurred, 'I'm just a bit pissed, you know.'

'I understand, Richard,' he said.

It took me a few seconds to cotton on that he had called me by my first name. My proper name, lovingly installed upon me by my mother and father. He smiled at me again. He seemed perfectly sober now.

'Do you think that we would agree to a job like this for any old Tom, Dick or Harry? We've had you vetted.'

I didn't know what he meant by this. Was I about to get shot? Which one of my lies was now blown?

He must have read the look of concern on my face. 'Don't worry,' he said, 'we know that you are Terry Hawkins' solicitor. The lads are happy about that. We know that only a total fool would double-cross him. We were worried that you might be representing those on the other side of the fence. But you're hardly likely to do that, are you?'

'Me,' I said, 'no, no way. Other side of the fence? No chance.'

I took the gun and a small box of bullets.

'Now,' Hunter continued, a sharpness to him, 'we'll carry out our side of the deal on Wednesday. On Thursday at 9am precisely you'll leave the rest of the money in the toilets of the Shell Garage just off the Huyton Road.' He looked at me carefully. 'You know the place?'

'Yes,' I said, 'I know it.' I did.

He kept my gaze for a few moments, then nodded. 'Good. You won't see us again.' He shook my hand.

I bade goodbye to the rest of the gang, who were now arguing with Wayne that if he chose to be a Kylie song, it wasn't the same as being Kylie or shagging Kylie.

I walked outside and back to my car.

I opened the door and put the gun on the back seat with the bin bags full of money and the six boxes of evidence in the case of The Crown versus Terrence Hawkins and then I drove home.

There I was driving home with an illegal firearm, one and half million quid in bin bags and the entire depositions in the biggest murder trial of the year in the back of the car, and I was completely pissed. The bizzies would have had a coronary if they had stopped me.

Thankfully, I made it home.

32

Then there was the weekend. It tick-tocked itself gently from Friday night through to Sunday.

I went for a pint with my brother and my dad. It was nice.

'Do you remember that band you used to play in?' said my brother. If only he knew. If only he knew that my whole existence was a shrine for the band I used to play in.

'Mm,' I said, trying to sound vague. 'What were we called again?'

'Yes,' said my dad animated now. 'What were you called?'

'The Sensationals!' declared my brother. He remembered. He knew.

'That's right,' I said, as though I hadn't given it a second thought in fifteen years.

'I saw Phil Needham's brother a few weeks ago,' added my brother.

'Did you?' I said. I was interested in this. I had lost contact with Ned, about the same time I started going out with Angela. She didn't like him; she was convinced that he was a gay drug addict. She spent a long time telling me that neither of these attributes were the reason she didn't like him. She just didn't like him. I liked old Ned though. He had courage. He had originality. I liked to think of him as a DJ in some trendy nightclub in Brighton or London. That was what he was into the last time I heard.

'What's Neddy Needham doing then?' I asked my brother.

'Jimmy his brother says he's DJing in some fancy clubs. He goes all over the shop - Brighton, London, even Ibiza and Agia Napa. Doing well, apparently.'

Fucking Ned, the bastard, I thought. Even Neddy's got closer to fame and fortune than me, the queer bastard. Still, he might be playing shite music to students and e-heads pretending to have a good time, but I am poised to save the world. In fact, I'm days away from saving the world.

On Saturday, I went for a walk with my mum. That was nice as well. We talked about things. She told me that I should phone Angela and sort it out with her. I wanted to say to her, 'Mum, I've got a gun and one and half million quid hidden underneath my old clothes in the wardrobe. I can't deal with Angela right now.'

'Yes, Mum,' I said. 'I just need to get this trial out of the way.'

She asked me how Ellie Smith was. I didn't answer; I just shot her a look of incredulity. She smiled at me. 'You can't hide anything from me, Richard Strafe,' she said playfully, 'I am your mother.' She smiled again. 'And besides, I saw you coming out of her car the other night.'

'Bloody hell, Mum,' I exclaimed, 'you don't miss a trick.'

She gave me a rueful look. 'Well, how is she then?'

'She's good,' I said. 'She's off to teach in a school on some island off the coast of Africa.'

'Typical of her,' my mum added cynically and without a great deal of sense.

I had forgotten that my mum had never really liked Ellie Smith. She had blamed my mediocre 'A' levels on Ellie - she had this unfounded and completely daft notion that I could have got into a top university if I hadn't been 'gallivanting' with 'that Smith girl.'

We walked over the beach. I found myself wanting to open up to her. I wanted to tell her everything that had been going on, and everything that was about to happen in the next few days.

But I couldn't.

On the Sunday my brother John, his wife Sam and their kids little George and little Whatevertheotheronesnameis came round for lunch. It was a traditional affair. We all sat round the dining table as my mum produced roast chicken, potatoes and all the trimmings. We sat round and watched my dad carve the chicken with his shaky hands, clasping onto the same carving knife he had used since time began for us.

John noticed. I knew he did by the way in which he decided to speak in an unfeasibly upbeat way. He spoke of the future in broad-brush strokes, like a child's drawing. We would all be going to George's Sports Day on the 14th of next month. We would all be going to the caravan for a weekend in Wales in August. We would all be watching the Cup Final on TV in a few weeks' time. There was no illness in the pictures John painted. I said nothing. But I felt love for him.

They asked me about the trial.

'Tomorrow's the big day,' I said. 'Just looking forward to getting it all over with.'

Did I think I'd win?

'That's up to the jury.'

Did I think that Hawkins was guilty?

'That's up to the jury.'

'Oh, come on, Richie. You've met the guy, you must have a view.'

I pondered for a second.

'I think that he is the single most scary bloke I have ever met. I think that he is the personification of all that is evil. He thinks of nothing but his battle with the world. He evaluates himself only in terms of how many people are scared shitless of him. I sincerely hope that he is convicted, and that they throw away the key down a hole that leads to a black hole that would take the person stupid enough to venture down it into a galaxy so far away that time has yet to be invented there, so that the key simply floats about in a mass void, forever lost.'

My family were at a loss how to react to that: even little George and Whatevertheotheronesnameis looked open-mouthed at me.

After a few seconds my mum asked someone to pass her the peas and my dad asked me if I would be joining them in the caravan for the weekend in Wales. I told him that I was very keen to.

Ah, the weekend in Wales. How much I wanted to say that I would be there with them and mean it. I knew that it was never going to happen.

That night I hid the money and the gun in my wardrobe underneath a load of old seven-inch singles. I was happy with that.

Monday morning. I shined my shoes. I drove over to the Liverpool Crown Court, parked in the car park nearby and made my way to the concourse outside the court building.

There were police everywhere, police and journalists and film crews frantically casting an eye over anyone who might have anything to do with the feature of the day: the case of the Wavertree Executions.

I strode purposefully past the film crews and the armed police officers and into the building, stopping only for my ubiquitous body search. I was enjoying this. I was enjoying the fact that the journalists and film crews, police and public didn't have access to the places I was allowed to go. In the trial of R v Hawkins, I was a player. I was Hawkins' special solicitor. I would be the person he confided in, the person he asked for when he wanted special jobs done. I might hate him. I might be petrified of him, but at least he had given me the opportunity to play at being the most important bastard in the whole world, at least for a little while.

McPhee, Fox and Phillips had kindly sent me an office junior to help with the boxes and do the running. Elliot - I later discovered this was the name given to him by his hapless parents - didn't say much, and showed all the initiative of a bag of cement. Still though, he helped me carry those bloody boxes from my car into the room especially put aside for the defence.

We sat there and I tried to engage Elliot in a bit of fraternal bitching about various people in the office. 'So what do you think of Howard, then?'

'Alright,' he said, in an insipid London accent.

'What about Julie from typing, eh? Has she shagged Martin from accounts yet?'

'Dunno,' he said.

I gave up. Anyone who had worked at McPhee, Fox and Phillips for more than five minutes who didn't have an opinion on whether Martin from accounts had shagged Julie from typing wasn't worth talking to.

We waited in silence for our barristers. Eventually I realised that it was not done for a barrister to come and find his solicitor; it had to be the other way around.

I told Elliot to speak to no one and to stay where he was, and skulked off to the find the barristers' robing room.

I hate barristers' robing rooms even more than I hate barristers. The barristers' robing room is a den full of egotistical self-important pompous wankers.

I found Golightly QC and Parker-Manly sitting drinking tea surrounded by a gaggle of other dark-suited knobheads. Golightly was loudly playing the rôle of the alpha male. In tones that would have been audible from Scottish Highlands, he was telling the crowd of sycophants what a weird psychopath Hawkins was and how he hadn't even given him any instructions.

'He has, though,' said Parker-Manly, 'the cunning of a street weasel. It wouldn't surprise me if he still had something up his sleeve.'

They all seemed to find this extremely profound.

I wanted to piss myself laughing. If only they knew what Hawkins had planned. There they were, so grand in their wigs and gowns, uttering their profundities about the people they were happy to take the piss out of, when the truth was that the man they were patronising was powerful enough to arrange for another man's life to be ended, simply because his living was an inconvenience. I hated Hawkins, but I had to respect him.

Golightly spotted me. 'Ah, Mr Strafe,' he said. I was impressed that he remembered my name.

'Shall we go and see our beloved Mr Hawkins?'

I nodded, as Golightly rose like a king amongst his court and followed me out of the robing room and down the stairs.

Hawkins didn't want to see Golightly and Parker-Manly. He told the security guard that he wanted to see me first, alone. I shrugged my shoulders at the two learned barristers and told them that Hawkins was 'a weirdo', and, that I'd go and see what he wanted; it was probably nothing.

When I arrived in the cell, Hawkins was in a fit of mania. His usual quiet menace had been replaced with a frantic pacing of his cell.

'Well?' he said, as I entered the cell. 'Well?' he repeated with even more force. His eyes were dark and being pushed out of his head by the muscles in his brain. 'What's going on? Is everything sorted? What is happening? I've heard from Maria. She says everything is okay. Is it?'

He was ranting. He tripped over the words as they jumped out of his mouth like a parachute regiment.

I held my hand out to indicate that he should be quiet. He stopped talking and pacing, but his eyes refused to go back into their normal slots either side of his nose. He stared at me.

I realised how much power I had over this man. I realised how he had probably spent the last few nights counting the hours before he could ask me if his conspiracy was working out. I realised that the moments when I had been drinking with my dad and brother and playing with my nephews, he had been fretting, pacing his cell, refusing to eat or come out for exercise. Suddenly he didn't seem quite as scary. He just seemed desperate.

I looked at him. 'Don't worry, it's all taken care of. Our expert witness will be doing his thing on Wednesday.'

'Wednesday,' repeated Hawkins, his hysteria growing. 'What if it is too late by Wednesday? What if Rutland has already given.....'

I put my hand up to stop him from continuing. If his cell in prison was being bugged, there was a good chance that his cell in court was being bugged as well. 'You'll just have to trust us, Terry,' I said. It was the first time I had ever called him Terry. I wouldn't call him that again.

He looked at me. For a few seconds we stared at each other in silence. He calmed.

'What's going to happen today then?' he asked.

'Today we get the jury in, and the prosecutor opens the case.'

'And tomorrow?'

Ah, tomorrow. That was my day.

'Don't worry about tomorrow,' I told him. 'There's nothing you can do about tomorrow.'

I was right. On that Monday very little of interest happened in the case of R v Terry Hawkins. The courtroom was packed: the journalists and voyeurs, police and staff were all crammed in next to one another, elbows touching, knees banging as they shifted in their uncomfortable seats. Golightly for the defence tried manfully to make a fuss about various legal issues, that, if I'm going to be honest, I didn't really understand. He made his submissions as the judge, lawyers and assembled scribes noted down his words and Hawkins looked on in menacing silence. Perkins QC for the Crown made his submission. The judge made a few jokes that only barristers were supposed to understand and Golightly sat down, defeated.

The jury were then brought in, blinking and unnerved by the packed courtroom. They were oblivious to the fact that they were about to try the case of the Wavertree Executioner until they were told by Perkins, who gave them every gory detail of the Crown's case, as Hawkins sat silently looking on, hating the thought that these twelve had such power over him.

Not much happened the next day, either. The Crown showed photographs and diagrams and read out statements from various witnesses.

I sat in my place on the third bench from the front with Elliot beside me looking bored and emitting a smell of aftershave and last night's lager.

'You went out last night then, eh?' I asked him in whispered tones. 'Sampled a bit of the old Liverpool nightlife?'

'Yeah,' he said and looked away.

Fuck him.

Halfway through the morning session the usher came up to our bench and leaned in towards us. 'Mr Strafe?'

'Yes, that's me,' I said.

He handed me a folded note. I assumed it was from McPhee and put it straight into my pocket without reading it.

We went to see Hawkins that night, before we left. Golightly and Parker-Manly sat down in front of him, and I stood by the door. They told him of their plans and tactics for the next day. As they spoke, he looked past them directly at me. Imploring me to tell him that the plan was in hand and that everything would be okay. He stared at me, not his usual vicious stare, but a different, desperate look, like a child imploring his teacher to pick him for the school team.

I smiled at him as I left. 'Don't worry,' I said. 'Everything's going well.'

As we trudged back up the stairs from the cells, Golightly turned to me; he was interested in me now. 'You seem to have a profound effect upon Mr Hawkins,' he said, a note of puzzlement in his voice.

'Do I?' I replied. 'I don't think so.'

'Oh yes,' added Parker-Manly. 'It's as though he's depending upon you.'

'I don't know about that,' I said modestly. 'He probably finds it easier to speak to me than a barrister.'

Predictably, the two bewigged advocates were content with

this appeal to their ego.

I drove home.

I went upstairs.

I took out some paper and a pen. I perched on the little desk in the corner of my room, just as I had when I was a boy doing my homework, just as I had when I wrote my lyrics that I thought were going to make me immortal.

I wrote three letters.

I went downstairs to where my mum and dad were sitting watching the early evening news.

'I'm off to Manchester then for this concert,' I said.

'Okay,' they muttered from their chairs, barely turning to look at me.

I kissed my mum on the cheek and squeezed my dad's arm, then left the house, bound for Manchester. On my back was a rucksack I had bought. Inside the rucksack was my Webley handgun, the rest of the money and various other items I thought might come in handy.

33

I didn't want to be at Freshers' Week, Southampton University in the penultimate year of the 1980s. I wanted to be in London with my girlfriend and my bandmate.

My father had driven me down to the concrete monstrosity that was my hall of residence. My new home. I looked around and saw dozens of other eighteen-year-olds embarrassingly bidding their parents farewell. The same scene was played out everywhere: new undergraduate standing clutching his/her stereo, Mum close by with a box of food and Dad a little further away struggling with an enormous trunk or suitcase. The difference between them and me, though, was that they all seemed genuinely excited to be starting at Southampton University - me, I was already sulking.

I sulked through Freshers' Week, although you'd never really have known it as I entered fully into the drinking, dancing, conversations about 'A' level results and the ritual slagging off of our friends who had gone to Oxbridge.

I phoned Ellie every night. On the first night she was excited to hear me. She declared how much she missed me, how she thought everyone on her course and in her hall was a dickhead. On the second night, she rambled on about whether she had made a big mistake choosing modern French poetry as one of her core modules rather than French Literature and Twentieth Century Philosophy - which everyone else appeared to be doing - before telling me she was looking forward to seeing me at the weekend. On the third night, she couldn't speak for very long because 'a load of us are going to see a film at the Scala in King's Cross' (The load of 'us' - Who the fuck are 'us'? What about me?). On the fourth night, she wasn't in.

On the fifth night, I travelled up to London. We went out - me, Ellie, Danny and Ned - to see a band called The Inspiral Carpets who were the latest thing to come out of Manchester. They were depressingly good. They made me mad. I wanted The Sensationals to be the newest fucking thing to come out of somewhere; I didn't care where.

I was tetchy all weekend. I didn't want to go back to Southampton with its unfeasibly happy Freshers and their Beer Club and Neighbours Appreciation Society, their Stalinist League and Athletics Union. I didn't want to go back to the bitter conversations about how there was more to life than getting good 'A' level results. I wanted to stay here hanging out with Danny and Ellie, discovering life.

Danny was at near stratospheric level of excitement. He talked non-stop. He talked about the people he had met - crazy art-school types who wore weird clothes, listened to fantastic new music that we on the Wirral would never have heard of, and took avant-garde drugs that made them do avant-garde things. Bollocks.

Danny told me of all the bands he was going to see. The Stone Roses were playing soon and they were going to be huge; and had I heard the new Happy Mondays album?

Of course I hadn't, I had been too busy brooding about in bloody Southampton. Even Neddy was way ahead of me; he talked of the new scene in Brighton which was called Indie/Dance crossover that was going to be 'absolutely fucking mega.'

Indie/Dance crossover? What the fuck was that? What was Ned talking about? I had visions of unwashed, long-haired Indie kids trying to dance. Indie kids didn't dance, they just sat around in a circle ignoring one another or looking at their shoes. Indie kids shouldn't dance. In fact most of them should be legally prohibited from dancing. Ned was surely talking bollocks.

Ellie and Danny knew exactly what he was talking about though. They agreed with him. Things called raves were the places to be. Ecstasy was the drug to take.

Raves? They sounded ridiculous. It sounded like an expression your dad might use at an embarrassing moment, like when he asked if you were going to the school hop or the scout club dance.

Still, Ellie seemed to have missed me. We had for the first time the chance to spend the night together unimpeded by parents. That was brilliant. For the first time, sex became something more than an act to be accomplished as swiftly as possible to ensure that no one would discover us. We could now spend time slowly discovering each other. It was brilliant.

On the Sunday she took me to the train station. We kissed and held each other. She told me she didn't want me to leave. I believed her. I would have stayed like a shot. I got on the train back to Southampton with a huge dark cloud hovering above me. When I got back, I refused to go to the pub with everyone else, preferring instead to lie on my bed listening to The Cocteau Twins.

I phoned her at around ten o'clock. She was out.

Danny was keen to get the band back up and running as well. He would get us a drummer to replace Pim and some gigs.

Fair play to him, he was as good as his word. When I went down next time he had got a new drummer called Jude, who was a sculptor and had a ponytail and a goatee beard. He didn't say much, but seemed alright. We practised in a special room at his college.

Some of his new mates came and listened. They quite liked some of our stuff, but took the piss out of our choice of covers.

'I can't believe you're still playing Billy Idol covers,' one of them said. I felt embarrassed. Danny though, he was angry. He told us he wouldn't play any more covers. I agreed. I was cool with that.

I came down the next week. The bloke who had made the Billy Idol comment was there again. This time he had a guitar with him. His name was Patrick. He was Southern. He was clearly too good-looking for his own good with hair like Brian Jones circa 1967.

Danny introduced us. 'This is Patrick,' he said to me. 'He wants to jam along with us.'

In my mind I screamed out, 'Why?' Why did he want to jam with us? What was the point? We were The Sensationals, there was no room for another guitarist. I nodded though, and we played. The twat was a good guitarist. Of course he was.

That was the last time Ned played bass with us. He didn't come down to the next rehearsal; he phoned up on the morning declaring himself unfit with a cold. Unfit with a cold, my arse - he'd been out partying the night before and couldn't be bothered getting the train up from Brighton.

Patrick played bass. He was good at that as well. Twat.

Ned phoned me during the next week and said that he couldn't make the next practice as he was going to a 'rave' somewhere in Manchester. 'Come after it,' I had suggested innocently. He told me I didn't understand. He told me that the rave might not end for days. I told him that we had a gig soon. I asked him if he minded if we got someone in to play bass. He said he didn't.

That was that. Ned, my mate who I had practised with back in the fifth form, the lad who I had dreamed with, was now more interested in going to dance with Indie kids than play. I felt sad for him.

We had a gig, though. And that was what the most important thing.

Patrick learned Ned's bass parts. We wrote some new songs. Well, to be honest, Danny wrote some new songs. Somehow, mine didn't seem quite as important. By the time the new set had been completed, there was only one new Richard Strafe composition, *'I want to talk to Jesus'* - a poignant, three-minute, four-chord rant about a single mother living in a high-rise. I had been inspired by the sights I viewed as my train from Southampton travelled through the London suburbs, snaking past the towering blocks with their glimpse of humanity through dim light that escaped from the grimy windows.

Our gig was at a place called The Powerhouse in Camden. I loved this venue. There was no Indie/Dance crossover here: this was a dingy venue with guitars and leather jackets and acne and Snakebites and Black. This was my type of place.

The Sensationals took to the stage as third support act to a band called Kingmaker who would be famous for about five minutes a few years later.

There wasn't the same feeling of excitement as there had been in the old days; there wasn't the same feeling of camaraderie. I couldn't bully and scold the new supercool bassist Patrick in the same way I had always done with Ned; and the drummer Jude didn't have a new anecdote describing his latest sexual conquest in the way Pim always had. Danny didn't seem to care, though. He was more interested in making an impression. 'This is London now,' he said, as though everything that went before was of minor importance.

Our relationship was changing. He didn't look at me for support and affirmation in the same way as he used to. I remember asking Ellie about it.

'Do you think Danny has changed a bit since starting art school?' I asked.

She reassured me that he was the same. She told me it was just *me* being sensitive. She told me she loved the sensitive side of me. I was happy with that.

We were greeted on stage at the Powerhouse by a few meagre claps and the overwhelming sound of students queuing to get a drink at the bar. I could see a whole expanse of dark sticky floor where people should have been standing watching and dancing.

We played alright though. Well, I thought we had. We went through all the old songs -'Meet Me By The Bus Stop', 'Billy Don't' - which Patrick seemed to play with a smirk on his face - 'Watch out World Here Comes the Kid', plus some new ones we'd written. We did our cover of 'West End Girls' as well because Jude and Patrick thought that was brilliant, brilliant and 'postmodern', whatever the bollocks that meant. And as before, we finished with 'Everything's Sensational'.

Danny did what he always did when we were faced with adversity - he went into his 'fuck you' routine. This meant a defiant, high-octane, high drama performance, directed as much at those who were not listening as those who were. I had first seen it at the Rock Ferry Working Men's Club, when he sang exclusively to a fat tattooed bloke who had shouted 'Get off, you bunch of poofs,' just before we had started. He had been brilliant that night, and was brilliant tonight. By the end there were more people standing in front of the stage than had been at the start. True, most people were still in the queue for lager, but, hey, this was our first London gig. The Who got bottled offstage in their first London gig, so mild disinterest from the crowd was a victory as far as I was concerned.

We came offstage and went into a little room set aside for the third support act. I passed Ellie on the way; she smiled a strange reticent smile at me. I put it down to the fact that she didn't think much of Patrick and Jude. We had to grow to get to know them together.

Inside the little room Danny was hyper. He walked to and fro across the floor.

'We need to practise more. We need to be tighter, and cleverer,' he snarled, as he paced the three or four metres from wall to door. 'It's fucking pointless playing a venue like this and being shite.'

I stood silently. I had heard him like this before. I knew he'd calm down in a little while.

'We need to drop some of the songs,' said Jude who was sitting nonchalantly rolling a spliff.

Patrick agreed. 'Yeah, absolutely.' He paused as an expression of pain grew on his face. 'Like that "Billy Won't" song. That's got to go; it's an embarrassment.'

'Billy Don't,' I said, correcting him. 'It's called Billy Don't.'

'Whatever,' said Patrick. 'It's still a fucking abortion of a song.'

I looked at Danny, hoping for some kind of support. Billy Don't had been my first song. It was the song I played to Danny way back at the beginning. It was the song about school and the kids we grew up with. It was a part of me. Part of us. Danny would surely back me up. He would understand the importance of 'Billy Don't' to the Sensationals. It was part of where the band had come from. Instead Danny just nodded. 'Okay,' he said.

That was it. A nod and an okay and Billy Don't, my song, was binned.

I felt like crying. Danny turned to me. I hoped that he was going to explain about the song, perhaps say a few words to placate me.

'We need to practise more,' he said, as a dark and resolute expression jutted from his face.

His expression stayed like that until we were at the bar. Then suddenly he changed again. He talked to blokes from A&R companies and record companies, promoters and people from other bands. I stood by him and sulked, or stood by the bar and sulked or talked sulkily to Ellie. They had liked the Sensationals, they told him. Then they would proffer their opinion on which band they thought we sounded like. 'The Bunnymen,' said one. 'Early Teardrop Explodes,' said another. One particularly camp bloke told Danny he was like Jim Morrison. Danny liked him. In the past, being compared to anyone else would provoke a collective red-misted teenage outrage. 'How dare they compare us to someone else? How lazy to simply dismiss our sound?'

Now, though, Danny was standing there cheerfully agreeing with them. 'Well,' he kept saying, 'we have been heavily influenced by them.'

No one talked to me.

I got the call two weeks later.

That moment will be forever etched upon my memory.

I was sitting in the tiny brick-walled cell that was my Hall of Residence home. There was a system where a buzzer would sound in your room when there was a telephone call for you. You would then trudge down to the telephone at the end of the corridor to speak. Usually to your mother. The telephone was by the kitchen area.

I heard the buzzer and my heart jumped. I hadn't heard from Ellie for a couple of days and presumed it was her. I skipped along the corridor to the kitchen area where the phone was ringing for me. A small Chinese guy, who was studying maths and always seemed to be cooking, was busy frying something in a wok.

I picked up the phone. It was Danny. I hadn't expected Danny.

'Rich? Hi, it's me,' he said. The tone of his voice immediately troubled me.

'Hi,' I said, adding immediately, 'hey, Danny, have you seen Ellie at all?'

'Ellie? Eh, yes,' he said.

'Oh,' I said. I don't know why I didn't ask him any more questions. Perhaps it was because I didn't want to know the answers.

'Are we still on for the practice next weekend?' I said as cheerfully as I could, 'and that gig in Hackney?'

'Listen,' he said, 'we're going to have a practice on Wednesday.'

'Wednesday?' I said. 'That's going to be difficult. I mean, I'll do my best, but I've got lectures.' In my mind I was already thinking of the excuses I would make to my Jurisprudence teacher, who was already in the process of giving up on me.

'Don't worry about it, Rich.'

Don't worry about it. What the fuck did that mean? They couldn't have a practice without me. The Sensationals *were* me: me and Danny. I was one half; I was Keith Richard to his Mick Jagger, Brian bloody May to his Freddy Mercury. Why would they want to practise without me?

'What do you mean?' I asked.

'Look,' he said, then paused. In the background I could hear music playing and people talking and laughing.

He continued, 'It's just not working as it is. What with you in Southampton and everything. There's no point in doing things half-baked; we need to get a really good sound. We need to be playing all the time.'

'I don't understand.' I didn't.

'What are you saying, Danny?' I asked desperately.

'I've got a really good chance to make a go of things,' he said, 'but I can't do it without practising regularly, without playing with people who I see and socialise with all the time.'

That was it then. The Sensationals were no longer *our* thing, they were *his* thing. Me being in Southampton was an inconvenience to *his* chances. I wasn't going to socialise with him, therefore I wasn't going to be in the band.

I bit back tears. I looked at the Chinese guy whose food was hissing blue flames on the stove. He ignored me.

On the other end of the phone Danny was still talking. 'You can form a band in Southampton, Rich. You're a great songwriter. It'll be so much easier for you down there.'

This was the equivalent of the *'it's not you, it's me,'* part of the speech you get when you are being dumped by your girlfriend.

I put the phone down. I didn't want to hear anymore. I went back into my room, lay on my bed and put The Sundays on my stereo. For about twenty minutes I felt numb. I tried to make sense of it all. Then I got up and went to the bar. It didn't seem that bad. Not then. There was so much time left, back then. Perhaps I would form a new band.

I had a few pints and tried to phone Ellie again. She wasn't there. Her room-mate didn't know where she was. I left a message. I went back to the bar. I got talking to some of the Socialist Worker crowd. They were organising a bus to go down to London the next day to rally against student loans. I asked if I could go along with them.

'Of course, comrade,' they said.

They liked me, because I had what sounded to them like a Scouse accent, and therefore was automatically working class, oppressed and potentially a revolutionary.

I decided that I would travel down with the revolutionaries, but skip the march and head straight to see Ellie. I needed to talk to her. I needed her to tell me that everything would be fine.

34

I felt a little uncomfortable on the evening train from Liverpool to Manchester. I had never, after all, been on a train with over a million quid in my possession before.

I kept my rucksack on my knees, but that was uncomfortable. So I tried to put it under the table, but it wouldn't fit. It wouldn't fit on the overhead luggage rack either. So in the end I decided to go and sit on the bloody thing in the corridor by the bog.

I looked outside as the evening sky turned from blue to its mongrel shades of crimson, orange and purple. I watched as the shadows darkened across the fields and the cars on the nearby roads put on their headlights and made their slow journey home through the traffic.

I thought of the three letters I had written. I had left my mum and dad's on the kitchen table. They might have got it by now. A letter in a large jiffy bag stuffed with fifty-pound notes: two thousand fifty-pound notes to be precise. Donated by the kind heart of one Terence Hawkins, the Wavertree Executioner.

I had left the letter deliberately vague. I couldn't tell them the truth about my intentions or the source of the money.

Dear Mum and Dad,
I have come into a bit of money - don't worry about how, it's a work thing, these things happen from time to time in my job. I thought though that it might come in handy for you Dad. There's not a great deal of point waiting to have your op done

on the NHS when this little stash of cash can pay for it to be done privately. I know, it's not a big op, but still, might as well have it done quickly and with better food and prettier nurses, eh. So make sure you spend it on your health.

One thing though, I have to get off for a little while. I've got a big job to do - it's kind of undercover, I can't tell you much more than that. Don't worry though, I'm quite safe, and as soon as I can, I'll be in touch.

I'm sorry that I haven't always been a good son, I've meant well.

I love you both very much,
Rich.
PS. Whatever you do, don't tell anyone about the money

I gave my brother the same amount, but I was a bit more candid with him.

Dear John,
Fuck me, I'm in the shit.
I've made a couple of decisions that mean I have to lie low for a little while. In this jiffy bag is £100,000 - in the immortal words of Jim Bowen, mate, 'that's yours, that's safe.' Don't worry where I got it from, it's a legitimate work thing: sort of someone else's insurance policy that has been cashed in. I thought that you might use it to spend on your lads' education. No, fuck that, don't send them to a posh school, buy them some new trainers and take them to Disney World for a year or something. Life's too short not to be reckless.

I've given Mum and Dad the same amount, I've told them to spend it on Dad's operation, please see that they do. I'm not trying to buy my way out of being a shite son for the last sixteen years - I'm just trying to do the right thing.

I'll be in touch as soon as I can.
Love to Sam, and George and Thingy,
Rich

He would get his letter in the morning. My third letter would take longer: it was going to Ellie's school on her island off Africa, where the children wanted to learn and the fishermen wanted to fish and the mothers wanted to cook and everything was right and in its place.

Ellie would be surprised to receive an envelope with over a hundred thousand pounds in it. I had tried to explain as best I could. And, I have to confess, I had explained things in a way I hoped would nicely jog the area of her soul that was marked 'guilt' or even its neighbours 'jealousy' and 'regret'.

Dear Ellie,

You mentioned the other day about the chronic shortage of pencils on your island. I might not have shown it at the time, but the thought of those lovely smiling faces not being able to write made my heart almost burst with emotion. What a fucked up world we live in, when we can spend billions of pounds on weapons of mass destruction but can't afford to provide a little pencil for the needy children of Africa.

Ellie, quite incredibly, the very next day, I came into a bit of a windfall. I won't bore you with the details of how it came about: let's just say it was so big that I immediately got drunk on the very best French Champagne and woke up with a hangover and a couple of loose women from Bootle.

It wasn't enough for me, Ellie, how could I live in a world of hedonistic bliss, with those little children splashing about in a pool of ignorance for want of a pencil or two?

Please find therefore enclosed - £100,000. I know that you will use it properly.

I have to say that when I told you that I had hardly thought about everything that happened all those years ago, I wasn't being strictly honest. I have in fact thought about it quite a lot. But hey, we were all young and a bit daft ~ I won't say any more than that.

Good luck.

Richie.

It had felt wonderful writing the letter to Ellie. I had blown the final whistle on that particular chapter of my life.

I tried to get comfy on my rucksack, but each time I moved something long and hard always seemed to stick me in the arse. Eventually I realised that it was my loaded handgun. To be shot up the arse on my way to carrying out my mission to save the world would be too embarrassing for words. I gave up sitting on my bag and stood by the train door looking out of the window. We were entering the outskirts of Manchester now. The fields had given way to suburban estates, roads and high-rise blocks of flats. The speed of the train caused the artificial light to streak against the darkening sky.

I wondered what Danny would be doing now.

Getting ready for his concert no doubt. Choosing which designer outfit to wear, which supermodel to shag, which drug to put up his nose. I stopped imagining it. Since my own bit of excitement dealing with Hunter and Hawkins, Danny Cappaldi didn't seem quite so important. Perhaps I was getting bored of hating him?

Before I could consider it, I heard the toilet in the corridor flush and the bolt on the door slide open. Strange: I hadn't even realised anyone was in the toilet.

Doctor Costas emerged, still pulling up the zip on his pea-green slacks. He smiled at me. I had long given up being surprised to see him. I smiled back.

'How are you feeling?' he asked.

'Weird,' I replied.

'Nonsense,' he said with enthusiasm. 'This is the first day of the beginning of time for you.'

I tried to make sense of that. As with everything he said to me, it made both absolute sense and no sense at all.

He continued, 'You know, I was talking to my boss about you.' I screwed up my face, imagining Dr Costas with a boss, and an office, and perhaps an office Christmas party where everyone got pissed and did bad dancing to songs by The Spice Girls and Kylie Minogue.

'Oh, yes,' he added, 'I have a boss - the Senior Archivist, ProfessorAndreas.'

'Professor Andreas,' I repeated unnecessarily.

'Yes. He is a fine man; he has been working at the Library since time began.'

I nodded as though I knew what he was talking about.

'Do you know, when I started this mission, he didn't hold out much hope. Do you know what he said to me?'

I had no idea.

'He said that Richard Strafe was not of the calibre to achieve the status of legend and myth.'

I wasn't sure how I was supposed to take this: I had been dissed many times in my life but never by the Senior Archivist at the Great Library of Myths and Legends. 'I spoke to him last night though, and he had to eat his words.'

Costas' face broke into a broad smile as he said this. He seemed proud of me. It was very strange.

'Do you know what he said this time?'

I had no idea.

He said, 'Richard Strafe's legend might achieve five century status. Imagine that – five century status.'

I didn't have a clue what he was talking about.

'What does that mean?'

He looked surprised, then his face changed to one of fond pity. 'Oh, my dear boy,' he exclaimed, 'here you are, about to embark on a wonderful act that will touch all of us, and you don't even know the repercussions.'

'Well, I thought about one or two,' I said, 'like life imprisonment, or the rest of my day counting the stains on my pyjamas after I've been locked up in a mental hospital.'

He ignored this comment.

'Five century status is where a myth lives on in the minds of people for five centuries. It's our way of organising myths and legends. Putting them in order. Naturally, the Greeks are at the top of the scale. Greeks from Hercules to Ulysses have achieved five thousand year status.'

I nodded as though this all made absolute sense.

'Jesus Christ - ten thousand year status. Robin Hood - seven century status, and so on.'

Was this man mad? Was I mad listening to him?

'What does Danny Cappaldi score?' I asked. 'Danny Cappaldi - he is on a different scale.'

'What scale is that?'

'That is the generation scale.'

I looked puzzled, so he explained. 'At the moment The Beatles have three generation status; Pele, two generation status. Do you see?'

I did, kind of.

'What will his status be if I kill him?'

Costas could see where I was going with my questioning.

'True,' he said, 'an untimely death at the height of his powers will expand his status a generation or two, but yours, yours will be huge.'

'What do you mean?'

'Let me be straight with you, Richard.'

'Please,' I said.

'When I first met you, I had no idea just how successful you would be. I thought that you and Cappaldi would probably end up with a similar impact in terms of your stories - a bit like JFK and Lee Harvey Oswald. But your work in the last few weeks has taken me by surprise. At the end of this you will far surpass anything that Cappaldi can do.'

'How?' I said. 'He's had twelve hit albums; he's had affairs with actresses and supermodels; he's spent more time in rehabilitation for one breakdown or another than I've spent at work. How can my status end up surpassing his?'

His fond look returned. 'My dear boy,' he said, which spooked me a little. 'Think of your story. You have ripped off the most reviled man in British criminal history to the tune of two million pounds, you've organised the assassination of a prime witness in his trial, you've given money to your ill father, your brother and your first love, and then you kill the

278

person you hate most in the world.' His eyes burst with pride. 'It is a wonderful story; it is a legend.'

I hadn't really thought of it like that. We stood in silence for a few moments as I contemplated what he had said. It made sense. It was mad.

The train gently pulled into the station.

'I've still got to kill him though, haven't I?'

'Yes,' said Costas, 'that is the arrangement; that is how it must be. But you will do that,' he added confidently. 'You will do that because you have always craved the immortality it will give you, and because you really, really hate him.'

The doors opened and people got in and out of the train. In the melée I lost Costas. I wondered if I would see him again after it was all over. Perhaps I would get invited to some kind of special awards ceremony at the Great Library itself? I imagined it: Elizabeth Taylor would be handing out the awards, with Jonathan Ross presiding as compère.

'And the award for saving mankind by brutally killing a popstar goes to..*(contrived hush)*..Richard Strafe.' *(applause, cheesy music, camera close-up on me smiling and shaking hands with various pissed celebs).*

Costas was right about one thing, though. I did really, really hate Danny Cappaldi.

35

I had been forced to get up at some ridiculously early hour to catch the minibus to London with the University of Southampton branch of The Socialist Workers' Party. They picked me up last. I got in bleary-eyed and hungover and sat at the back. Incredibly, the Socialist Workers were all bouncing around like a troop of border collies on the way to their favourite woods for a walk.

Their leader was a Glaswegian mature student called - I kid you not - Michael Carmichael. He welcomed me into the van with fraternal and comradely greetings.

The next two hours in the van were weird. I had never before in my life spent such a long period of time with such an assiduous and intense bunch of people. Every banner had been carefully made and handed out, every loudhailer was checked and double checked to ensure maximum volume, and each chant and slogan was carefully inspected for political correctness, class soundness and Marxist credibility.

There was an intense discussion about whether a song about building a bonfire and putting all the Tories on it was in some way offensive to Catholics, as it alluded - albeit in a roundabout way - to Guy Fawkes. The discussion went on for an hour and involved a number of impassioned speeches, before Carmichael declared that it probably was offensive, as Fawkes - though flawed in his revolutionary ideal - was Catholic, and that a good many Catholics had been oppressed by the Capitalist Imperialist Bourgeois Fascist Right, and that we as Socialists should do what we could to include them, not exclude them. Everyone nodded along in agreement.

'Thatcher, Thatcher, Thatcher: Out, Out, Out', was deemed perfectly suitable, indeed should be encouraged, as should a song about putting a boot up the then Education Secretary Kenneth Baker's arse, sung to the tune of 'Oops Upside Your Head'. This was deemed an acceptable threat of violence: after all, didn't Comrade Trotsky have to resort to violence to quell the Capitalist Imperialist Bourgeois Fascist Counter-Revolutionary White Russians in 1919?

By the time we reached London I was very tired but strangely enthused with revolutionary fervour.

I had another task though. I had to find my girlfriend and I had to resurrect my band.

I bade farewell to the Comrades at Parliament Square and walked towards Tottenham Court Road where Ellie's Halls of Residence were situated.

I walked up the steps and turned to press her buzzer. For a few seconds my fingers hovered over the button - why? I was just calling unannounced on my girlfriend, wasn't I?

I pressed the buzzer. A female voice, groggy with sleep answered.

'Hello?'

It was Ellie's room mate Beth, a pleasant and wholesome American student.

'Hi, it's Richard.'

'Richard,' she repeated for no particular reason. 'Hi.'

'Is Ellie there?'

She paused. 'No.' I could hear a note of concern in her voice.

'I don't know where she is,' she stammered, 'she must have stayed out last night.'

'Okay,' I said.

Her words had landed like cluster bombs and exploded inside me. 'She must have stayed out last night.' That meant only one thing: she has been out shagging behind your back.

I couldn't believe it.

I buzzed again. 'Beth, I'm sorry, it's still Richard. When you say she must have stayed out last night, and you don't know where she is, what exactly do you mean?'

There was a pause at the other end of the line. 'Richard, I really don't know what to say. She isn't here.'

'Okay,' I said, realising how sad and desperate I sounded. 'Tell her I called.'

'Sure.'

I took a step back. Everything seemed final. Pain swept through me. I knew I wouldn't ever stand on these steps talking to this pleasant American undergraduate ever again.

That bothered me. Not because I liked her particularly - hell, I didn't even know her - but because it meant things were spiralling out of my control. I needed to find Ellie. I needed to regain control. Maybe I was wrong. Surely I was wrong. Yes, fuck, she was a nineteen-year-old girl. Just because she had stayed the night somewhere else didn't mean that she had been up to no good. God, what kind of possessive, sexist dinosaur was I? This was the girl I loved, and she loved me. She told me, maybe not recently, but she had told me, lots of times. I trusted her.

I decided to go to Danny's. At least I could confront him in person about the band. It wasn't right to chuck me out over the phone. I was going to tell him this. I would hook up with Ellie later, after seeing Danny.

He had a flat with a couple of his art school buddies in Chelsea. I walked to the tube station. Fuck it, I hailed a taxi. It was my first ever London taxi ride. I gave the taxi driver the address and spent the next twenty minutes worrying that I didn't have enough money. At least that took my mind off Ellie and Danny and The Sensationals.

His flat was over a restaurant. The door was round the side. It was open. I entered and walked up the stairs. It was the first door. I knocked. As I knocked, I felt my pulse accelerate and my heart start to beat heavily inside my chest. I tried to calm myself.

The door opened.

Danny stood there. His jaw dropped. His eyes betrayed him. The blood ran away from his face.

I didn't know why he looked so shocked to see me.

I didn't say anything. Nor did he. He just stood there, wearing a ridiculous silk dressing gown.

In the background I heard a voice.

'Who's there, Danny?'

It was a female voice.

It was Ellie's voice.

'Is that Ellie?' I asked him tentatively.

He nodded.

I didn't know why she was there, why he was looking so guilty and wearing a silk dressing gown.

'What's she doing here?' I asked.

He took a deep breath and opened the door for me.

I could hear Ellie repeat her question.

'It's Rich,' he shouted back.

There was silence from the room where Ellie's voice had called out.

I walked into the room. Ellie was in bed. Danny's bed. I looked at her. I was nineteen. I didn't know what to think. I didn't know how to react. I didn't want to hit him. I didn't want to call her a slag. I didn't know what to do.

She looked at me. Her brown eyes pricked with tears. She felt sorry for me. Danny started to speak. 'Look, Rich.....' he said. I wouldn't let him continue, I didn't want to hear his bullshit. I put my finger up and pointed it at his chest then turned and walked away towards the door.

Things would never be the same.

I saw Ellie a few times when she came home at Christmas, but we didn't really speak. I knew she left her London University a few weeks after the incident and started studying in Edinburgh. Someone had told me that - I can't remember who. We only really talked, properly talked, in the pub on the night she told me about her job in Africa. Even then, though, that incident, which lasted less than a few minutes, that incident, which has shaped my life so much, was hardly alluded to at all.

I didn't see Danny again after that. He never came back to the Wirral like the rest of us to get pissed en masse during the Christmas holidays. He had bigger fish to fry. Bigger plans.

The Sensationals would never play again, with or without me. Danny - so the documentaries on MTV and numerous biographies and autobiographies said - formed a band called simply 'Cappaldi', and was signed to an Independent Record Label. You know the story as well as I do: Cappaldi's first album, ingeniously entitled 'Cappaldi', was huge. And the rest is history.

And me, I limped back to my university. I spent a couple of days of wonderful, inconsolable, solitary sadness, then I spent a couple of days wallowing in the attention I received, having declared in a particularly drunken and melodramatic way to all my student mates that my girlfriend had run off with my best friend. After that I kind of got on with life.

The 1990s went by in a flash. Indie/Dance crossover became Madchester. Raves became clubs. Madchester became Britpop. The Stone Roses became the 'next big thing' and in turn were replaced by the 'next big thing'. Nirvana kicked Guns'n'Roses into the long grass, thank God, before Oasis erupted with great songs we'd all heard before, then died in an embarrassing heap. Radiohead gave us deep, wonderfully crafted songs to slit our wrists to before disappearing up their own arses in their desperate desire to stay real.

I loved them all.

I finished my degree - predictably taking a lower second - took a couple of years out, doing very little but amassing debt, met Angela and started work for McPhee, Fox and Phillips. I discovered jazz and Bob Dylan. I discovered wine, and as my twenties faded into the light, I thought about pensions and mortgages.

I lost my guitar. It got left behind when I moved from my

first London flat. I knew I'd left it there. At first, I decided I would go back and get it. But somehow I never did. Weeks became months became years. I wouldn't buy a new one. I had no desire to play.

36

And now here I was, standing at the back of Old Trafford Football Ground watching and waiting along with fifty thousand others for Cappaldi to take the stage for the Manchester leg of their Worldwide Tour. Here I was with my gun strapped to the inside of my thigh and my rucksack containing one and a bit million pounds, poised to take up the promise of immortality I had been offered by a strange Greek bloke with a penchant for awful slacks and chunky knit pastel shades.

Something wasn't right.

I stood with all the others and tried to make sense of it all. I did hate him, just as Costas had said. It was a good story too, just as Costas had said. But I hadn't meant for it to become such a good story. I hadn't asked to be assigned to look after Terry Hawkins. I hadn't asked him to let me arrange for Rutland to be whacked. It hadn't even taken me long to figure out how to con him out of a million quid. It had all just happened.

I still wasn't sure what I would do when he found out about my little scheme with the money. It was just too tempting. I hadn't even thought for long about giving money to my family and Ellie; that had sort of just happened as well. Perhaps that was what was at the heart of what Costas had been saying all along - my fate meant that I had got myself involved in this, well, this weird situation.

I had enjoyed it, though. I was even enjoying it now. I had

enjoyed knowing that I had a handgun concealed between my legs when I had entered the Stadium. I enjoyed knowing that there was more to come in this whole strange business. I had enjoyed carefully selecting the CD that I was going to leave behind on Cappaldi's body.

Well, I assumed that was what was going to happen.

The crowd around me were singing Cappaldi songs. I fought against joining in. He had released some good songs, the bastard. They loved his songs. They loved him. I looked around me; there was adulation everywhere. They were an interesting crowd. They weren't the teeny-boppers and gay men he used to attract. This crowd were a mix of people in their late twenties and thirties who listened to him on CD players in their nice cars. They weren't the weirdos, druggies and teenage geeks that I had always wanted The Sensationals to be adored by; they were nice mums and dads enjoying an evening out without the kids.

Danny Cappaldi wasn't living my dream. My dream was to write songs that would be ingested into the souls of solitary teenagers listening in their bedrooms whilst worrying about whether they were in fact the only real living thinking beings in a world where everyone else was a robot.

My dream wasn't families in four-by-four Jeeps phoning the babysitter before the band to make sure that little Johnny was happy. This made things better. Somehow.

At last Cappaldi arrived on stage. Just as he used to do with us all those years ago, Danny waited for his band to go into their first song before entering the stage himself. Just as he did all those years ago at Jenny George's party, he put his hands out to the crowd and lapped up the applause. And the crowd did applaud. They loved him. They sang along as he played all his hits. They laughed along as he told them about his adventures in therapy. They whistled as he gyrated, they lit matches and fired up lighters above their heads as he crooned the ballads that they had danced to on their wedding nights.

It didn't move me. This wasn't immortality. This was

entertainment. I didn't hate this. This wasn't going to achieve five century status.

I felt confused. I felt hot. My gun burned into my groin. Everywhere I turned there were smiling happy faces.

I made my way to the side of the stage and showed a bouncer my backstage pass. He directed me to a doorway by what was usually the players' entrance. I wandered down, showed my pass again to another bouncer and was waved through. It was all so easy. Everything had been. Perhaps Costas was in some way making things happen in this effortless way. Perhaps I had no choice now but to carry out my part of the deal.

I turned into a toilet and moved the gun from my thigh, ripping off the sellotape and taking off most of my hairs in the process. I squealed. I put the gun in my inside pocket.

Outside the toilet, I wandered into another corridor, up some stairs and into a room where there was a bar. I was surprised to find the bar quite busy even though the band were still doing their set. The people in here were older than the crowd outside. I realised that it was full of corporate hospitality types. Awful people, all trying to wear young people's clothes and get as much free drink down them as possible.

This wasn't how I thought things would end up when I wrote songs in my bedroom. This wasn't what I imagined would become of Danny.

I got myself a free drink and stood by the bar. Beside me, a man in a leather jacket was telling an attractive young female that he was in 'finance' and asked her if she was enjoying the gig. Enjoying the gig! How could she be enjoying the gig when she was standing in here listening to him try and shag her?

Where were the stage divers and pissed-up hippies? Where were the students pretending to be off their tits on acid? Where were the plump young girls with angelic faces who stood around, too shy to look at anything but their own shoes? There was none of this here. Danny Cappaldi and his eponymous bunch of knobheads had become corporate hospitality fodder. I wasn't jealous of this. I wasn't so enraged by this that I could kill.

Or could I? I would in some ways be doing him a favour. After all, he had once shared my dreams. He was probably pretty miserable in this environment. A heroic rock 'n' roll death might be the greatest service I could do for him.

I walked towards the end of the bar. A busy-looking woman with a clipboard, an earpiece, and a voice that sounded like she had a whole orchard's worth of plums stuffed down the back of her throat was talking to another eager-looking woman with a clipboard and earpiece. I listened in to their conversation.

'Jaqui, have you sorted out Danny's flight tickets for tomorrow?'

'Yes, Bea.'

'Good. Now, be a darling and drop them into his room. When you see him later, make sure he knows that it's a six thirty start tomorrow and no messing about. Don't take any shit from him: we've got to be in Dortmund by lunchtime.'

I watched as Bea gave Jaqui that dreadful patronising false smile that superiors give to their minions.

'Okay, Jaqui. Chop, chop.'

'Chop, chop.' That was priceless. 'Bea' was a female version of McPhee. I expect that if I had listened for longer, I would hear her tell Jaqui that she had her 'piss flaps in the door about Dortmund.'

At least I now had a chance to discover Cappaldi's room. I followed Jaqui out of the bar and into another corridor.

Strange, I felt that I had played out this scene before.

I could hear the music of the concert in the background, like a murmur, like a rumour of something that was going on elsewhere. To anyone else it would have sounded exciting. Anyone else would have wanted to seek it out. Not me. I was going in the opposite direction.

The corridor was quite dimly lit. There were those small

round ceiling lights above me, but they weren't giving out much light. I followed Jaqui, but the funny thing was, I kind of knew exactly where I was going. I knew exactly where I'd find Danny Cappaldi. I didn't need lights or signposts or anything.

I watched from a safe distance as the young woman went into a room. I waited for a few moments before she re-emerged and walked off in the opposite direction.

I walked up to the door she had gone to. I opened the door. It was his room. His dressing room. I knew that. Don't ask me how. For a few seconds part of the room was illuminated. Well, I say illuminated; it was more like a triangle of light thrown onto the far wall. As I opened the door wider, the triangle got bigger. I could see most of the room now. I knew it was his room. His dressing room. Fucking hell: dressing room. We once got changed in Jenny George's parents' kitchen.

I waited for him.

The show ended.

There was a lull, then the crowd started chanting his name, 'Danny, Danny, Danny,' in a meaningful rhythm. They wanted more.

They got more. They played an encore, came off, then went back on and played 'Everything's Amazing'. The first guitar chords were vaguely mine. It was a sanitised version of the three minutes of merry hell we had once created with our own, 'Everything's Sensational'. It was the only trace of me left after all these years. No one would know that I wrote the tune. No one would know except me and him. It was a better song when it was 'Everything's Sensational'. It had an edge then.

This time there were no more encores. The PA thanked everyone for coming and reminded them to have a safe journey home. They all filed out. No one was so moved by this that they wanted to riot or fight or spit. No one was so moved that they wanted to fuck or cry or scream. They smiled and made their way out in an orderly fashion. They smiled because they had been entertained.

I waited for him.

I knew he was coming here.

After a while the door opened and in walked Danny Cappaldi with a girl.

He saw me. His face changed from incredulity to concern to recognition.

He squinted as I sat expressionless and calm in the corner: he knew it was me.

Perhaps he had always known that one day I'd come back.

The girl spoke. 'Who the fuck are you?'

I ignored her and looked at Danny. He was wearing a vest that was glistening with the sweat from his performance and a pair of skintight leather trousers. He looked older than his thirty-six years. His face was more wrinkled than I had seen in the pictures, and his hair was dyed. He looked tired. He shook his head.

'Richie? Richie Strafe. Fuck, how did you get in here?' He seemed fairly happy to see me.

The girl wasn't. She tugged at Cappaldi's arm. 'For Christ's sake, Danny. Can't you get him out of here?'

'How long has it been?' he said.

'Fifteen years,' I told him.

He shook his head again. 'Fuck me, fifteen years.'

The girl tugged at Danny's arm again. 'Danny,' she whined.

He ignored her, so she threw her head back, puffed out her cheeks and went and sat by the dressing table.

'So, how are you?' he asked. He did seem genuinely pleased to see me. I didn't know what to say. The gun felt heavy in my pocket. I had hoped that he would be alone. I hadn't factored in the possibility of a witness to this. The girl looked pissed and had her head down on the table where she had cut up lines of cocaine. She started to audibly snort them one after the other.

'I'm fine,' I said.

'Good. Now, Rich, seriously, how did you get in here?' His

292

voice was different now - it had a tone of concern about it. He was sensing that I wasn't here to get his autograph.

'I got a ticket from Ellie,' I said.

'Oh, she's still getting those, is she?'

'What?'

'Yes, my PA sends tickets to a group of old friends and family. Ellie is on that list.'

'You fucked her and she was my girlfriend,' I blurted out. I even surprised myself with my bluntness.

At this, the girl put her head up and turned towards me. I recognised her now. She was from a girl band who had had a Christmas Number One last year in collaboration with Tom Jones. She looked awful. She was smashed.

'I'm sorry, Rich. Perhaps you'd better go. I've got to get changed. Maybe we'll catch up later.'

I pulled the gun out of my pocket and waved it at him.

'Fuck me, Rich. Is that real?'

'Yes,' I said, 'it's a Webley Mark IV handgun.' I'm not sure why I felt the need to tell him that.

'What's this all about?' said the girl who was starting to shake.

'This is about unfinished business,' I said.

'Don't mess about, Rich,' said Danny. 'Put the gun away and we'll talk about this.'

'Talk,' I said, 'I don't remember there being much talking when you chucked me out of the band, and then fucked my girlfriend.'

I pointed the gun at him and wondered if I was about to fire it. I didn't know. I assumed that I would, that fate would somehow conspire to make me. But I wasn't sure.

'What do you want me to say? It's fifteen fucking years ago. Believe me, Rich, there's been an awful lot of water gone under the bridge since Ellie Smith.'

He talked about her like she was some kind of river scum. I aimed the gun at his head and turned my own away from him, screwing my eyes shut; I didn't want to hear or see the gun go off and the effect the bullet would have.

I waited for the noise. I waited to feel the vibration in my hand. But everything was stuck. I couldn't make it fire. My fingers felt like they were wading through a pot of treacle; in fact all of me felt like I was wading through a pot of treacle.

The girl screamed, 'Danny!'

I opened my eyes again. I looked at him.

'Sit down,' I said. 'Lock the door.' I could hear a tone of exasperation in my own voice. Why hadn't I shot him yet? I should have just done it – bang, bang.

Reluctantly he did as I had commanded.

'I've come here to kill you,' I told him calmly, and the girl screamed again. She was starting to do my tits in.

'Why?' he asked. 'Surely not because of Ellie and our old band?' He was shaking now.

'No,' I said, 'I've got to kill you because......' Suddenly I felt really stupid. I couldn't tell him that I had to kill him because it was my mission to save mankind from losing the will to live.

'It's not straightforward,' I said. 'You might not understand the reasons.'

'Oh God, Danny,' sobbed the girl.

I really had hoped that she would disappear, but I couldn't just let her out. Perhaps I would kill her as well. I mean, she was a shite popstar, just like Cappaldi. Perhaps that would gain me extra Brownie points at the Great Library of Myths and Legends.

Danny turned to her. 'Shut up, Candice, for fuck's sake.'

I was impressed; he was being quite cool about it.

I allowed myself a chuckle. He tried to smile back. He was such a cliché. Standing here with his smacked-out girlfriend and his leather trousers and dyed hair.

'So, why did you do it?' I asked him. 'Ellie and the band?'

He shrugged. 'I don't know.'

'Oh come on, you remember, you must have some idea why you slept with your best mate's girlfriend, then deprived him of the thing that you knew was more important to him than anything else. You must know.' I shouted the last three words and pointed the gun at him again.

'I don't know. I suppose,' he paused, 'I suppose, it was because I could.' He took an intake of breath, as though he was trying to find the right words. 'You took everything so seriously. Everything had to be important. Everything had to have meaning.'

'So you wanted to make everything meaningless?' I asked him.

'Not meaningless,' he said, 'just not so bloody serious. I just wanted to experience everything for its own sake, not worry about the consequences.'

'Everything has consequences,' I said.

I pointed the gun at him and went to pull the trigger.

The girl screamed and there was a knock at the door.

I couldn't do it. Not with this bloody manufactured magazine pop girl in the room.

There was another door that led, I presumed, to some kind of bathroom or toilet.

I waved the gun at Candice. 'You go in there,' I snapped at her. 'And you,' I said to Danny, 'tell whoever's at the door that everything's okay.'

They looked at each other, desperately urging the other to do something, then did as I had ordered.

Now it was just the two of us. This was the moment I had been waiting for. This was the moment I had longed for all the times I had to watch him on Top of the bleeding Pops, every time I saw his face smiling at me from the cover of a magazine. I was five feet away from him. I could see into his eyes, into his face. Some kind of stage make-up was running from his eyebrow down his cheek towards his twitching mouth.

I waved the gun at him again. Danny cowered, his eyes closed. Fuck me, I still couldn't pull the bastard trigger.

'Nothing is meaningless,' I said, I wasn't entirely sure I

knew what I meant. 'Nothing is meaningless,' I repeated. 'It can't be.'

I could hear a voice from outside. It was the posh drawl of Bea.

'Danny, I don't care what's going on in there, just as long as you're ready for Dortmund in the morning. Okay? Okay?'

'Do you know, Danny,' I said, 'I've watched your career over the last fifteen years and I've resented you, hated you so much. But now, funnily enough, I don't give a shit. I used to think that you sleeping with Ellie and throwing me out of the band made me a failure. But it didn't. It just made you a twat. I've got friends and family who go on caravan trips to Wales – they try to be happy, they mean something. And to them, I mean something.'

He nodded, though I didn't know if he had a clue what I was on about. Mind you, I wasn't sure I had a clue what I was on about either.

I sighed as Danny looked at me, powerless. I sighed again.

'Tell her you'll be there,' I said. 'Tell the woman you'll be in bloody Dortmund.'

'Okay, Bea,' he said weakly.

I looked at him. Sweat was pouring down his face.

'I can't do it,' I said. 'It's too daft. *You're just* an entertainer. You're too old now to touch people, to really mean something to people. You're jaded and embarrassing.' He said nothing, though in fairness he was being subjected to abuse by a bloke waving a handgun at him. 'And if I kill you, I'll never find out what's going to happen to us.'

I continued, 'Do you remember when we had our photos taken by Ellie before we played Jenny George's gig?'

He nodded. I did not doubt that he'd remember it.

'At that second you were beautiful and pure. We both were. I remember you saying - and I knew it was bullshit, but I still believe it - that you wanted to die before you were thirty, because there was nothing worse than a rock star over thirty. Do you remember saying that?' He nodded again, though I'm not sure he did.

'Now you've become what we always said we hated.'

I paused. There was a sound of sobbing from the toilet.

'I can't kill you, Danny. You've got to carry on decaying. That's worse than death for you. And me. I've got to carry on regretting. That's what it's all about. And both of us have got to find our meaning wherever we can.'

I put the gun down on the table. We both looked at it. For a second I thought that Danny was going to grab it, but instead he grabbed a decanter from the table and started to slug whatever was in it.

He proffered the drink to me. 'Do you want some?'

I shook my head.

He was shaking now, shaking and making eyes at the line of cocaine that was on the table.

I turned my back and walked towards the door.

'One thing I do remember though, Rich,' he said, and I turned round to face him. 'I remember you saying that you wanted to write one song, just one song, that people would hear on a jukebox in a pub and immediately forget everything about their humdrum boring lives and be transported to somewhere else. Do you remember saying that?'

I did. I nodded.

'Well, I have done that, haven't I?' His voice was still shaky, his eyes were wide, as though he was beseeching me to answer in the affirmative.

He wanted reassurance. Here was the aging star and he wanted reassurance from the man who had just waved a gun at him. The man who he had treated with contempt all those years earlier. It was victory, of sorts. I didn't respond. I walked away.

37

By the time I got to Manchester Airport it was midnight and sleepy. I went up to the British Airways desk and asked for a ticket for the first flight on which they had seats available. It turned out to be Dortmund, which was the last place I wanted to go. I asked about the second flight, which was Warsaw, which I didn't fancy much either. We eventually settled on a flight to Cairo. I was happy with this.

I would live in Cairo until my money ran out. I would buy a white suit and spend my days in the bazaars drinking that strange tea stuff they drink through a bong pipe. I would learn Arabic and tell stories. I might adopt a little monkey that would idolise me and live on my shoulder.

I bought my ticket and made my way to the departure lounge. I had an hour to wait for my flight. I bought myself a cup of tea and a sandwich and sat down. The restaurant was totally deserted. I thought about Costas. I knew I wouldn't see him here. I knew I would never see him again.

I was glad that I hadn't killed Cappaldi. I was free of him now. I sat and wondered about my dad. I would lie low, but find some way of making contact with my brother - he would let me know how my dad was. I'd cross that bridge when I got to Cairo.

A couple of men walked into the restaurant and sat down. One of them looked at me. I became suspicious. Perhaps they were something to do with the police. I hadn't given Maurice Hunter and his mad mates much thought - but tomorrow they would be carrying out a killing at my instigation. Fucking hell.

I needed to get to Cairo to work that one through. Rutland was probably deserving of a nasty end in some way. I'd leave it at that for now.

I fancied a chocolate bar. I put my hand in my pocket to get some loose change. I pulled out a handful of coins and the note that the usher had given me from McPhee earlier in the day. I opened the note out of curiosity. To my surprise it had nothing to do with McPhee. It read simply:

Angela has called. Please phone her today, it is absolutely, absolutely urgent!!!

Two absolutelys and three exclamation marks! What did Angela want? I had been putting off phoning her for weeks. I thought about it; this sounded serious. If she had just wanted to bin me, or tell me that my entire possessions were now in the Cancer Research Shop, Streatham Branch, she wouldn't have phoned me in court, and she wouldn't have instilled that same sense of urgency in the receptionist who took her call.

I decided to phone her.

I found a payphone and dialled the number of her mobile. I still knew it by heart. I mouthed the numbers to myself as my heart started to pound. What did she want? I hoped that everything was alright.

She answered.

'Hello, Rich?' she said immediately, a note of urgency easily detectable in her voice.

How did she know it was me? Why did she presume it was me?

'Yes. Hi,' I answered, 'I'm sorry it's late. I've been kind of busy.'

'Where have you been?' she said. She sounded tearful now.

'It's a long story,' I said. 'I'll tell you later.'

'Okay.' By now she was sobbing, deep sobs.

'Angie,' I said, trying to console her, 'Angie, what's the matter? Don't cry. I'm sorry it's late.'

'Rich,' she said, in a breathy staccato voice, 'Rich, I'm pregnant.'

Fuck me.

Suddenly all the world seemed to stand still and stop what it was doing. Suddenly everything that had once hurried around in my head and body went into slow motion. Angela was pregnant. Fuck me.

'It's yours,' she said, though I hadn't actually thought that it wouldn't be. I didn't know what to say. I didn't know what to do. This was beyond weird. A few minutes ago I was waving a gun at a popstar as I came to terms with what life really meant for me. A lifetime being bitter I had said. Perhaps that wasn't quite right.

'Richard, please say something,' she begged from the other end of the line.

'I don't know what to say,' I said unhelpfully. 'I'm such a prick.'

She laughed and then snorted away the tears. 'Yeah, you are.'

I laughed with her now.

'I've been trying to contact you for weeks. I don't know what to do.'

'What do you mean?' I said.

'Well,' she continued, 'I don't want to be a single mum. I've got to make decisions.'

'Fuck,' I said, 'fuck. Don't get rid of it. Don't have a, you know, an abortion.'

It came straight out. It was spontaneous and heartfelt. I wanted her to have the child. I wanted her to have our child.

'Okay,' she said, 'okay.'

I smiled at the phone. A big, beaming smile. It was the first time I had properly smiled in ages.

Then I remembered. I remembered that I was about to go to Cairo to live with my adopted monkey. I remembered that I had arranged a murder conspiracy and ripped off a psychopath at the same time.

'Angela,' I said tentatively, 'things have been a bit strange.'

'What do you mean?' she asked.

'Well, I've done a few things that might have some serious repercussions.'

'Like what?' I knew that she was imagining I had had some kind of affair or something.

'Don't worry, it's nothing to do with anybody else. It's, well, it's kind of weirder than that.'

'What?' she said, in that tone she usually used when I was telling her that I wouldn't be around on Saturday afternoon because I was going to the football with my mates. Then her voice changed, became softer, as she added, 'Do you think we can work it out?'

'I don't know,' I said. I didn't.

'I hope so.' I did.

'Then that's a start,' she added.

It was.

'Are you happy?' she asked.

Was I happy?

I would be lying if I said I was happy. I would be misleading you if I said that suddenly the clouds lifted and the sun beamed its yellow rays of loveliness down on Richie Strafe. I wasn't unhappy though. I was shocked and felt a complete prick, but I wasn't unhappy. And, significantly, I wanted to see her. Into my mind like little blossom petals falling gently from a tree were lots of lovely thoughts about Angela. How she used to curl up in her pyjamas on cold winter nights; how she smiled to herself when she was reading a book she liked; her awful taste in music that I would not tolerate in anybody except her.

We made an arrangement to speak again the next day. I hoped that that would be the case.

I walked around the airport. I walked past the shops that sell exciting holiday items that you only ever think about buying when you are waiting for a plane: sunglasses, fancy CD players, video cameras and multi-coloured shorts.

My ticket was in my inside pocket. I could walk away. I could get on that plane and start a new adventure. I would never save the world from losing the will to live, but I could embark upon a journey into the unknown, far away from the mundane things I had spent my whole life battling against. I could run away and never be forced into growing up.

I continued to walk around. I looked at the large dot matrix board showing the status of departing flights. My flight to Cairo was boarding from gate 14. My flight to Cairo would be leaving in half an hour. There's hundreds of millions of people in Cairo, and many millions of them have got adopted monkeys and a tall tale to tell. No one would ever find me. I could leave. I could leave.

I walked over to the pay phone. I picked up the same phone I had used to phone Angela. I dialled the Directory Enquiries. A ridiculously enthusiastic voice answered.

'Hello, Directory Enquiries. This is Andy. How can I help you?'

I paused. I took a deep breath.

'Hello. How can I help you?' repeated Andy, who was probably new to the job.

'Can you give me the number of Merseyside Police, please?'

It didn't take long for the police to arrive. Indeed some might say they were there with indecent haste. Mind, you when I spoke to the desk sergeant and told him that I was Terry Hawkins' solicitor and that I had some information about another conspiracy to murder charge, it didn't take him long to put me through to the sleeping detective inspector who was in charge of the case against Terry Hawkins.

DI Lambert clearly jumped straight from his bed and into his car. He looked terrible, God love him, and his halitosis was a disgrace.

We sat down in a tiny interview room in the deep recesses of Manchester Airport.

'I'm sorry to drag you guys out of bed,' I said, 'but I've got some information that might be of interest to you.'

DI Lambert was very excited. 'Okay,' he said, wafting a cabbagy aroma in my direction.

'But before I say anything, I need some reassurance that if I help you, and if I give evidence against Terry Hawkins, you are going to protect me.'

Lambert nodded.

'Me,' I continued, 'and my girlfriend,' I paused, 'and our baby.'

I told him and his colleagues everything.

Well, nearly everything. I didn't tell them about Dr Costas or the Great Library of Myths and Legends. I've kind of decided to keep that to myself. I didn't tell them about Danny Cappaldi either. I think I'll let Danny get on with his life and watch him, without envy, as he makes his way down the list of celebrities. I didn't think he'd press charges against me. He owed me that and he knew it.

I did tell them about Maurice Hunter and the plan to kill Colin Rutland. I told them that it was going to be a 'motorbike job'. They seemed to know what that meant. As soon as I said it, they all nodded sagely to each other. I guessed that that information would save Rutland's life. I was sorry to grass on Hunter - but hey, I had a baby to think of now, and Hunter and his gang of nutcases could look after themselves.

After almost three hours of questions and answers we left the airport. I sat in the back of Lambert's car. He was in the front, with one of his men driving. They didn't handcuff me, or charge me, or do that thing when they push the suspect's head down as they put him the back of the car.

By my side was my rucksack. It still had all the money in it.

I felt small in the back of the car. Small, but comfortable and safe. I was tired, but my head was racing with everything that had happened and everything that was about to happen.

I leant over to Lambert.

'Hey,' I said, 'when I'm on this witness protection programme, can I choose my new name?'

'Yes,' said Lambert. He didn't seem too sure, but I got the

feeling that at half past five in the morning, and with the information I had just given him, he would have promised me just about anything.

I was satisfied with that, though, and sat back again in the comfort of the leather back seats of his car.

I looked out of the window: the world was waking up. The workers and slackers, the young and the old, the happy and depressed would all open their eyes to a new and unique day.

I rummaged around in my rucksack. Lambert glanced behind him, but without a great deal of concern. He knew that I had no weapon in it or posed any great threat to them.

I found what I was after near the top, underneath my washbag. It was my CD, the CD that was to have been left on the dead body of Danny Cappaldi. I didn't need it now.

Not for that purpose anyway.

I leant over again and handed it to Lambert. 'Do me one more favour,' I said, 'play this for me.'

He sucked in his lips. I could tell that he didn't want to play the bloody thing. I could tell that I was starting to irritate him.

'Please,' I said, 'it's just one track.'

'Alright,' he said reluctantly, and pushed it into the CD player in his dashboard.

'This has to be played loud,' I said, and he shot a sideways glance to his driver before turning up the CD player.

'No,' I said, 'really loud.'

He touched the dial again.

I sat back and smiled as the familiar drum opening to Teenage Kicks erupted over the car's CD player. Fergal started to sing:

Teenage Dreams so hard to beat,
Everytime she walks down the street.

I sat back and listened. I had heard the song a million times. It is only three minutes long. It's perfect. It can't be improved. It says everything that needs to be said about the energy and desperate naïvety of youth. It has instinctive understanding and profound ignorance.

I was glad that I hadn't placed the CD on the dying body of Danny Cappaldi. I was glad that I hadn't destroyed its innocence by linking it with one man who simply couldn't escape his teenage dreams and another who took his and crushed them under the weight of his own ego and sense of self-importance.

I'm not sure what Lambert and his driver made of my request. I didn't care.

I thought about the name I would adopt.

I considered Johnny Sharkey: Johnny after Marr, Sharkey after Derry's finest singer. I quite liked that - Johnny Sharkey, his girlfriend and newborn child Jimi. Some others popped into my head: John Morrisey, Shane Paige.

Or perhaps I should just keep plain old Richie Strafe, the man who would never write a song that would be played forever, but who was poised, now, for the immortality of fatherhood.

Printed in the United Kingdom
by Lightning Source UK Ltd.
133646UK00001B/7-21/P